Once a Runner

John L. Parker, Jr.

Cedarwinds Publishing Company
Tallahassee, Florida

The author wishes to emphasize that the characters in this book are fictional, with the exception of those competitive runners whose names are easily recognized by those who follow distance running.

The author is aware of certain anachronisms and geographical quirks in the story, and to those diligent souls who ferret them out he says: A hearty well done!

The Southeastern University of this book, naturally, is in no way related to a school of that name in Washington, D.C.

Published by Cedarwinds Publishing Company
P.O. Box 13618
Tallahassee, Florida 32317
Orders: 800/548-2388
Editorial: 850/224-9261
Fax: 850/561-0747

Library of Congress Cataloging in
Publication Data

Parker, Jr., John L. 1947-
Once A Runner
I. Title.
Library of Congress Number 78-59993
ISBN 0-915297-01-9

Printing history
1st printing   June, 1978
2nd printing   October, 1978
3rd printing   November, 1978
4th printing (author's revised edition)   November, 1990
5th printing   April, 1993
6th printing   August, 1995
7th printing   October, 1997

V 10 9 8 7

Thanks...

The author, as with all those who struggle to realize a dream, incurs the tenderest of debts. These are mine:

Richard Endris and John O'Bannon, fellow runners whose graciously and unhesitatingly offered dining room table became the birth stool for this impoverished literary child.

Ron Wiggins, a fellow writer whose editorial advice proved so helpful as to nearly entitle him to a share of the by-line.

Dr. Alan Beyerchen, a fellow author, and wife Marila, whose last-second, crusading efforts were extraordinary, and will not soon be forgotten.

Erica, Doug and especially Ann Arbogast, whose loving encouragement was simply a *sine qua non* of this book.

Know, all of you, that you are loved.

Dedication

This book is for Jack Bacheler and Frank Shorter, old friends, great runners. In fond remembrance, fellows, of many Trials and many Miles . . .

How did I know you ran the mile in 4:30 in high school? That's easy. *Everyone* ran the mile in 4:30 in high school.

—Frank Shorter, *out running somewhere*, circa 1969

1. Once . . .

The night joggers were out as usual. The young man could see dim figures on the track even in this pale light, slowly pounding round and round on the most infinite of footpaths. There would be, he knew, plump, determined-looking women slogging along while fleshy knees quivered. They would occasionally brush damp hair fiercely from their eyes and dream of certain cruel and smiling emcees: bikinis, tennis with white-toothed males, wild tangos in the moonlight.

And men too of various ages and levels of dilapidation, perhaps also grinding out secret fantasies (did they picture themselves a Peter Snell held back only by fat or fear as they turned their 90-second quarters?).

The young man stood outside the fence for a few moments while moths attacked the streetlight dustily, leaving him in a dim spotlight of swirling shadows. He loved early fall in Florida's panhandle. Leaves would be turning elsewhere but here the hot breath of summer still held forth. In the moist warmth there was a slight edge, though, a faint promise of cool air hanging in the treetops and close to the moss. He picked up his small travel bag and went in the gate, walking clockwise on the track towards the white starting post at the head of the first turn. The joggers ignored the stranger in street clothes and he likewise paid them not the slightest attention. They would always be there.

The high jump pit had been rearranged, a new section of bleachers had been added, a water jump installed for the steeplechase. But mostly it looked the same as it did four years ago, the same as a four hundred and forty yard oval probably will always look to one who knows a quarter of a mile by the inches.

The Games were over for this time around. He knew quite well that for him they were over for good. Four years is a very long time in some circles; in actual time—real-world time, as

1

that of shopkeepers, insurance sellers, compounders of interest and so on—it is perhaps not long at all. But in his own mind Time reposed in peculiar receptacles; to him the passing of one minute took on all manner of rare meaning. A minute was one fourth of a four-minute mile, a coffee spoon of his days and ways.

As with many of the others, he had no idea what he would be doing now that Montreal was over. It was such a demanding thing, so final, so cathartic, that most of them simply never thought beyond it. They were scattered around the world now, he supposed, doing pretty much what he was doing at this moment: tallying gains and losses.

He was going to have to pick up the thread of a normal life again and although he did not exactly know why, he had to start by coming back here, back to the greenhouse warmth of the Panhandle, back to this very quarter-mile oval that still held his long-dried sweat. Back to September, the month of promises. He put his bag down by the pole vault pit, looked uptrack to make sure no one was coming, and then walked up to the starting line. God, he thought, one more time on the line.

In lane one he stood very still, looking down at his street shoes (joggers now going around him with curious glances) and tried to conjure up the feeling. After a moment a trace of it came to him and he knew that was all there would be. You can remember it, he told himself, but you cannot experience it again this way. You have to be satisfied with the shadows. Then he thought of the second and third laps and decided with a little twist of a smile that shadows were sometimes quite enough.

He was 26 years, five months and two days old and though as he stood there on the starting line he felt quite a bit older than that, the muscles that rippled up and down inside his trouser leg could have only been the result, biologically speaking, of more thousands of miles than he cared to think about all at one time.

He tried to focus blurred emotions, a metaphysical photographer zeroing in on hard edges to align in the center square. What was this, nostalgia? Regret? His mind doubleclutched, asked the musical question: am. . . I . . . buh loooo?

He could not tell. He realized again how adept he had become at not being able to tell such things. His emotions had calluses like feet.

The starter would tell them to stand tall, so he stood tall for a moment there in the night. There would be the set command and then the gun. He took a deep breath and began walking into the turn in the familiar counterclockwise direction, the way of all races, and thought: The first lap is lost in a flash of adrenaline and pounding hooves . . .

2. Doobey Hall

Doobey Hall was one of those ancient resonant wooden buildings that seemed to hold the oils and essences of those who had lived there. Like an old cloth easy chair, it was musty but comfortable.

As with many structures that had at one time been someone's home, it managed to retain a certain familial warmth amidst the current institutional clamor. It thumped and boomed hollowly rather than clicking in the bony staccato manner of more modern, more efficient dwellings.

Having once housed Kernsville Mayor Hiram "Sidecar" Doobey and his various clamoring kindred, during recent years the large friendly house had been used to shelter 30-some odd members of Southeastern University's grateful track team. Located a merciful two blocks from the campus proper, the edifice emitted from morning to night a steady if unpredictable cacophony of barely human yelps, primordial shrieks, righteous bellows, and off-key fragments of current hit songs, all courtesy of a singular group of young *sapiens* whose main function in life was to run, jump, and toss heavy objects about. And hopefully to do so far better than, well, ordinary mortals. The net available energy required to produce a 70-foot shot put or a seven-foot high jump just occasionally would not be contained by mere wood and plaster.

Walls trembled and there were eerie goings on.

Old Sidecar Doobey himself would have been tickled pink. Dead since 1959, his nickname derived from those carefree Depression days of yesteryear when on a Saturday night for pure diversion Hiram would sample about three quarters of a jar of the local untaxed stock, let loose a mighty wail, scoop up his tiny startled wife—a pretty, round-eyed thing named Emma Lee—deposit her in the sidecar of his

4

1932 Harley Davidson 74-inch flathead, and proceed to more or less terrorize many of the large herds of local grazing cattle.

"Woman," he would tell her, "we fixin' to do some *night ridin'!*" His wild green eyes held her for a moment like a light.

"Eeeeee!" she said.

This is not to imply that Sidecar was an outlaw exactly, since he owned most of the cows in Kalhoun County (and a good deal of the land, and several very sensitive mortgages for that matter). He was just what some folks might call loose. Sidecar was one of those raw, energetic men who understand very early in life which levers and pulleys really work and which are just for show. And he also understood that the whole shebang was most certainly going to come to a shrieking, grinding halt one fine day. Irretrievably, he suspected.

The only time he found himself in any kind of trouble worthy of the name was on one of the nights when he got particularly rowdy, broke down some fences and (Emma Lee squeaking like a wounded bat) went roaring into downtown Kernsville to "strafe the golldanged pigeons" while sad-eyed old negroes around the courthouse square watched in wrinkled amusement. Sidecar made his own fun.

"Lawd, Sheriff, I su*wanee* . . . I *lawd* don't know why I get so mean sometimes," he said with true regret the morning after his actual arrest. He held his shaggy, throbbing head in his hands.

"Well, Daddy," said the sheriff, "people is beginning to talk, and that's a fack." Sheriff William "Boots" Doobey was his eldest.

"What I cain't quite figure out," continued the lawman, "is why you always want to go and take mama with you."

Sidecar perked up suddenly. "Why," he cackled savagely, "she enjoys the *pure T hell out of it!*"

It was perhaps a tribute to the university town's collective sense of humor when it elected Sidecar mayor a year later. He had run on a platform of throw the bastards out, interesting only because the bastards were without exception his own blood kin. True to form, he threw the bastards out.

Sidecar's election had been like much of his life, a prize thrust upon him almost without the asking. The old man's one deep hurt came when his youngest boy, born when Sidecar was 52 and Emma Lee nearly 40, turned out to be something of an ordinary klutz. Boots could have had a West Point appointment, Sheryl Ann was Georgia Tech homecoming queen (before dropping out to marry a pulling guard). It touched a deep, painful place in his breast when Sidecar moistly watched the youngster, more like a grandson really, trying to master the elementary gear shift configuration of the big John Deere. When the child was stymied at a simple card game by a cousin half his age, Sidecar wandered out into his fields and wept with rage.

At that moment Sidecar decided, being a man of large concepts and a true patron of irony, to get for this slightly addled child that which his other children lacked (and didn't want for that matter): academic status. Years later, this curious task would be accomplished in the way that difficult/impossible objectives are generally accomplished amongst men of great power and integrity; which is to say on the sly. He deeded over to Southeastern University (which desperately needed space for an entomology laboratory) the house he had occupied for seven years as mayor "in exchange for ten dollars and other good and lawful consideration . . " The nature of the other good and lawful consideration was known only to Sidecar himself, his lawyer, and the prospective president of the school, the Honorable Stephen C. Prigman. At that time Emma Lee was five years in her grave and old Sidecar wanted to get away from "downgodamntown politics" and back to his ranch where he said he could "at least godamned well die with the honest smell of fresh dung in my nostrils." Actually he was toying with the idea of reincarnating the ancient and beloved Harley, then rusting under a paint-spattered canvas tarp in the barn.

His youngest would have to go through the motions of attending the university, so the formal conferring of the degree did not take place until four years after the house was donated.

Meanwhile Sidecar mucked around the ranch, got in his foreman's hair, was finally persuaded to purchase a package tour deal to several Mexican cities of interest. He returned raving about the regenerative properties of certain cactus distillates and hinting darkly about the "im-and-ex port bidness." On the scholastic scene things went without a hitch and the old man lived to see his boy, dazed, in cap and gown.

Entomology outgrew Doobey Hall and in 1958 the track team, delighted to a man, inherited it. Sidecar passed on soon thereafter but it was said he tried to kick his way out of the coffin on the way to Jesus Walks Among Us Acres.

A good bit of Doobey folklore was known in and around Kernsville and accounted for no small amount of graffiti scattered about the campus. Bold red letters on the side of the women's gym warned ominously: *SIDECAR LIVES AND WILL NAIL YOU YET!* And his youngest son, he of the dim wit, bogus degree and unaccountable penchant for hurting insects, his youngest son, Dick Doobey, ended up as the head football coach.

3. The Morning Run

On the third floor of Doobey Hall was the room in which Richard Doobey had slept as a child. Now, in 1972, its battered oak door held two three-by-five index cards neatly thumbtacked one atop the other. The top one said in Smith Corona pica:

If you can fill the unforgiving minute
With sixty seconds' worth of distance run—
Yours is the Earth and everything that's in it,
And—which is more—you'll be a Man, my son!
—Rudyard Kipling, 1892

The other card read:

Rudyard Kipling was a 4:30 miler.
—Quenton Cassidy, 1969

Inside the room, the one true Quenton Cassidy slept fitfully as dawn approached. In a damp orb of his own worst fears, he nightmared with a certain grace. It was an old and familiar theme with him: The last lap of a footrace found him being methodically passed by every runner in the Western Hemisphere. He was running in peanut butter as they all glided by easily. What was wrong here? Was his training inadequate? Where was his kick?

Mercifully, he awoke. Before the alarm, moist from his fretting, but forgetting the dream quickly. He sat on the edge of the bed wiggling his toes thoughtfully as the cobwebs of anxiety melted away in his shaggy head. In the waking world his whole being centered around covering ground quickly without benefit of Detroit technology. At this he really had no equals save a few dozen others scattered about the country and world who also woke to such disquieting dreams. Quenton Cassidy knew every one of them by name.

Wearing only the weightless nylon shorts he slept in, he ambled stiffly to the dawn-lit window and stood momentarily, drowsily enjoying the pale orange-yellow glow that suffused the blackjack oaks outside his room. A slight breeze was chilly enough to raise goose bumps on sleep-warm flesh. He did not much like this early-morning business, but the idea of foregoing the ritual, even for one morning, never crossed his mind.

Quenton Cassidy was 6-2, his meager 167 pounds stretched across his frame in a manner dictated by the searing daily necessities of his special task. Beneath the tight skin, a smooth musculature glided with fluid ease, giving the impression of elastic, lightweight power; a featherless view of a young falcon.

There were no inefficient corners or bulges; the form was sharply chiseled as if from sand worn driftwood, fluted with oblique angles and long, tapering ridges, thin products of his care. Even now, standing perfectly still in the early morning glow, inverted teardrop thighs and high bunched calves suggested only motion: smooth effortless speed.

Stretching with a lovely kind of pain, he turned from the window and sat again on the edge of the rumpled bed to put on his worn Adidas Gazelle training shoes. His face was ruddy, even in the soft light, with a Scandinavian nose and sharp cheekbones; its attractiveness was debatable. Ragged brownish hair, bleached by hours of sun, tumbled in no particular pattern as he double-knotted his shoes. He washed his hands in the sink (the shoelaces, repository of ancient sweat, smelled like something that had died behind the refrigerator) and, with a grunt he was out the door and gone.

Quenton Cassidy was a miler.

Out in the early morning streets, the small group of runners made its way down University Avenue and turned north on tt Street; they would traverse a large seven-mile square known interchangeably as "The Morning Loop," "The Seven-Mile Course," or "The Bacon Strip" (for a series of undulating hills). Cassidy ran in the back of the pack with a loose stride that approached awkwardness. For a miler the 6:30 pace was a stumble, but with his accumulated fatigue he wanted nothing more stimulating. He conversed quietly with Jerry Mizner, a thinner and darker runner who had the look of a true distance man. He and Cassidy had been through what they now called the Trial of Miles. As with shipwreck survivors, hostages and others in dire circumstances, duress fosters familiarity, sometimes love. At times Cassidy and Mizner seemed to be able to read each others' minds.

"I don't think it can be done, really," Mizner said.

"It's absolutely true. I can sleep for at least the first half mile. I'm sure of it. They say soldiers can march when . . ."

"Nah . . ."

"Well, it *feels* like I'm sleeping, that's good enough for me."

"Feeling and doing are different. Plato said that. Or Hugh Hefner. One of the philosophers anyway."

For Cassidy there was no joy in this morning ritual. He slept hard and woke slowly. The easy wakers who found the morning workout a lark annoyed him to distraction. But the gentle conversation made it easier, a social occasion of sorts, for just as rank has its privileges so indeed does the barely comprehensible conditioning of good distance runners. They gab like magpies.

At paces that might stun and dismay the religious jogger, the runners easily kept up all manner of chatter and horseplay. When they occasionally blew by a huffing fattie or an aging road runner, they automatically toned down the banter to avoid overwhelming, to preclude the appearance of showboating (not that they slowed in the slightest). They in fact respected these distant cousins of the spirit, who, among all people, had some modicum of insight into their own days and ways. But the runners resembled them only in the sense that a puma resembles a pussy cat. It is the difference between stretching lazily on the carpet and prowling the jungle for fresh red meat.

"Suppose we'll soon know who's nice and rested from the weekend," Cassidy said. They were nearing the halfway point.

"Three guesses," said Mizner.

Despite the standing prohibition against racing during overdistance runs, a practice that rapidly got out of hand, occasionally a younger runner would cultivate a wild hair and light out for faint glory.

"Get a load," Cassidy said a few minutes later. Mizner looked up ahead and gave Cassidy an I'll-be-fucked shrug.

"Monday Morning Scalders," he said simply. Reference Jack Nubbins, 20 yards ahead of the group and still pressing. A freshman from the scrub pine territory around Orlando, he had been courted by a number of schools until his transcript revealed another example of functional illiteracy being turned loose by the republic's secondary educational facilities. When Nubbins arrived at Southeastern on special probationary status, he proceeded to inform his other first year colleagues at Doobey Hall: "Nubbins is the name and I cut the mile in 4:12.3 but I ride a horse better'n that 'n in the fall I hunt wild hog with my grandaddy, sometimes employin' a whepon, sometimes not. Nice ta meetcha."

The others, albeit distance runners and accustomed to certain amounts of weirdness, quickly pronounced him looney as a gull and accorded him temporary legend-in-his-own-time honors. Cassidy liked him okay, but figured he laughed too loud and tried to get too much mileage out of idioms like "hog-tied" and "gut-shot." Additionally, he appeared to lack a certain . . . *respect.*

"I don't think he is going to be able to restrain himself this morning," Cassidy muttered irritably. Some of the other runners were trying to pick up the pace and the group was starting to string out. The unspoken rule against racing had a sanction: those who persisted would be privileged to take on either Cassidy or Mizner (or both, if they couldn't decide who felt worse).

"You did 27 yesterday, didn't you?" Cassidy asked.

"Yup."

"You wouldn't want to come along anyway, would you? Just for grins?"

"Nope."

"That's what I thought. See ya."

"See ya."

A runner develops after a time a deep and powerful sense of pride. There was no question that Nubbins had been a prodigy of sorts; he had run the mile in 4:12 and had very nearly broken 9:00 for two miles. These were impressive accomplishments for a high schooler and gave Nubbins a certain automatic status among his young peers. A strong runner such as he, unfettered by a sense of unity and left unrestrained, would quickly destroy a team effort by simply pummeling his teammates day after day. Soon he would represent to them the pinnacle, the ultimate competitor; he would forever be the ceiling of their accomplishment. If his were a certain kind of personality (as Nubbins' was), he would accept this responsibility with love and great modesty. As long as he was indisputedly their vanquisher, he would laugh and joke with them and pound their backs in ribald camaraderie; then daily on the trails or roads or Tartan he would cruelly stomp them into submission. Mizner called it the Top Dog Syndrome. Everyone was subject to it to a certain extent (being bested in a daily workout by one's teammates did not portend well for the time when one went out to meet the rest of the world). But Cassidy had a genuine desire to bring the younger runners along without resort to humbling daily comparisons. He was stronger than they were; he wanted them to know it, but not to dwell on it. There is time, he would tell them; time and time and time. He wanted to impart some of the truths Bruce Denton had taught him, that you don't become a runner by winning a morning workout. The only true way is to marshal the ferocity of your ambition over the course of many days, weeks, months, and (if you could finally come to accept it) years. The Trial of Miles; Miles of Trials. How could he make them understand?

Nubbins was nowhere near a slouch. He was fast and courageous and mentally tough. Like all good runners, he gave away nothing. Cassidy knew he took winning for granted. He was accustomed to looking over at an opponent with a kind of detached pity before surging off with great style.

The gradual sinking despair of hitting what Nubbins figured to be a pretty damned hot pace and still finding a non-negotiable shadow on his shoulder was an altogether new and discomfiting experience for the young runner. Quenton Cassidy (his t-shirt read: GAUNT IS BEAUTIFUL) just looked over at Nubbins and smiled back pleasantly.

"You feeling pretty good, Jack?" Cassidy asked on the exhale.

"Not too bad, I reckon." Nubbins tried to grin.

"Good," Cassidy said. "Real good," as he kicked the pace down about 10 seconds. A minute later, just as Nubbins was getting accustomed to the alarming speed, Cassidy threw in a 32-second 220 to blow out the tubes and see what would happen. Nubbins' face was both blank and concerned. He looked like a man with a problem.

They flew along the early morning sidewalks of Kernsville at sub-five-minute pace, quite fast enough to startle pedestrians. They blew into the last mile, came upon and passed on either side of a sleepy coed bound for first period class: reams of biology notes filled the air.

Mizner trotted up to the front porch steps of Doobey Hall where Cassidy sagged in repose.

"Another convert to the no-race policy?" he asked.

"Hell if I know. Jeez, he's getting tough. Next time he's all yours. Did you see him back there anywhere?"

"Yeah, passed him half a mile back. Said he only turned off because he had to go lift weights at the field house. That what he told you?"

"No, all he said to me was: 'aaack.'"

"Aaack?"

"Aaack. And then he bent over, grabbed his knees, and commenced serious air sucking."

In the world of the runner, as in the ocean, there is a hierarchy of ferocity. The swift blue runner is eaten by the slashing barracuda, which is eaten by the awesome mako shark. In track, such relative positions are fixed more or less in black and white and are altered only at great and telling expense. Pride necessarily sprouts and grows; a pride that can only come from relentless kneading of unwilling flesh, painful ages of grinding and burning away all that is heavy, all that is strength-sapping and useless to the body as a projectile. The runner becomes, alas, haughty. He looks to those stronger with respect and fear, to those slower with sympathy or tolerance (they trod ground he has long since covered). The jettisoning of but a single second is announced like the birth of a first born.

Quenton Cassidy had run one mile in 4:00.3 and despite the studied indifference of the sporting world, four-minute milers are still very nearly as rare a breed as, say, successful heart transplant patients. The name "Cassidy" appeared in the school record books eight separate times counting the various relays. Though Jack Nubbins was extremely talented, Quenton Cassidy had viewed the Specter; when he reached down through the familiar layers of gloom and fatigue he generally found more there than a nameless and transient desire to acquire plastic trophies. He and Nubbins were not even in the same ball park.

"Good morning Captain Cassidy," called Roger Mobley, the All American shot putter. He surrounded his table as if it were a toy.

"Good morning Captain Mobley," Cassidy called back. "Join you in just a moment." Cassidy had probably started this exaggerated politeness among the tri-captains. He had a helpless affinity for harmless traditions.

The dining room at Doobey Hall was suggestive of what might happen if a cargo plane full of raw sirloin were to crash in Lion Country Safari. Several dozen athletes screamed, laughed, cajoled and punched each other in the easy fond intimacy that sports give to young men in groups and that they would consciously or subconsciously miss during the rest of their lives.

The good-humored pandemonium was considerable as they consumed the daily caloric requirements of several small nations. The relatively thin distance runners ate more than you would expect (Cassidy loaded his tray with three scrambled eggs, two pancakes, sausage, nearly a quart of milk, and two donuts for later). A colossus like Mobley, however, simply ate with a vengeance. With unswerving deliberation and concentration, he sat and *consumed.*

"Got to keep up my strength, right?" he would say. "Otherwise you gotta go to anabolic steroids and I don't want my little 'ol nuts to shrivel up like withered peanuts, right? Be fairly disappointin' to a number a' young ladies I'm acquainted with." He laughed like a bass drum.

The weight men were cocky, masculine and gentle; they never needed to bully, such was their looming physical presence. These specimens made their particular way in the world by heaving 16-pound iron balls great distances, tossing fiberglass plates out of vision, whipping sharpened aluminum shafts to the horizon. They were the most direct throwbacks to ancient times when such arts were cultivated to bash and puncture the armor of one's enemies; to spill blood from a distance. The confidence of those who do such things well is enormous and needs no bravado for support. They feared only each other.

The distance runners were serene messengers. Gliding along wooded trails and mountain paths, their spiritual an cestors kept their own solitary counsel for long hours while carrying some message the import of which was only one corner of their considerable speculation. They lived within themselves; long ago they did so, and they do today.

There was great unspoken respect between the weight men and the distance runners that was understood but never examined closely. They all dealt in one way or another with the absolute limits of the human body and spirit, but the runners and weight men seemed to somehow share a special understanding.

The sprinters and jumpers were quite another story. Their art revolved around a single explosive instant during which all was gained or lost. They were, perhaps, the spiritual descendants of the assault troops who leaped trenches and scaled barricades to lead the attack. They were nervous, high strung; either giddy with success or mired in swamp funk. They were the manic depressives of the track world. They constantly puffed themselves up with bravado, either to bolster their own flagging courage or to intimidate their opponents. The intensity of their competition was ferocious, almost cruel. A high jumper is in the air less than a second and a half. A sprinter's race takes ten seconds. A pole vaulter stands with fiberglass catapult in hand and contemplates his task far longer than the three seconds he struggles in the aspic of space. Cassidy pitied them the intensity of their contests, but at the same time was envious. One would grunt with the enormous effort, elastic muscles responding from years of weight training and explosive exercise, soaring up, up, and turning on an axis of perfect technique (so quick you would miss the beauty of it if you did not know what to look for), an awful moment of hate-filled glaring at the dread black and white bar—a fragile, shame-bearing obstruction, loathsome to the touch—and then a free fall (throwing your fist with joy and relief) back to earthly cares. Yes, there was something to that, Cassidy would think, particularly on a hot spring day when he had to run 15 or 20 quarter miles on a sticky track shimmering with heat.

It can be appreciated that Cassidy's table companions made for lively dining. He and Mizner, still damp from the shower, finished filling their trays and sat across from Mobley, who gave the impression of eating with both hands.

"Heard you guys were scalding dogs this morning," Mobley said, without halting the intake.

"Now just why the details of a morning workout would be of interest to a member of the gorilla corps is certainly beyond me," said Mizner, who well knew that Mobley reacted to no brash comments. The giant, all 6-6, 265 pounds of him scarcely stopped chewing. He looked up with an expression that didn't quite rise to the level of annoyance.

"Just be sure to keep those little shits in line, please Captain," he told the miler, shoveling in half a pancake. He gulped. "We've got a chance to win some big brass at conference this year and your pond birds are gonna have to come through for some points."

"Pond birds is it?" said Mizner, pounding his spoon like an impatient child. "Pond birds? I have a good mind to pump up for a couple of months and take your young ass on." The imagery evoked by such a notion caused considerable merriment around the room.

4. Cross Country

Cassidy's year, a runner's year, was divided into three parts. Fall was cross country, a season of six-mile races that stretched from the heat of Indian Summer to the frozen slushiness of November. Winter was the indoor season, a time of exciting races on the little banked wooden tracks in the large cities of the northeast. Spring and early summer were for what Denton called "real track." During the bleak expanse of fall and winter, however, "real track" was too far off to think about.

Cassidy did not like cross country; the distance was too long for a miler, he disliked not being able to "feel" the finish line during the race. Six miles seemed interminable to a runner accustomed to the blissful unyielding symmetry of four quarter miles run in nearly 60 seconds each (in his own specialty he never felt the first lap, the second and third were pure hell but still quick, and the last went by in the giddy excitement of the sprint and the locked-up zombie gait of total oxygen debt).

"What's wrong with cross country?" Denton asked. Warmdown time was slow luxury, an easy mile of deep, aching satisfaction.

"Some weird people like it, I know that. I'm very aware of that," Cassidy said. A muted glance passed between Denton and Mizner. They had heard this before.

"Six miles . . . 10,000 meters," Cassidy said disgustedly, "over hill and dale out in the middle of nowhere. Spit freezing on your godamn chin. Five hundred complete wild men in the mud, running up on your heels with long spikes. Oh, I love cross country all right. I also like being flayed alive with a rusty straight razor."

"Why, Quenton, you were *county champion* in high school. I saw it in your scrap book. You had a clipping from the morning paper and a clipping from the evening paper. Don't you remember?" Denton asked seriously. Mizner bit his lip.

17

"Sticking my tongue in a light socket, that's a lot of fun too," Cassidy said moodily.

"But you *did* win the . . ."

"Yes, and for your information it was my *mother* who cut out those clippings, you can tell by how neatly they are trimmed. I don't operate that way."

"Quenton Cassidy, *cross-country champion* . . ."

"It was a two-point-five-mile race and the competition was fierce, lads. Several local entries could have been real trouble if the race had only been two and a quarter miles shorter. They were the kind of guys who yell and scream for the first hundred yards, you know, like they are having a good time and all . . ."

"But they couldn't hold the pace, eh?"

"It kills me when they yell and scream like that, or talk back and forth to each other real nonchalant like it's not bothering them at all," Cassidy looked genuinely puzzled.

"But tough cookies nonetheless?" Denton wouldn't let him off the hook.

"To a man," Cassidy grinned at Mizner. "I leaned at the tape and nipped second place by about half a mile. Maybe they sent the wrestling team by accident. Anyway, Palm Beach County is not noted for its cross-country strength."

"Half a mile is what Mize usually gets you by, isn't it?"

Cassidy feigned hurt. "You don't need to rub it in. I *told* you I don't like it. You distance animals can have it. Milers are too fine tuned to enjoy that pastoral crap."

"So are road runners, race walkers, orienteering nuts and a bunch of other folks looking to avoid real confrontation," Denton said.

"Right," Mizner said. He liked watching Cassidy having to take it for awhile.

"Real confrontation is four laps and a cloud of . . . Tartan dust," Cassidy said.

"That's clever."

"Tartan dust?" Mizner asked.

"Oh yes, that's really clever," Denton shook his head.

"You guys can just blow it out your . . ."

"Steady big fellow," Denton said in his mock deep voice, the Lone Ranger calming old Silver down after a hard day of chasing desperadoes. Cassidy laughed and threw a half-hearted elbow at Denton, who dodged and rolled his eyes.

Coach Benjamin Cornwall was getting into his car when he saw the three of them jostling each other at the door of the field house. Weary from his own work, he never could figure out what it was about a 20-mile day that made some people so playful.

"Three more?" Cassidy asked.

"At least."

He and Mizner did 100-yard striders in the grass, trying to build up some lactic acid resistance and get the systems moving. They wanted to be well into what some people call "the second wind" before the race started. The runners usually referred to it by the physiologists' term, "homeostasis." Whatever it is called, it entails a good hard warmup. They had already run three miles at an easy pace.

Dual meets were not at all hectic and Cassidy didn't really mind this miniature version of cross country. A single team would not usually have enough talent to present much of a challenge, even to Cassidy. Neither he nor Mizner considered this particular Saturday important enough to slack off their training in the slightest. They had both run 16 miles the day before, a gambit known as "running through" a meet. When you are beaten by an athlete running through, it means you are owned by him body and soul. The Fixed Order will have been established in a most definitive way, to be altered only by some kind of felonious conduct, possibly involving Claymore mines.

Bruce Denton ran up from behind them and fell in with their strides. Even at this quick pace his legs moved with a ghostly lack of effort. Runners from the other team stole glances at him. Cassidy thought: the little sons of bitches are experiencing true awe.

"You doing your morning?" Mizner asked.

"Yep. Thought I'd come over and watch the fun."

"I hate racing in the morning like this," Cassidy offered.

"There's not a whole lot about this deal you *do* like, is there sport?"

Denton smiled at him.

"Not much, I guess," Cassidy admitted gloomily. "My gut goes crazy . . ."

"Do these guys have any horses?" Denton asked.

"The redheaded fellow," said Mizner, gesturing. "The one so very obviously not looking at us. That's Eammon O'Rork his own self, a genuine imported Irishman. Guess they couldn't afford themselves an African." Mizner was unconsciously mimicking Cassidy.

"Gave you a scare last year indoors, didn't he, sport?" Denton turned to Cassidy.

"Scare isn't the word. It was the Mason-Dixon Games in Louisville. The score was, the Kid: four oh three point two; the Irish Upstart: four oh three point two. But it was closer than it sounds."

Denton laughed as they started another strider. O'Rork's freckled face was clouded with concentration as he did his own warmup. He glanced constantly at his watch, timing it to the minute. They had about eight minutes before assembling for the starting instructions.

O'Rork was older than the rest of his team; older and far more mature. His talent and courage had delivered him from the rigors of life in Northern Ireland and he went at distance running with the uncomplicated ardor of the truly hungry. Denton appraised the Irishman's stride as he went by and thought: there is always something, isn't there fellow? With us and prizefighters, the wounded and the fleet . . .

O'Rork was thinking about Cassidy's cloth-thin victory the previous season. It still rankled him. The American was all right, he supposed, but perhaps just too blithe a spirit for his own good. A few weeks after the Louisville meet O'Rork had picked up an intestinal flu and was all but incapacitated during the outdoor season. It had been a bad December: a telegram (hanging in a serious looking plastic envelope on his dormitory room door) brought the bad news from home. He had sat quietly for five minutes looking at the sad little yellow message, then he pulled on his training shoes and went out to run himself into a blubbering mush in the hills surrounding his Tennessee campus. Then he was in bed for two weeks and really wouldn't have minded dying. Cold Decembers, he thought, watching the carefree American. I have known too many of them.

They were less than a half mile from the finish; Cassidy ran slightly behind O'Rork off his left shoulder, eyes fixed on the freckled neck. He was drafting without malice or humor. If O'Rork minded being used in this manner he gave no sign.

Somewhere up ahead of them Jerry Mizner sauntered into the finish chute with the more tolerable fatigue of victory on his face. He had employed the simple expedient of running away from everyone. Similarly isolated from the rest of the runners, the two milers bruised each other in the tensionless grind of those who struggle for second place.

Cassidy was *in extremis*. They had gone through the first mile in 4:37 and Cassidy thought with alarm: *godamighty that hurt.* The heavy training of the past several weeks had sapped him; when he reached down for an extra surge just to hold pace, he found only a searing strained feeling with which he was intimately familiar: red line city. He was not enjoying his weekend.

Hanging onto O'Rork these past two miles had been possible through a dreary combination of will power and wishful thinking. Coast, you bastard, Cassidy told himself. Then he put his mind into neutral, locked onto the freckled shoulder and obtained his mental abstracts: gliding, floating, covering ground. He balked unashamedly at the remarkable discomfort he was living through at the moment. He even thought of tossing it in, not an unusual sentiment, but knew it wouldn't happen. He also kept telling himself that they wouldn't all be this bad because if they were he surely couldn't live with it. He didn't consider himself particularly brave.

A long path led up the hill through Beta Woods and onto the track for the finish. The hill was steep; it numbed the legs and discouraged fast finishes. O'Rork intentionally worked Cassidy hard on this hill, surgically removing the sting from a kick he remembered very distinctly. Pumping hard, he pulled away. With, great distress, Cassidy reeled him back in. This isn't so bad, Cassidy thought, I'm just dying is all. But hang on asshole and maybe you can be a hero at the end. The self-loathing was genuine and when he thought about it later it always mystified him.

Every stride now caused him the most profound regret. Spitting fluffy wads of congealed saliva, his thinking soon came only in staccato bursts: 200 yards . . . keep him near . . . keep him near . . .

Within sight of the finish he could vaguely see Mizner doing a silly bounce and yelling something as Cassidy began to lock up. Andrea would be there somewhere but he didn't see her. A white haze—a normal phenomenon—clouded everything, like looking through the dirty window of a long-abandoned house. Funny how your mind works at the end like this, he thought. The excitement was all outside as he watched quietly from inside his raging skull.

A hundred yards to go he thought *oh christ* and threw the remainder of what was left into it; now *that* really cost him.

O'Rork burst away from him quickly and won by ten yards.

Cassidy was bent over at the waist, hands on knees, doing a little circle stagger that in other circumstances might have passed for amusing. The other runners were noisily starting to come in. Mizner stood with his arm around Cassidy's waist, providing balance. "Easy, easy," he said in quiet empathetic tones. Cassidy could not speak; his eyes bulged insanely, breaths came in greedy rasps and his face was a splotchy violet color. "Yack!" he said, trying to straighten up. It was too soon; back to the hands-on-knees death grip, fetal rest of the totally blown-out runner. The white haze had thickened into a heavy fog; he felt faint but knew his conditioning held all horrors at bay except in extreme heat. These were the worst few seconds and he understood better than anything else that like the tail fin, the Nehru jacket and the republic itself, they too would pass. The drained elation, special property and reward of those who have been to the edge and back, would come later. But for now he had a while longer to hurt.

Andrea, who had never seen such things, stood close by, almost afraid to touch him, hands fluttering around each other and over to his wet singlet. The rasping, dripping, violet-shaded runner studied intently the moist earth between his spiked toes and seemed unaware of her presence. Was he all right?

"Sure hell, he's all right," Mizner said, surprised by her question. "He's just run himself a race is all." Seeing that Cassidy had his own balance, Mizner went off gaily to check the team scores. Finally straightening up enough to stumble for a few steps, the runner looked at her and said again: "Yack." But this time there was something that could almost have passed for a smile on his hot face. To her he looked near death—not a mysterious wan passing, but a demise culminating in hot bouts of fever and hallucination, fearful and soul-wrenching. The smile brought her considerable cheer. "Yack?" she smiled back.

"Gee, that was un*com*fortable," he said seriously, as he began to make himself walk; he was unaccustomed to long spikes, one caught, he stumbled as he gripped her hand. "What did you think?"

"I thought you were going to die there for a second. I was afraid."

"Well," he said jovially, "that's cross-country biz."

Denton stood 20 yards away, chatting with the coaches. But his eyes followed Quenton Cassidy very carefully.

Half an hour later the three of them trotted off, laughing, on the eight mile course to get in some mileage for the day.

5. Bowling for Dollars

erry Mizner was an admitted obsessive compulsive, probably an absolute necessity for a true distance man; his mind adapted well to the distance runner's daily toil. Cassidy was far more impulsive by nature and had to painfully teach himself the record-keeping, ritualistic, never-miss-a-mile mentality of a dedicated runner. Mizner and Denton, like Jim Ryun or Gerry Lindgren, were natural runners who had never even attempted other sports seriously. Cassidy had good speed, and like Peter Snell had done well in other sports before concentrating on middle distances. At times he felt like a spiritual interloper with the other two; occasionally he was actually jealous of the way they casually handled the stress. Slowly, slowly, he learned the lifestyle of the compulsive personality in order to survive the grind. But at times he tottered. Mizner felt truly sorry for him during these periods of blue funk and strange behavior. Cassidy would tell him:

"The kid is largely unhappy."

"There there."

"Got caught in the rain and muh green stamps got all plastered to muh Sweet'N Low."

"It'll be okay . . ."

"Bet muh money on the bob-tailed nag . . ."

The friction produced by superimposing alien psychological traits on his own behavior occasionally burst forth in interesting manifestations: Cassidy arranging a quadruple moon shot (the famous Four Way Pressed Ham) out of the tailgate of a duly licensed state vehicle; Cassidy presenting a series of unauthorized awards at the cross-country banquet in mixed company (". . .and now a very special presentation, the Zazu Pitts Memorial Plaque to the runner who most infrequently committed flatus on the morning run . . ."); Cassidy, as Nubbins put it one night in absolute bewilderment, "just plain walkin' around *talkin'* funny."

Whatever outward form his inner disquietudes took, his odd energies held Doobey Hall like a spell. In this tiny society where the extreme was commonplace, Cassidy's mystique affected everyone. He was often sought out for counsel and his apparent reluctance to render it only added to his aura. His opinion was solicited on matters scholastic, financial, romantic, and mechanical, though he disavowed expertise in all these areas.

He had the gifted athlete's innate sense of timing, a sense of providence, of fantasy, an intuition into the art of the Proper Moment, where the escape velocity of frivolous lunacy triumphs over the mean gravity of everyday life. By way of example, the doldrums of summer were approaching at the end of his junior year when Cassidy, bored with the hot, ennui-stilled Sunday lunch, posed a general question to the drowsy dining room: "I wonder if Spider can jump over a Volkswagen."

Spider Gordon looked up sleepily from his vegetable soup.

"Of course he can jump over a Volkswagen," said the giant Mobley, his mouth full as usual. "You ought to know that."

"Yes. Yes, of course he can. Spider can easily jump over a Volkswagen," Cassidy said. Mumbling, everyone turned back to the unexciting lunch, clearly disappointed. What had gotten into Cassidy?

"The *real* question," Cassidy continued after a proper pause, "the real question *here* is, whether Spider can jump over *two* Volkswagens!"

The philosophical extensions of this problem became quickly evident and the dining room emptied like a barroom shooting. The neighborhood was scoured for a certain make of foreign car and the entire affair went down in Doobey Hall folklore as "The Day Spider Gordon Busted His Ass On The Fourth Volkswagen."

New members of the team, freshmen or transfer students, were given no special warning about Cassidy. They found out, as everyone else did, in the best way they could.

"Gentlemen," Cassidy would say, rising at dinner and tapping his glass for silence, "we have got to have a plan. We must have a plan even if it is *wrong.*" There would come scattered, polite applause.

Chairs scraped as everyone turned their attention to Cassidy's table. Some veterans muttered approval at these odd sentiments while the new guys looked around in stark confusion. After waiting for the buzz to die down, Cassidy continued:

"I realize World Team Bowling is a relatively new concept. But gentlemen (a small chuckle here) as our attendance figures indicate, it is a concept . . . *whose time has come!*" Cheers from the veterans. New guys aghast.

"Now we have made some mistakes. No one denies that." Negative mumbling; certainly no one was going to deny that. "When our Eye-talian all-star here, Jerry Mizerrelli, split his pants on network teevee going for that spare in the sixth frame against Akron, well gentlemen, it was a bleak moment for our fledgling organization as well as for sports in general. Certainly no one is faulting Jerry for that one, but I'll tell you that all of us, players and management alike, were keeping our fingers crossed. All of us except Jerry, of course, who was doing a medium-slow crab walk with a new Brunswick double ball bag jammed in his crotch . . ."

Well, it was just old crazy Cassidy of course, and maybe the moon was full or something. But he had eaten their bread and salt (and was always walking over exhausted from his race to inquire just how *was* the pole vault going anyway?) and to put it simply he could get away with just about anything with them.

At times he swiveled the spotlight and its harsh glare fell on those not quite so ready for wholesale craziness; it was in this way Mizner had been "discovered." As a new distance man, Mizner had sat around with a dour expression through his first of Cassidy's Bowling Banquets, and had generally been marked off as an old maid until Cassidy suddenly presented him with some mythical honor one night. Mizner stood timidly as Cassidy handed him a Dr. Pepper can fashioned into a ridiculous trophy with a scrap of tinfoil. The new runner stared with wide eyes at the bemused, expectant faces around the room. He cleared his throat. A few veterans looked at each other; this was going to be good.

"I, uh, would like to thank Mr. Cassadamius for this here award and I'd like to say something else while I'm standing here. You know, I wasn't really nobody at all when Mr.

Cassadamius found me in that little three-lane alley in Pittsburgh. Sure, I mean I was a local hotshot and all, rolling 210, 215, and just, you know, getting along. But I wasn't no serious contender is what I'm trying to tell ya. Never made the cut or nothin' like that. And then one day Mr. Cassadamius comes in and be watches me roll a few frames, no more'n that, just a few frames, and then he comes over big as day and says 'Son,' he says, 'Son, if you get rid of that limp wrist of yours and learn to come *over* the ball on your follow through, you just might knock yourself over a few a' them pins.' I mark that as the turnin' point in my career which has led me to the point at which I am at today." He started to sit down, changed his mind and stood back up, clearing his throat.

"That, uh, and going to the 25-pound composite ball. Thank you."

They sat stunned for several seconds, finally breaking into rowdy applause that quickly became a standing ovation. Mizner looked around the room with a faint smile on his dark face, making little bows with his head.

Cassidy, sitting across from him all mooney-eyed, fell smack in love.

6. Bruce Denton

Quenton Cassidy would have thought it amusing had someone described him as a great runner. He wasn't even the best in the neighborhood. Nor was Jerry Mizner, who could claim to be an All American at the six-mile distance. It wasn't even close: the best runner around Kernsville was Bruce Denton, a methodical, dryly humorous doctoral candidate in botany. While both younger runners were considered formidable talents in collegiate circles, Denton's place in the hierarchy of distance running was lofty and secure. The others held him in secret awe and reported his words to comrades with the solemnity of one reading from the Dead Sea Scrolls: "Well, now Denton says you should warm down like blah blah . . ." Such pronouncements could halt the most vociferous arguments.

As an undergraduate at a small school in Ohio, Denton had not been a spectacular performer (he ran the mile in 4:08), but as with many runners he began to improve with age. He took up graduate studies at Southeastern and started training again with a scientifically precise vengeance. On the altar of Consistency he offered up no less than two portions of his life per day, seven days a week, 52 weeks a year. His neatly filled calendar diary told no lies; the symbolism of the unmissed workout—ritualistic with him—took on an importance he did not like to admit, even to himself.

On a rainy day in November he was so sick with the flu that his wife, Jeannie, felt constrained to stay home from work to look after him. He threw up regularly and had diarrhea so badly his stomach muscles began cramping. Nonetheless, he arose and ran two eerie miles at a stumbling pace, pale and shivering the whole way. His wife was aghast. Again in the afternoon he repeated the process, this time nearly fainting as he staggered back into the apartment. Dr. Stavius—whose claim to fame was that he had once punctured a blister on the foot of Roger Bannister—stormed into Denton's sickroom and pronounced him a madman.

"What crazy?" Denton asked, trying to make his parched lips resemble a smile. "After today I'm 16 miles behind for the week."

Over the course of several years at Southeastern, as Denton's reputation grew, a number of undergraduate runners decided they would train with him, thinking to pick up on The Secret. The new man showed up the first day expecting all manner of horrific exertion, and was generally stunned and giddy to find he could so easily make it through one of Denton's calendar days. Showing up the second morning at 6:30 he would be of good cheer, perhaps trying to imagine how he would handle the pressure of his incipient fame. That day also went well enough, but he would begin to notice something peculiar. There was no let-up. The tempo was always moderate but steady. If a new guy decided to pick up the pace, that's where it stayed, whether he finished with the group or not. You showed off at your peril.

On the third day (assuming the new man made it that far) his outlook began to bleaken. For one thing, he was getting very, very tired. No particular day wore him out, but the accumulation of steady mileage began to take its toll. He never quite recovered fully between workouts and soon found himself walking around in a more or less constant state of fatigue-depression, a phase Denton called "breaking down." The new runner would find it more tedious than he could bear. The awful truth began to dawn on him: There was no Secret! His days would have to be spent in exactly this manner, give or take a mile or two, for longer than he cared to dwell upon, if he really wanted to see the olive wreath up close. It was going to be the most difficult, heart-rending process he would endure in the course of his life.

At that point most of them drifted away. They searched within themselves somewhere along a dusty 10-mile trail or during the bad part of a really gut-churning 440 on the track, and found some key element missing. Sheepishly they would begin to miss workouts, then stop showing up altogether. They would convince themselves: There must be another way, there *has* to be. The attrition rate was nearly 100 per cent.

Only Cassidy and Mizner made it through and learned about the Trial of Miles, though in fairness they already had discovered much of it on their own. When Denton saw that they were different, he opened up to them and they discovered for the first time that the silently gliding machine at their sides all those months actually had a personality. Accustomed as they were to the flamboyance of their teammates, they were captivated by Denton's penchant for understatement. Once, upon returning from the large international road race at Springbank, Canada, they gathered around his locker, waiting for details. Well, they wanted to know, how did it go?

"Not too badly, I guess," said Denton, dressing in his quick, methodical way. "I got in a token mile in the morning and then ran a few after the race so the week's total won't suffer too much. Jogged around the Atlanta airport, too." He added the last thoughtfully, scratching his chin.

"Well godamn, Bruce, all the Europeans are usually there, Aussies, even some Africans. Who the hell won?" Cassidy was impatient.

"Oh I won it," Denton said breezily, apparently still thinking about the coup of getting a couple of extra miles at the airport.

"Christ, you won it! Ron Hill, Dave Bedford, Frank Shorter, all those guys usually . . ."

"Yeah . . ." Denton said, pausing in the middle of tying his shoelace as if remembering something pleasant from his childhood, ". . . nicest bunch of guys you'd ever want to meet."

When during his first post-graduate year Denton came from relative obscurity to run 27:10 for six miles at the Drake Relays, knowledgeable distance buffs were mildly surprised that such an undistinguished performer could run an international caliber race out of the blue. However unlikely it seemed in retrospect, at the time the phrase "flash in the pan" was bandied about. There are scoffers, it seems, in every line of work. Later that spring when Denton made the U.S. Olympic team, nearly everyone professed surprise. Everyone except Dr. Stavius and a promising young miler named Quenton Cassidy, who watched the U.S. trials on television.

True to form, Denton powered across the finish line in the 5000 meters and simply jogged past the cameras over to his sweats and departed the stadium. Everyone had ignored him for so long, it seemed to Cassidy a delicious gesture.

Now, two years after that Olympiad, though they had survived the Trial of Miles and knew his "Secret," and though they were championship collegiate runners, Cassidy and Mizner knew better than anyone that Denton played the game on an entirely different level. He was unencumbered by such things as team standings, dual meets, conference titles; as a graduate student he ran for himself (nominally for the Southeastern University "Track Club," of which he was the sole member). His fare was paid to large meets all over the country by promoters who wanted his name for their posters. During the indoor season he would likely be found in nearly any large city in the country on a given weekend, running either a two-mile (which he called a "deuce") or a three-mile race.

He knew or had run against most of the top runners in the world; he had raced Ron Clarke on the grass in Australia (winning with a big kick), he had suffered through a high-altitude two-mile against the smiling, fierce Kip Keino (losing to a big kick). He had spent several weeks in Eugene with *The Pre*, listening thoughtfully to the Bowerman/Dellinger school of thought (tempering his awe with miler Roscoe Divine's confession that he snuck out and ran extra workouts because the assigned ones were too easy). He had listened to Gerry Lindgren say "*bad berries*" about three thousand times during a hot 20-miler outside Spokane. He had had a long, pleasant argument with Kenny Moore as to the real value of the Mileage Ethic as opposed to the hard/easy theory, which ended when he told the great marathoner: "You may not *believe* in mileage, but you sure as *hell* run mileage."

There was little wonder Bruce Denton had more quiet confidence than Cassidy or Mizner in the distance runner's little rigid hierarchy of black and white numerics, and little wonder why they held him in awe. In his apartment there was an overburdened second bedroom used as a combination study and trophy room. In the corner was an ancient filing cabinet with locking drawers. In the bottom drawer, the only one that still locked, was a flat oblong leather box.

In that box was an Olympic gold medal.

7. Andrea

I'm in love with her I tell you," Cassidy said.

"You don't even know her."

"I don't care. If I knew her it might spoil it. Did you see her little forehead, how it was all wrinkled and sweaty?"

"Come on . . ."

"She was concentrating on her *pace* fer chrissakes . . ."

"Awww . . ."

This was how it all began, back at the very start of the school year. The scrap of red yarn she carelessly tied her hair up with might have had something to do with it. Or perhaps it was the *very* sincere look on her face as they trundled by her on the warmup course that day. Even Mizner commented on how pretty she was.

Southeastern University sported, like many southern schools, any number of mind-numbing pharmacists' daughters with hard little asses, dairy maid complexions, and the general instincts of a wounded animal in the forest.

Cassidy had no idea what made her seem so different, but he sensed that she had survived 20 years as an attractive female in the republic without having had her mind reamed out by teevee, Gloria Steinem, or Helen Gurley Brown.

Several days later on the three mile warmup they saw her again.

"Try to smooth it out a little," Cassidy suggested as they passed. He demonstrated with an exaggerated version of the classical running stride (a stride that he did not use himself when the chips were down).

She looked up, her damp forehead wrinkled with concentration, and stared at Cassidy as if he were some aquatic parasite that had attached itself to her ankle while she was wading in a creek. Cassidy nearly swooned.

"You're crazy," Mizner told him.

"She appreciated the advice," Cassidy decided.

"She thinks you're crazy, too."

"How do you figure?"

"What would you do if some guy out of the blue just up and starts critiquing your stride?"

"Challenge him to a race."

"If his t-shirt said 'Pittsburgh Holy Rollers' and he started prancing around like this . . . you'd think he was crazy, too. And you'd be right."

"Mize, the girl was deeply moved. She appreciated the advice," Cassidy repeated, troubled.

"The *girl*," Mizner was annoyed, "has a gimpy leg. I saw it yesterday when she was stretching up at the track. She probably not only didn't appreciate the advice, she probably thinks you're an asshole."

"Oh."

But giving up quickly was not one of Quenton Cassidy's foibles. A week later he saw her in his haunt, the Gay Nineties (a rather unfortunately named and remarkably heterosexual tavern). Her blond hair was down, but there was no mistaking her. The sight of her made his heart hurt. He waited around until her two girl friends got up to play foosball, then he made his slew-footed entrance. She saw him coming.

"Well, well. The coach," she said. It was only faintly sarcastic. She even smiled a little, he thought.

"Ah yes, well I . . ." He spilled a trickle of beer as he started to make some expansive gesture. Idiotically, he began licking foam off his wrist.

"Don't do that," she said.

"Right. Uh, look, I'm sorry if I . . ."

"That's all right. I was a little annoyed, but then I figured you might have taken a class or something and maybe even knew what you were talking about."

"Not really," he said happily, sliding into the booth across from her, "but I know a bunch of guys who are real good."

"Are you on the track team or something?"

"Yes indeed," he said, feeling slightly looney watching her green flame eyes in the pale tavern light.

"Don't stare like that. What event do you do?"

"Decathlon," he said.

"Really?" she asked. "How far do you throw it?"

They drifted. Dappled by the hard cyprus shadows, out into the burning September sun, they drifted. In one of those pleasant cool eddies life provides the young in fall or spring, they drifted, quite unaware of the not-so-far-off rattle of bones...

"I didn't ask to see the movie," she said. "I thought the book was sophomoric. Baroque and sophomoric. The movie was your idea."

"It was my fault. But your friends wanted to know . . ."

"My friends think *Love Story* is the finest literature to come down the pike since . . . *The Prophet*. You should have eased up on them. Some day they will be producing babies and not causing anyone any trouble at all."

"All I said was such cornpone has a way of co-opting real life. I mean it's fun to talk snazzy and run around and play in the snow with *yur girl* for chrissakes, but I don't know if I'll ever be able to do that now without seeing myself as an out-take from some godawful movie . . ."

"Tear ducts raped. 'I resent having my tear ducts raped' I believe is just about how you put it."

"And were following up with something about the teensy weensy sexual members of dope-crazed screenwriters or something . . ."

"Well . . ."

"Mary Ellen Conastee was close to having a stroke. She's a harmless girl, Quenton. You're going to have to break in a little slower with some people."

He looked over and gave her what he thought of as his pixie grin.

"Don't give me that pixie grin crap," she told him.

They drifted. Cassidy was plopped without grace in his innertube, his white bottom now thoroughly chilled by the icy waters of the Ichnetucknee River. Andrea somehow accomplished a similar position without the same loss of dignity: on her it looked sultry. When she leaned back to take the sun he looked carefully at the two brown legs draped over the edge of her tube, but could hardly detect the difference between them that would forever put a little catch in her walk.

Of course there would be something like that; he lacked interest in the perfect item. Quenton Cassidy, unmoved by kittens, sonnets, and sunsets, was nonetheless given to tragic flaws.

In order to arrange this day of perfect drifting, an entirely traditional local pastime, he and Mizner (now floating up ahead with his date) had arisen at 7:30 and run no less than 17 miles. It was the only way they could spend their day in the sweet haze of Boone's Farm Apple Wine and still appease the great white Calendar God whose slighted or empty squares would surely turn up someday to torment the guilt-ridden runner. They went through such contortions occasionally to prove to themselves that their lives weren't really so abnormal, but the procedure merely accentuated the fact. There were several ways it could be done. If they were going to the beach, they might put it off and run when they got there, but contrary to popular opinion, beach running is only jolly fun for the first five miles or so. After that, the cute little waves become redundant, the sand reflects the sun up blindingly, seeming to focus it on the upper lip, grains of sand slip annoyingly into the heel of the shoe or flip up on the back of the leg. Fifteen hot miles on a long, flat beach is considered good sport only by those who haven't tried it. The ocean is too infinite; the run seems as if it will never end.

They could always put training off until they got back in the evening, but that just made things worse. No beer! None of the sticky wine! Their friends would slyly try to tempt them, see if they really took all that training stuff seriously. It was too much to ask. Better to get it all over with and then be able to drink beer like any other citizen.

Though he hated running in the morning worse than anything he could think of at the moment, at this moment Cassidy was glad to have it over. The oversized tubes floated along on the gin-clear river, meandering slowly under the spooky cyprus stands and pleasantly out into the sun. Even though it was Florida, it was north Florida and as winter approached, this kind of activity would become a fond memory.

Cassidy paddled over awkwardly to Andrea's tube and invited her to double up. Flirting with disaster for several seconds, she finally accomplished the difficult maneuver.

"Next time you do the transfer at sea, please," she said. Her warmth beside him was searing; she smelled of summer, youth, Sea and Ski, and moist, slightly sweet sex. Clearly edible. His head spun from the wine and sun. Muscles along the top of his thighs trembled from his morning exertion. In a month or so he knew they would carry him screaming around the track. He had the power.

"Ouch!" she said. "What's that all about?"

8. Dick Doobey

The head football coach pushed the sweaty baseball cap back on his bristly crewcut head, leaned way back in his $1,495 Execu-Kliner, plopped his rippled-soled coaching shoes up on his gigantic gleaming desk and wondered what in the world was becoming of him.

With mournful pride he surveyed the wide expanse of lush maroon and silver carpeting that displayed in the very center a custom-woven and very savage looking Daryl the Swamp Dawg; the office was so large as to invite speculation as to which indoor sports might or might not be accommodated.

The Rotarians had been most unkind that morning. Whereas several years ago he would have been treated with the unbridled respect and admiration due a United States senator or even a big money media evangelist, this day's luncheon had been laced with a certain ill-concealed nastiness that now knitted Dick Doobey's brow like a ten-dollar pot holder.

L.T. Doaches, owner of the Fat Boy's Pit Barbecue on Interstate 75, had posed the question: Since Doobey's first three years had allegedly been "rebuilding" years for the ol' Swamp Dawgs, and keeping in mind certain early and somewhat rash predictions, in retrospect how did the coach view this past season's 4-6 record? As L.T. put it: "I mean, are we gonna start rebuilding again without seein' what it was we got ourseffs built the last time?"

It was a mouthful of a question, L.T. having obviously practiced it some, but he delivered it without a flaw and, to the affirmative grumbles and guffaws of the group, replaced his pear-shaped bottom on the Holiday Inn folding chair, Dick Doobey meanwhile discerning all he wanted to know about the general mood of the brotherhood.

A little surprised by the brewing hostility, he babbled something about some real fine junior college transfers, some redshirts who would be "a real great help to us out there next year," and a few other favorite mouthworn Doobey maxims. Kernsville cynics suspected that the NCAA held yearly seminars for the purpose of allowing football coaches to swap these fluffs of wisdom back and forth. Doobey's favorite was: "In order to win you've got to avoid losing first." Things like that.

The same material that at one time would have at least won nodding approval now netted him a few muffled coughs. He was dying up there with a live mike and a glass of watery iced tea. He tried to tell some funny anecdotes, generally racially tinged, mangled one-liners uttered by one of "the boys," the punchline of which inevitably began: "Well gosh coach . . . "

As a last resort he told some of his My Daddy Used To Say chestnuts that always won chuckles of nostalgia for the old man if not admiration for his fumbling offspring. Nothing worked. Finally, one sports writer, a short Jewish fellow Doobey disliked intensely, asked Doobey's opinion of the "Dump Dick Doobey" bumper stickers that were showing up on cars in and around Kernsville.

Doobey cleared his throat. "Well, now, there has always been dissident elements, you see, in our American System, and while these people may think they are doing the right thing, and while they are certainly entitled to their opinion, you see, such disloyalty to the program can only . . ."

This tack also netted him little in the way of positive Rotarian feedback. It was becoming painfully obvious to him that many of these very Rotarians were themselves either among the "dissident elements" or were thinking seriously about enlisting.

Dick Doobey was discovering that a football coach in a small southern town walks upon hallowed ground only if he is either "rebuilding" or else whaling tar out of his weekly opponents. There is no middle ground called "Holding Your Own." And you can sell the "rebuilding" concept only so long before you find your career of about as much moment to the community at large as the blocked '48 Packard rusting in Grandma's back yard. Uprisings are fomented; Rotarians go on careful rampages; and—oh the infamy!—the very bumpers of automobiles call for your destruction.

Dick Doobey took his feet off the desk and pressed the intercom.

"Mary Lou, come on in here a minute, willya hon?" His mind reeled with daring, if half-baked, strategies. Mary Lou, hoping for hanky panky, bounced in, mini-skirted and primed for action; she sported an alarming beehive hairdo.

"Shall I get the key to the whirlpool?" she asked coyly.

"Uh, not now, hon. I need you to take something down for me." Frowning slightly, she left to get her steno pad.

"This will be a memo to all coaches from Dick Doobey as Athletic Director, not head football coach. You, ah, don't need to write all that down, hon, I mean word for word and all. Like when I said 'not head football coach' you didn't need to write 'not head . . .' Well, you know what to put." Her shoulders sagged impatiently. *What an incredible mind,* she thought. They went through something like this nearly every time.

Doobey waited self-consciously for a few moments as if to allow his words to fall from the air so he could start fresh.

"Ahem. New Rules on Hair Groomin' and Dress, uh, Procedures For Southeastern University Athletes . . ."

9. An Afternoon

The runners circled the big grass field in a slow, prancing jog, their shirtless bodies gleaming with sweat. As they trotted by Ben Cornwall, they all looked up at him almost simultaneously. Their rasping and coughing grew louder as they approached.

"One thirty eight. Two to go, guys," the coach told them. They immediately lowered their heads and continued jogging. They were on their rest interval, respite in the acid storm.

Cornwall started back across the field to catch the next 660 on his split-timer. A 330 jog wasn't much recovery time and he could tell by the strain on their faces that this was no lark for them. The last two would be quicker perhaps but Cassidy and Mizner had made sure the first six were evenly paced and fast. Cornwall studied his two star runners as he crossed the field to the opposite post. They looked less distraught than the rest, but not by much. He watched them carefully across the way, trying to judge by the sluggishness of their jog how badly it was going for them. Cassidy was saying something to Mizner, who replied with a thin smile. Cornwall couldn't hear it, of course, and wouldn't have understood if he had. The conversation, between gasps, went like this:

"There must be some mistake," Cassidy said. "I have not yet attained that sense of euphoria commonly reported by runners."

"You are speaking no doubt of the fabled 'third wind.'"

"I'm not sure. I haven't read *Runner's World* lately so I don't know what they are calling it this month."

When they reached the post Cornwall clicked the expensive timer and studied with admiration the easy power of the runners flowing into their long strides. The head track coach, oddly enough, didn't know a great deal about distance running (Cassidy and Mizner were constantly—though very unobtrusively—amending his workouts), having been a javelin man in college.

But Cornwall understood that the 880 men, the milers, and true distance men were the heart of a track team. They could run everything from the mile relay on up. It was imperative that he pay attention to their training.

He had learned very early, though, that the milers and distance men were like seeds: the good ones, given minimum care, just grew on their own. He had only a casual jogger's appreciation for their training—he knew from his own days of conditioning that what they were doing before his eyes was far beyond his ken—and he knew the daily grind took its toll. The attrition rate was startling. Even the most promising runners, disheartened by injuries or poor performances, would sometimes leave their scholarships on his desk. He never tried to talk them out of it; he knew that once they lost it, it was gone for good.

The runners entered the far turn, Cassidy and Mizner still leading. Up close their breathing would make a considerable racket, but from here they appeared to be gliding along without effort. From the middle of the pack a shorter runner moved up to their shoulders. Without even having to squint, Cornwall knew it would be Nubbins. If they didn't break him, Cornwall thought, that Nubbins might turn out to be something after all.

Entering the far straight, Cassidy and Mizner picked up the pace slightly and only Nubbins hung on with them. They seemed to sense his presence, but showed no sign of it. In an interval workout there was no objection to a hard finish so long as the early running had been even and taxing. Dogging in the early stages in order to shine later on was considered antisocial behavior. Cassidy saved his fiercest workout kick for such occasions.

But Nubbins had been conscientious and was now making a bid for status. He knew very well Cornwall was watching closely. Cassidy slackened somewhat and Nubbins went by, pulling up to Mizner as they came out of the turn. But when the freshman bore down in the last straight and tried to pull away, Mizner matched him stride for stride. Cornwall smiled as he clicked the split-timer for them. He looked down at the watch and thought: *Jesus.* They had run 1:28. Nubbins looked entirely washed out, a face without hope or humor, but he kept on jogging. Cassidy caught up to Mizner and they trotted along without speaking. Cornwall still did not understand that pairing; they were so different. Cassidy was breezy, almost light-hearted for a runner; Mizner was studious and serene. But they were identical in one respect: the haunting cast of their eyes as they entered a gun lap was exactly the same. The coach walked back across the field studying the runners as they stumbled through their rest interval. Those two, he thought. I'll never get another pair like them. Just read the watch for them, see they get fed, get them their plane tickets and keep them in shoes (no small expense), and they'll go out and win everything in sight. They were chugging up to him now, looking up from their despondent jog with the same expectant expression (it always amused him how interested they were in the numbers, no matter how exhausted—it was the first thing they wanted to know after a race, from the depths of their distress).

"Leaders 1:28, Cass 1:29.5, everyone else hit at about 1:33. Last one fellows." The runners were jogging especially slowly now; this was the way they always did it. Everyone would want to be as fresh as possible for the last one in order to end on an upbeat.

Actually, they would still be out of breath when they started the last one, and Cornwall thought again how surprising it was that after the first several intervals they looked as bad as they would get. The rest seemed to take no more out of them, though he knew each one had to be more difficult than the one before. But then they blew the last one like they couldn't think of a better way to end the day. They were a strange crowd, runners, Cornwall thought. They were strange in his track days and they were still strange.

They finally arrived at the starting post with their mincing little steps and with a deep gasp leaned into the last one as Cornwall clicked the watch. They flew into the first turn and Cornwall smiled again. Cassidy was already ten yards in front. By the time they were out of the turn and into the far straight, he was 25 yards ahead and still telescoping away. Mizner smoothly led the rest of the pack. Around the final turn and into the straightaway Cassidy powered on with crisp business-like strides. There was a lift in his stride and from his expression Cornwall could tell he was serious. Forty yards in front Cassidy flashed by the post and Cornwall flicked the watch at him in that strange little *gotcha* affectation of earnest timers everywhere. The coach let out a little grunt as he glanced briefly at the watch before catching the others on the second sweeping hand. Cassidy did not keep jogging as before, but curved back in a parabola of expectation.

"Whyn't you get your ass in gear, Cassidy?" the coach asked.

Cassidy was still gasping, not amused in the slightest.

"C'mon. Coach. What. Was it?" "You think I don't know when you guys are loafing?"

Cassidy rolled his eyes at that, but stood panting, hands on hips. Let him have his fun.

"You had 1:24.6," the coach smiled. "Everyone else was right about 1:29." Cassidy nodded, satisfied, and started to jog off towards Bruce Denton, who stood wringing wet, watching from the side of the field.

"That's about right," Cassidy called back, "Last year would have been 1:26 something about this time." Cornwall knew how accurate his training records were and that Cassidy wasn't guessing.

"You might even do some good in cross country pretty soon, you keep this up," the coach called out to him. He knew it was a sore point. Mizner had caught up to the other pair as they headed off for the one-mile warmdown course.

"Right," Cassidy called back, "and I might run the 100 in nine flat and play wide receiver for the Dolphins."

Cassidy slumped on the bench, draped immodestly with a towel, more or less savoring the deep itchy ache of the last 660 while apparently studying his toes with great interest. He would be losing another nail soon. *Ugliest feet in the world,* he thought, next to Denton's. He ran his hand up and down his left achilles tendon. Very tender; better pay attention to it and back off if it gets any worse. Maybe ice it. The old Injury Evasion Fandango. Did it ever end?

The afternoon workout had cost him seven pounds. He longed for cooler weather. In the shower Denton laughed: "It's the lean wolf that leads the pack."

"If I am captured in Indochina," Cassidy told him, "I will not last out the night in a bamboo cage."

"Just walk out between the bars," Denton had suggested. The older runner had been impressed with the 660 workout, but mildly disapproved doing hard intervals so early in the year. He had settled for a 12-mile run himself.

"It's easy for you to criticize," Cassidy said, still slumping on the bench while Denton dressed quickly. "You won't be doing the old one-mile run on some little 11-lap roller derby track in a few weeks. I need me some *get down* speed out there."

"When did you turn into a black sprinter?" Mizner asked, "What's this 'get down' stuff?"

"He's a miler person, you see," Denton said, "and he's explaining about how it's dog eat dog out there. Right, sport?"

Into the steamy and subdued post-workout atmosphere charged Daniel Hayes Ingram, a student trainer whose round face was a sad pink and white topographical map of adolescence. In high school Ingram had secured a place on the track team and set about accomplishing his lifelong goal: a five minute mile. Having failed (by 3.4 seconds) he learned how to tape ankles and apply ice packs and was thus spared exile from that intimate neutral world where the sounds were of rushing water, rough laughter and the click clack of brittle spikes on tiled floors. Substitute gratification does not vent completely the deeper yearnings, however, and Danny Ingram was known as a highly excitable person. He now clucked and sputtered with such energy as to gather a small crowd. If the news were not of interest, they would at least get to watch a trainer go mad.

"They got Walton!" Ingram gasped for the third time. The track men looked at each other.

"*John Walton you idiots! They got John Walton!*" Ingram was exasperated by their blank stares. They knew who he was talking about, but could not get the context. They calmed him with abuse and made him begin slowly. He had their interest now and they were going to get to the bottom of this.

"I was just in Cornwall's office . . ." he took a deep breath, ". . . and the telegram just came in from the New Zealand travel committee. Walton has agreed to run in the Southeastern University Relays this spring! He's on tour then and had the weekend open. Holy Jesus Christ John Walton running here! Won't that just be something else now? Can you imagine what he'll do to all these yokels around here when he . . ."

It was a particularly awkward thing to say for, as the import of the news had finally come across, the others had turned almost as a man to see what kind of reaction would issue from the distance runners' corner, where Cassidy and Denton sat watching them with great interest.

"Well, I didn't mean you of course, Cass, uh . . ." But the trainer was clearly into his own pit and scampering around only brought more debris down upon himself. It was very quiet. Big fans in the roof beat at the hot air.

"Who did you say was it coming to the relays, Danny?" Cassidy asked.

"Uh, Walton, John Walton, the miler from New . . ."

"John Walton? Is he supposed to be pretty good?" Cassidy maintained a countenance of innocent curiosity. Denton turned slightly and coughed.

"Yeah, well, he's *only* run 3:49 and all . . ." Some of the others were snickering but Danny had a very high embarrassment threshold. "Say, Cass," he was all curiosity now, "how do you think you'll, uh, handle, you know, the . . . situation."

Cassidy pondered. He looked at the ceiling and sphincterized his lips. Then his face lit up: inspiration!

"I think what I would do would be to hang right with him, see . . ."

"Yeah, well . . ."

"Check him out *real* close, like for a couple of laps. Make *him* take the initiative, see, make *him* run *my* race, see . . ." Denton was leaning against his locker, biting on a towel.

"But *John Walton*, I mean, when he . . ."

"Then going into the last lap, I'll be right on his tail, see, all the way into the last turn . . ."

"But they say his kick . . ."

"Then I'll take a short cut across the infield, sprint down the pole vault runway and lean at the tape. Works every time."

The assemblage dispersed in what might be called a good mood, but there was an eeriness in the air. Some names were uttered with reverence in that tiled sanctum and John Walton's was one of them. Surely Bruce Denton's name was accorded similar respect in other locker rooms around the world, but there was always something even more mysterious and exotic about those far-off heroes, rarely seen in person, whose feats were frozen for all time in irrefutable black and white numerals. Walton's aura, being the first human being to run the mile under 3:50, was that of almost total invincibility. To the public he may have been just one more in a long line of champions, but to those whose own numerals gave credentials of insight, Walton's name brought with it an unpleasant chill. A 3:55 miler would understand it better than a 4:05 miler. Walton was the best there was, but he was only an image to most of them. And now that he was to be viewed in person—take the form of flesh and blood-no one knew quite what to think. Bruce Denton was an Olympian. He was accustomed to unstable atmospheres where heady names such as Walton's were bandied about like so many harmless acquaintances, but these undergraduates clearly were not, despite their best efforts to act nonchalant.

"Aw, he pulls on his shorts the same way we do," said one of the freshmen. But it didn't dispel Walton's ghost in the least.

"That's right," Denton chuckled, "except he pulls *his* shorts up over legs that can run a mile in three minutes and forty nine seconds."

Some of them laughed as they finished dressing, but there was no further discussion. Cassidy still sat on the bench, towel draped across his middle, too weary even to clothe himself. He looked up at Denton and smiled. His 660 workout didn't seem like such hot stuff anymore.

An awesome creature—up until recently more a myth than anything else—was to assume human form and cross oceans to perform his magic right on the same track that held their sweat. In doing so he would necessarily devastate those who sought to test his power. That this force would be inexorably brought to bear on one they all knew, one they had come to respect for his own prowess, made everyone at the same time uneasy and strangely elated. They had rarely seen Quenton Cassidy lose a mile race, did not *want* to see him lose, yet the inevitability of the prospect was somehow exciting, in the manner of an execution.

Their lion was to be devoured by a greater lion.

10. Demons

It's demons, you see," Cassidy said seriously. He was on the floor doing his stretching. Andrea was propped on one elbow on his bed, looking up from her organic chemistry book, suppressing amusement, something she often seemed to do. She pushed a wisp of hair back from her glasses and looked entirely scholarly.

"Do they whisper moral imperatives in your ear?"

"Lovely. I try to explain the dark forces at work within me, and you amuse yourself."

"Oh, I'm sorry, please do go on. And on. And on."

He caught her by an ankle, the good one, and flipped her neatly onto the floor beside him. The back of her neck smelled like a parakeet's tummy, sweet hay and fluff.

"Yes indeed," he said, lost in the pale corn silk of her hair. She muddled simple thought patterns; he had difficulty studying when she was about. Colors muted and he lunged for her with neither premeditation nor guilt. He adored her and told her so.

She on the other hand had no handle on Quenton Cassidy. He said things occasionally that brought her up short. She would shake her head and say, queer duck. He acted not at all like the many boys who had sought her attentions. This one wore a great weariness about the eyes, yet ironically with an incredible well of silly energy bubbling just beneath the surface, barely contained by secret locks. He rambled at times, talking in streaks of lucid prose; then lapsed into deep silences from which he could not be retrieved without great effort. He cavorted. He played with her mind.

She had watched him race four times now. He tried to pass off much of this activity as trivial, but during those times especially he was lost to her. She wondered where he went, leaving her excluded, lonely and (could she admit this?) jealous.

She wondered what provinces she was not privy to and repeatedly asked him to explain what he was talking about.

47

This she knew: There were times when she drew only polite responses; she could have been for all the world a distant cousin come to visit.

"What do your demons make you do?" she said softly, holding his head and making curls absently with his ragged blond hair. He sighed.

"About sixteen, eighteen miles a day."

"Um," she started to push him away, perturbed at not being taken seriously.

"But sometimes when it is all going good, I mean when it's early- May warm and there's cut grass in the air and you've made it through winter okay, not bad sick or anything, then sometimes you can take a deep breath and feel your own heart jumping—*that's right don't look at me like that*—you can feel your own heart in there jumping around like a godamn bobcat or something; that's when you've just got to get yourself out somewhere and let them loose." Her head cocked at this; she watched him closely.

"Don't try to make me feel funny about this," he said. "You were the one who wanted to know. Besides, you've never been in four-minute shape, not that many people have, so if you think this is all just a crock . . ."

"No," she said quickly, "go on. I want to hear it. Please go on . . ."

"About the demons?"

"Yes, what . . ."

"They make you want to run through the jungle, baby," he said happily, "cover countryside at a clip, slide by in the night like a scuttling cloud." His eyes had the faraway cast, but his voice quavered in mock solemnity like a Southern tent evangelist. Sensing genuine interest, he picked up the tempo.

"They make you bolt awake in the middle of the night with an involuntary shot of your own true adrenaline, ready to run a hundred miles; we're talking when you're there, now, really there, four-minute shape or better. They make you jittery with the smell of forest, ready to hurdle fallen trees, run down game, leave gore in the bushes . . ."

Her eyes widened.

"And then when you get them all reigned in," he looked at her fiercely, "they make you lay back in the pack, coasting three laps on an old melody . . . and then they make you wail

out of the final turn and blow down the last godamn straightaway like *the midnight train to hell!*"

Although he said it humorously in his mock religious
voice, in his eyes nevertheless she could see but not quite
penetrate limpid ethers of a far-away Elysium, where the
unworldly citizens were without exception vessels of nearly
pure spirit: heavyweight prize fighters, rare-air mountain
climbers, soon-to-be-martyred saints, and other quiet, sadly
ironic purveyors of The Difficult Task.

"You are of course quite mad," she said softly.

"Come," he said, intentionally breaking the spell, "we
have to meet Mize at the Nineties."

"We are speaking of human endeavor and delusional
systems," Cassidy said, punctuating with a steady cracking of
pistachio nuts. Their second pitcher was almost gone; Thursday night foosball and pinball background noise nearly pre-
cluded conversation altogether.

"Everyone likes to think they have their own little corner,
it can be anything; needlepoint, lawn bowling, whatever.
Some guy may gratify himself by thinking he's the best
godamned fruit and vegetable manager the A&P ever had.
Which is fine. It gives people a sense of worth in a crowded
world where everyone feels like part of the scenery. But then
mostly they are spared any harrowing glimpses into their own
mediocrity. Pillsbury Bake-Off notwithstanding, we'll never
really know who makes the best artichoke souffle in the world,
will we?"

"Gotcha. Don't filibuster, tell me Demons," she said.

"Right. The thing is that in track we are painfully and
constantly aware of how we stack up, not just with our
contemporaries but with our historical counterparts as well.
In that regard it's different even from other sports. A basketball player can go out and have a great day and tell himself
he's the greatest rebounding forward to ever hit the hard-
wood, but he'll never really be troubled by the actual truth,
will he? Maybe he's just in a weak league. Maybe Jerry Lucas
would have eaten him alive 30 years ago. But he'll never know.
He'll just have to leave such judgments in the sorry hands of
the sports writers, many of whom it has been pointed out can

be bought with a steak." Mizner nodded vigorously from behind a pile of popcorn.

"In track it's all there in black and white. Lot of people can't take that kind of pressure; the ego withers in the face of the evidence. We all carry our little credentials around with us; that's why the numbers are so important to us, why we're always talking about them. I am, for instance, four flat point three. The numerals might as well be etched on my forehead. This gentleman here, perhaps you'd like to meet him, is 27:42, also known as 13:21, I believe."

Mizner bowed graciously, half rising. He seemed to be enjoying this immensely.

"A knowledgeable observer might ask yards or meters and it is most assuredly yards," Mizner said, "I'll not puff."

"What?"

"Never mind," Cassidy interrupted, "the point is that we know not only whether we are good, bad, or mediocre, but whether we're first, third or a hundred and ninety seventh at any given point. *Track and Field News* tells us whether we want to know or not."

"Assuming we make the lists," Mizner put in.

"That's right. Sometimes it is possible, despite your best efforts and a hundred godamn miles a week, *not to even exist.*"

"That bothers you, does it?"

"That, my dear, breaks my heart."

"But you can beat most of the people around, we know that, right? Isn't that good, isn't that what you want?"

"Well, sure. But in my own mind, I know that I'm what a newspaper sports person would call a 'steady performer.' And it really doesn't matter a whit how many races I win. I haven't even broken four minutes yet. Roger Bannister did that back in 1954. I've spent seven years of my life hard at this thing and so far I'm . . . average. It happens to others, concert pianists maybe, actors, and the like. But they aren't subject to the cold cruel numbers like we are.

"Let's put it this way," he continued, "There is a fellow right now in New Haven, one in Boston, one somewhere in Minnesota of all places and two—Mize is now indicating three—in Oregon who might very reasonably request that I launder their jocks for them. And that's just the United States. There happens to be a young man down in New Zealand right now by the name of John Walton who breathes actual air and eats human food and the son of a bitch has run one mile faster than any human being in the history of the world, 3:49.1 to be exact. I don't believe ol' John'd *let me* wash his jock, do you think, Mize?"

The other runner shook his head solemnly.

"Is there some kind of final point to all this?" Andrea was determined to get to the bottom of it all.

"Depends on what you call a point. It's a simple choice: We can all be good boys and wear our letter sweaters around and get our little degrees and find some nice girl to settle, you know, down, with . . . take up what a friend of ours calls the hearty challenges of lawn care . . ." Mizner was snickering, but Andrea was solemn. Cassidy stared into his beer.

"Or what? What is the alternative?" She leaned over the table, trying to get him back on the track. He looked at her surprised; his eyes lit up as they had earlier and his voice shook again with deep excitement.

"Or we can blaze! Become legends in our own time, strike fear in the heart of mediocre talent everywhere! We can scald dogs, put records out of reach! Make the stands gasp as we blow into an unearthly kick from three hundred yards out! We can become God's own messengers delivering the dreaded scrolls! We can race dark Satan himself till he wheezes fiery cinders down the back straightaway!" He was full into it now.

"They'll speak our names in hushed tones, 'Those guys are animals' they'll say! We can lay it on the line, bust a gut, show them a clean pair of heels. We can sprint the turn on a spring breeze and feel the winter leave our feet!"

Andrea leaned back in the booth, wide-eyed, and swallowed.

"We can, by God, let our demons loose and *just wail on!*" He threw his head back and let loose a low, eerie cry. Foosball, billiards, and pinballs all stilled suddenly. Mizner, unaware of the sudden quiet, pounded the table in animated agreement.

"Yes, yes, godamn, that's it! *Wuhail Owwwwnnnn!!*" When he had finished the cry he looked around at the silent blank faces of the various confused fraternity jocks and winced.

"My lord in heaven," she said, her eyes glistening. But she smiled as she said it, a slight woman's smile that said perhaps now here was something after all, and even though it was an admission against interest, she had to consider the possibility that there was something here a little . . . out of the ordinary. Later in her life, she always counted that as the moment when she truly fell in love with Quenton Cassidy, a madman who claimed to be both vexed and enchanted by ethereal barriers she did not understand, fell in love with him even as he sat, tired from his performance, absently drawing figure eights in the spilled beer.

They were all a tad drunk.

"That was nice," Cassidy said. Three days later they were walking back to Doobey in the dark, hand in hand. Though it was November, it was still pleasantly warm out.

"I don't know. It was a little eerie at first. But it was nice to look at the stars," Andrea said.

"People used to do it watching the stars all the time until Alexander Graham Bell invented the motel," he said. "But I told you no one would bother us. Very few people know that practice pit is out there. The main one gets a lot of use. I sometimes wonder what people used to do back in the old days when the jumpers landed in sawdust."

"Making love in a pole vault pit." she sighed, "If my mother only knew. She'd be sure to come up with something about 'passion pits' or some such."

"Mothers like those kinds of lines. As if there was automatic wisdom in corn pone."

"I suppose."

They walked as slowly as they could without the whole thing getting silly, both of them having an instinctive sense about preserving good moments.

As they neared Doobey Hall, he heard the commotion in back.

"C'mon," he grabbed her hand. "If this is what I think it is, it might be fun."

In the back of the house was a large garage building that had been turned into a recreation and storage area. There was a battered ping-pong table, a very old juke box, and some Sidecar Doobey-vintage furniture. Cassidy led Andrea through the door and they stood in the back of the small crowd. A space had been cleared out on the sandy concrete floor to make room for a miniature high-jump arena. Andrea was puzzled.

"What are they . . ." But Cassidy shushed her. Ron "Spider" Gordon was standing at the edge of the open space to their left, his eyes focused on the ridiculous makeshift standards. They had taken two large coat racks and taped coat hangers to hold the horizontal bar, which was an old cane fishing pole. A pile of mattresses made up a comfy looking landing pit. Cassidy thought of the pole-vault pit, looked down at Andrea with a loud sigh and was promptly shushed himself. Gordon was going into his routine now, in the manner of all jumpers, clenching and unclenching his fists, mumbling to himself, bending over at the waist and wiggling his hands like gloves with no fingers in them, in general doing the field man's Dance of High Anxiety. Except now it was overtly histrionic, for he was also doing his own voice-over, *sotto voce* like a golf match commentator:

". . .and so ladies and gentlemen the pressure is really on the famous Italian high jumper, Ron Don *Giordante*, here in the Olympic finals in this beautiful new stadium in Rome, Italy, in front of thousands of hopeful countrymen . . ."

Andrea did not understand what was going on. The makeshift bar was far over the head of the 6-1 jumper, and she knew he didn't have enough room to take more than two or three steps. She got on tiptoes and whispered to Cassidy, who was watching with a big grin on his face.

"Quenton, what's he going to . . ."

Cassidy shushed her again and just nodded at the jumper. "Just watch," he told her.

It was a startling thing to see, even though most of them had seen it before. Gordon finished his commentary, leaving off with: ". . .it looks like he's ready . . . yes, there he goes now . . ." The jumper loped in with three casual strides and simply floated over the bar, clearing it easily by several inches. Gordon was one of the last to use the western roll, which Cassidy thought far more aesthetically pleasing than the flop, and it was a beautiful thing to watch. Cassidy estimated the bar at 6-5, though one side was lower than the other due to the instability of one of the old coat racks. Though it was nearly a foot under Gordon's best jump, seen from up close and in such casual circumstances, it was mildly shocking. The

crowd was still applauding good-naturedly as Gordon
wallowed around on the mattresses, paralyzed with laughter.
    Stoned to the gills, Cassidy thought.
    Jim Beale, another jumper, took his place and began
going through the antics. Gordon, barely able to control
himself, very considerately crawled from the "pit" and began
to give the commentary for his colleague. Everyone seemed
to be having a wonderful time. Cassidy and Andrea slipped
out of the back.
    "Isn't that something?" he said, shaking his head.
    "Weird like everything else around here. I don't think I
get it."
    "I didn't either, for a while. I've seen the hurdlers, the
shot and disc guys doing stuff like that. Never made sense.
Then I figured it out. What they're doing is they're *playing*
track."
    "Playing?"
    "Right. See, when you're doing the actual thing itself, it's
so competitive and serious, I don't think anybody really has
much fun at it. Rarely in practice or *never* in meets. Oh, they
like the *idea* of it all right, they like going to competitions, and
they like being on a team and the general hullabaloo of being
a jock. But when you get right down to it, while you're doing
the thing itself, it's not a lot of grins. I can't remember a mile
race in my life that was even mildly amusing."
    "So what was all that back there about?"
    "Well, sometimes Spider or one of the others will be
sitting around here and suddenly realize that he *likes* doing
what he does. He may have turned it into a compulsion or a
job, but it was once something he did as a kid just for the neat
sensation it gave him. So Spider will have a few tokes and
suddenly realize he *loves* sailing through the air without
having to hand someone a boarding pass. I've seen Mobley
drink three pitchers and go out and heave his godamn shot
around a playground by moonlight all night. *Weird* stuff like
that . . ."
    "But they do this every afternoon. I don't see why he
would want to go out in some garage . . ."
    "It's very simple. Though it looked pretty remarkable to
us, for him jumping 6-5 is like strolling around the block. He
could do it in his sleep. So, for him to make it play, all he had

to do is drop back several notches off his true capabilities; he puts on a pair of cut-offs, rigs up a stupid cane pole for a bar, and he does . . . *what he does*. It would be like me going out and running a 4:20 mile. I don't know how else to explain it. They do it all the time. Everybody likes to watch, particularly when the high jumpers do it. They make up these fantastic situations, give themselves glamorous foreign names, pretend it's some great vendetta in the Olympics or something..."

"I didn't understand that stuff about the foreign names..."

"One of the half-milers, Benny Vaughn, started that. Everyone on the team now has some foreignized version of his own name. It's a kind of fantasy they seem to get a kick out of."

"Do you have one?"

"Of course. Made it up myself. I am Quintus Cassadamius, the famous Greek miler. I'm also somewhat renowned on an imaginary pro bowling tour, but that's another story."

"How about Jerry, does he have a funny name?"

"Sure. Mizerelli, another famous Italian athlete. I was responsible for that one, I guess."

"And how about Bruce Denton?"

"That, my dear, shows how much you know. Bruce Denton is Bruce Denton, the famous American clock cleaner."

11. A Fan's Notes

The tremors woke Andrea.

She blinked, startled by the unfamiliar surroundings. The tremors continued, rhythmically, far-off, yet deep and powerful, shaking the whole bed. She peered around in the thin yellow dawn light, alarmed but still drowsy, trying to figure out where she was and whether she was in danger. Her hand fell on something warm. It was Quenton Cassidy; she was in his room.

But what was going on? Did they have earthquakes up here in north Florida? She stayed very still, scared, trying to make her sleepy mind work.

Then she figured it out and got really scared.

"Quenton," she shook him gently, groggily. He didn't stir.

"Quenton."

"Hmmmff?"

"Is there something wrong? Baby, wake up, please Quenton, your heartbeat is shaking the bed . . ."

One bluish-green eye opened and studied her carefully. This was his morning to sleep late. The team would be driving to Jacksonville to catch a plane; the morning run would be just a token.

"Shhh," he murmured softly, "go back to sleep." She did. The little tremors continued rhythmically; steady liquid drumbeats at precisely 47 to the minute.

They did indeed shake the bed.

Now that some of the questionable benefits of the lifestyle were inuring to her, Andrea was far from pleased. She wasn't crazy about the idea of staying home on a Saturday night, Mary Tyler Moore or no Mary Tyler Moore.

The team had left at noon and would be gone for days. The USTFF meet was Monday at Penn State, the AAU championships the following Saturday in Chicago. She fretted around her room like a cat on diet pills.

Some of her dateless sorority sisters came by, full of good will, not at all unhappy with their plight, and made a pitch for pizza and some tentative prowling around. Andrea demurred as pleasantly as she could.

She was actually pretty miserable, but what really annoyed her was that she didn't know exactly why. She got out a pair of scissors and some old jeans and began to make cut-offs, but tired after one leg and threw the stuff in a corner in a heap. This wasn't like her; not at all. If this was what it was all about, she wanted no part of it.

She cast about her room, distastefully taking in the cute pastel artifacts that had always been her joy. The giant stuffed Snoopy seemed pretty stupid when she thought about it. She felt like giving it a swift kick right in its smiling kisser. Why hadn't she gone with the girls? She knew why. It would have been worse.

Finally she wandered down the hall to the drink machine, came back with a Fresca, sat down at her neat white desk and took out a legal pad. She had never liked normal girl-type stationary; perhaps because she wrote prolific, rambling, philosophical letters rather than bright, quick, newsy ones, and it was embarrassing to stuff 20 or 30 of the little sheets into a small envelope.

In her flowery, nearly illegible handwriting, she wrote:

Dear Alicia,

How are things at horny old Randolph Macon? If you get this during the middle of the week and don't like to be reminded that the nearest boys are 35 miles away, sorry about that.

But don't feel too deprived because here it is Saturday night and little Andrea is sitting in her room at the university voted by Playboy magazine last year as the number one party school in the country, drinking a Fresca, barely able to hear several nearby live bands and feeling like (excuse the expression) crap.

And would you like to know where the sports hero is? Okay, but I'm going to tell you anyway because you've probably already figured out this letter is a bitch session. Well, right now he is at the Nittany Lion Inn at Penn State probably trying to charm some Yankee girl with his ridiculous fake Southern accent. Whoever heard of a West Palm Beach drawl? Well, he's got one, but he only trots it out every now and then. He says he got it during the summers at his grandparents in North Carolina. Oh well, he tells me there is really not much fooling around on these trips and why would I have reason to doubt anything said with such sincerity?

He also told me he hated cross-country meets like a plague of boils, but you've never SEEN such a happy traveler packing for a sojourn. Singing, whistling, trying to decide which of those strange little spiked shoes he will take (he has about 50 pairs of them and they all have little stories). Oh yes, he was really upset about leaving, all right.

Leece, what's wrong with me? I've never acted like this before, have I? I wish you were here now. Why did we ever decide to go to different schools?

When he's around I'm not really even conscious of being particularly happy. It just seems kind of normal. But when he has to go off somewhere it's like I cease to do anything but exist until he's back. And it's not like we see each other all that much during the week, either. We're both taking a lot of hours this semester and we agreed a while back that it could really get silly if we let it. So we usually study apart. Still, there's just something about knowing he's not far away.

He says it is going to be worse during the indoor season. He could be gone every weekend if he's running well. And right now he is.

I can't figure it out. It's not that he's beautiful. Sometimes he looks so thin it seems he must be sick or something. And if I say anything, he comes out with these smart ass comments, like "It's the lean wolf that leads the pack, baby." Honestly, he can be so condescending I want to just slap him. But then I look in his eyes, and Leece he's always so tired, so frail looking, it just breaks my heart. Sometimes he catches me looking at him and says, "What?" I say, "Nothing, just thinking."

He says he's "smitten" with me, and I guess he means it. But if there's ever a question of a running thing or Andrea, guess who's second fiddle? Have I ever put up with a boy like this that you can remember?

I wish I could drag him home over Thanksgiving so you could get a look at him, but as usual he's going to be gone. Can't you just see him with Daddy? What if they got into the war or something like that? But I guess they could talk about fishing—Quenton knows all about fish from skin diving in West Palm.

Leece, am I sounding like a little lovesick puppy? Me, the Ice Maiden of Coral Gables High? Brother.

One thing I'll say about him, he didn't flinch when I told him about medical school. Most of the guys I've ever mentioned it to just give me this weak little smile. They're right on the verge of saying something like, oh, you're much too attractive to blah blah blah and if I had a gun right then I would shoot to kill.

I must say Quenton took it right in stride. But then, I guess delusions of grandeur don't startle someone whose real goal in life is to set a world's record (he told me not to EVER EVER tell a soul in the world about that, but telling your twin is not really like telling someone else, is it?)

I don't know, maybe I'm crazy, too. I just don't seem to be able to do much of anything about it. Has your date ever wandered around the dance floor at a disco place with a five-dollar bill in his hand telling people he wanted to tip the band but he couldn't find them?

Leece, I was paralyzed. I was the only one, but I couldn't speak, I was laughing so hard. And he didn't care about the weird looks he got, not at all. What is it about this one?

Am I in love, Leece? For true this time, for real?

Love, Andy

12. The Indictment

It was a do-nothing Thursday afternoon. With a junior college meet coming up the freshmen and sophomores were constrained to playfully jog five miles. Cassidy and Mizner elected to go the ten-mile course with a few others. The pace would be brisk, around 58 minutes, so extended conversation was necessarily restricted to the first three or four miles. The group headed out on a loop they called "Tobacco Road" because the unpaved road wound through a wooded section south of town replete with shacks, wincing dogs and barefoot children; it was rumored that the course had been named by Marty Liquori years earlier when he was down for the Southeastern Relays. It was like running back in time 40 years. But the runners waved to the locals and the locals waved right back. There was a friendliness born of familiarity and although two entirely different worlds eclipsed each other at that point, by some process of emotional osmosis each had come to respect the other's struggles; there was the homey aroma of inexpensive foods in preparation; greens, fritters and such.

Someone wanted to know what was to be done about Nubbins.

"What about him?" Cassidy asked. "I thought he had become a pillar of the community." They spoke in quick bursts on the exhale.

"Old wine, new bottle," said Hosford, a pale, literary type.

"Haven't you heard the latest?" asked Mizner. "Oh, this is too good. Last Tuesday night, after he won that freshman meet against Old Miss, he got to feeling pretty full of himself. He got on his High Plains Drifter kick. He dolls himself up in his godamn Roy Rogers shirt and his shit-kicking boots . . ."

"I don't see anything so wrong . . ."

"Wait a minute, let me tell it," Mizner was starting to snicker breathlessly, remembering. "And he had this blanket that he stole from the plane when we went to Atlanta. No lie, this is the honest-to-god truth. He cut a godamn hole in this piece of Eastern Airlines property to make himself a poncho, see, and then he proceeds to the State Theatre with that birdbrained girlfriend of his, that Betty Sue . . ."

"Aw, come on . . ." Cassidy was not averse to certain brands of extemporaneous craziness.

"Well, trying to be objective, now," Hosford interrupted, "he was making even more of an ass of himself than usual. There was a big crowd in the lobby waiting for the first show to get out. Nubbins kept cavorting around doing his Clint Eastwood material—which is pretty silly considering the little shit is only 5-8. Anyway, someone in the crowd would get nervous and giggle, like, you know, from sheer embarrassment. So then Nubbins would get even more loud and rambunctious, thinking he was, you know, *entertaining.* I mean, I was *there.* I wanted to *hide,* man . . ."

"I think I get the picture," said Cassidy. "Let's pick this pace up a little bit."

The shower room was a fine place for deep, conspiratorial thinking. Cassidy slumped in the weariness that was his chosen mantle, lost in the hot torrent of water. Mizner, more chipper, sang a gurgling aria at the next nozzle.

"Are you still doing the Honor Court thing?" Cassidy asked from inside his waterfall. His left knee was tormenting him.

"Yeah. Clerk of the Court. That means I get to man the tape recorder and perform other taxing duties. Sure looks good on the résumé, though."

"But you have physical access to the courtroom itself, right? I mean, can you get in whenever you want to, get ahold of letterhead, stuff like that?"

"Sure, that's the job. What's the deal?"

"Oh, just a Classic," he bubbled, "just an All Time Classic is what it is. . ."

The Honor Code at Southeastern University followed in that fine old American tradition of overcoming defeat by 1) pronouncing some unmitigated disaster a resounding triumph and then 2) smiling pleasantly in the face of even the most crushing contrary evidence.

Cassidy figured such addlepate stubbornness helped to explain more than a few of such amusing collective national lapses as the electoral college, the Eighteenth Amendment, and "our efforts" in Vietnam. This curious process is necessitated by the perversely unrelenting and self-damning refusal of the ruling classes to admit that somebody important fucked up. But rest assured, Cassidy would say, that if things get really squirrely—the meltdown *was* a possibility after all, the warhead *could be* armed by accident—some clerk/typist somewhere is definitely going to lose his or her job.

If such a principle can sustain a war or a nuclear energy policy, it could surely sustain a student conduct code in a land-grant university in the deep south. The Southeastern University Honor Code, in brief, commanded far more in the way of belly laughs than respect from the student body.

The program was based upon the presumption that the Honest People were the best sentinels for guarding against Evil and generally preserving The System, whose morality was defined broadly by our Christian Ethics, our American sense of Fair Play, and our sincere conviction that Cheaters Are Only Hurting Themselves. After all, who knew when, some five or so years from now at some important cocktail party, your boss from J. Williston Beckman Widget Co. might wander over and request the dimensions of the Parthenon? And then where would you be?

The way it worked was, when you saw someone cribbing, you were supposed to turn them in. There would follow a kind of doll house due process, which the law students used as a kind of practice court.

It was all in good fun, of course. Good fun for everyone except the few unlucky "defendants" who were actually dragged before the child-tribunal, slump-shouldered and highly chastened. Generally, however, the Chancellor, exercising his sound discretion, would order something like "15 make-up credits," thus swelling the rolls of courses like GEO 101 (Rocks for Jocks), MUS 101 (Mozart on a Stick) and other cake walks. The defendant could then graduate on schedule and go to work in the regional purchasing department of Wal-Mart, feeling not only had he paid his debt to society, but also that in a pinch he could identify a feldspar or hum a few bars of *Le Pathetique.*

But just as an aircraft that won't fly is a failure by definition (no matter how soft the seats or snazzy the tail design), so Southeastern's Honor Code was a failure for the simple reason that it inspired more criminality than it prevented.

The wide and airy gulf between ideal and reality was in no instance more clearly demonstrated than the day Cassidy saw an angry student standing, hands on hips, by an "Honor Fruit Stand," an instantaneously bankrupt attempt by student government True Believers to sell apples, bananas, and oranges in convenient bins around campus by attaching containers for bright-eyed students to drop their coins into.

The stunned student Cassidy saw that day was upset, glaring at the empty fruit bin (the program had been abandoned quickly for lack of, ah, cash flow), for he turned on his heel and stalked away, exclaiming to no one in particular: "Godamn! No more free fruit!"

Cassidy was bewildered by the honor system and he generally resented the kind of education he was getting, especially during his first two years at Southeastern, a university large enough to insist on grading humanities examinations by computer.

The way he saw it, mechanical testing per se was not so bad, but the requirements of binary logic coupled with a faculty wholly devoid of imagination led to exam questions that bordered on high comedy. He would never forget one such question. The second quarter of Humanities had concerned itself with the early Greek philosophers, basic religion, architecture, and art (no one ever accused the department of being unambitious). One nearly senile question writer, an associate professor who lived with several cats and was said to be a hoot on a concertina, in a giddy attempt to syllogistically mix his various marbles, offered this poser: *Plato was to Jesus Christ as the Parthenon was to: A. The Appian Way, B. St. Peter's Basilica; C. The Aqueducts, D. None of the above.*

Cassidy cared little whether he won such contests, left exams in a blind fury, and plotted dark revenge. Time after time he asked instructors about the lunacy of such a system and they were generally sheepish in attempting to defend such vapid academic skullduggery.

Once he was in a section taught by no less than the head of the department. After the midterm exam, Cassidy angrily pointed out the specific page in *Madame Bovary* that demonstrated his answer to a very obscure question was just as correct as the one espoused by the department (and, more importantly, the computer). The department head, a defeated, grey-headed and somewhat confused old man, looked up from his unkempt notes and, without the grace of any sort of humor, said between thin white lips:

"No one promised you there would be universal justice, you know."

Cassidy thought: This addled old fart has lost the ability or will to teach, perhaps, but he can still impart useful knowledge. Obliquely; always *obliquely*.

It was late at night and an unmistakable edge of conspiracy excited the air in Cassidy's room as he unfolded The Plan to Mizner and Hosford. Their jobs would be relatively simple for the now; help to be recruited and casual gossip to be chummed around the training table.

But after the scenario was laid out *in toto*, in spite of Cassidy's frantic efforts to maintain control, his room sounded like a loosely muzzled chihuahua paratrooping into a pack of highly vocal piglets.

Nowhere on campus was the Honor System more stoutly defended than Farley Hall, the main athletic dorm, where football players in particular professed for it nothing less than True Love, spiritual and enduring. Using the vernacular of the horse track, they discussed at great length the opportunities presented them by such a grab-bag of situation ethics. They were cheating their asses off, of course, and doing so with the general high spirits of any playful and energetic group of n'er do wells who discover to their great merriment that someone has wandered off and left the tap unguarded.

The term they used was "riding," which is to say that if one were going to copy from someone else's paper, one would be "riding" that person through the exam. Such a technique was not hard to perfect in the crowded rooms where tests were given. One would, yawning immensely from the strain of all that heavy *pondering*, easily turn one's body this way or that (just trying to loosen up, you understand) and return to one's answer sheet with a string of pure knowledge: 3,2,2,2,1,4,2,4,1. Or was it 2,4,2?

Whether the answers were right or not was entirely the rider's responsibility. One was on one's own in selecting one's "mount." On occasion the mount was a predetermined matter. Generally though, the selection process was impromptu. A nervous footballer would study appearances carefully as students wandered into the exam room.

"A fat ugly girl is the only horse for me," insisted Harold Sloate, a pig-eyed maniac left guard who eventually made the Atlanta Falcon suicide squad. "Some folks swear by skinny guys with slide rules in they belts, but give me a ugly girl and I'll win the fuggin' Kentucky Derby. One with acne's even better . . ."

The whole process had become more or less a culturally ingrained institution that the athletic department looked upon with a kind of confused admiration (how could the boys, on their own, have come up with this grand way of eliminating expensive tutors?) It reached a point of outright hilarity when some of the more imaginative players showed up at the Farley training table on exam nights with cowboy boots and sterling silver spurs and waited in line for their feed yelling *"Yippeeyi O Kiyaaaay! We gone Riiiide ta-night!"*

Old pig-eyed Sloate topped them all one night by bringing in a 45-pound hand-tooled imported brass-horn western working saddle, complete with fittings and reigns. Dragging it up on the coat rack, he ripped off his 10-gallon Stetson and exclaimed to the silently waiting multitudes paused mid-bite: "Make way you varmints, there's an EN 201 final tonight and the Pony Express is *comin' through!*" He received a rather nice round of applause, but the next day Dick Doobey called the head dorm counselor and told him in no uncertain terms that although he thought the, uhm, horsing around was in its own way quite humorous, it was about time to call off the shenanigans. Word was getting around, and some of the more shall we say unathletically inclined faculty members were beginning to make references to measures which, if allowed to gather momentum, just might represent the hatchet that would separate from the body politic the head of the proverbial golden goose. In short, it was time to quit pissing in the soup.

Thus it was that the fevered and unexplained local penchant for Western dress that had blossomed so suddenly in Kernsville, died just as suddenly, leaving overstocked haberdashers once more bewildered by the unfathomable vicissitudes of college fashion. The more entrenched trend of jocks "riding" through school, however, remained very much a part of the subculture.

That Jack Nubbins was not getting through exams on his own steam was not in question. In fact he talked about his indiscretions in a booming voice around the training table, mimicking the football players whom he admired greatly: "Sheeit. I thought he was a thoroughbred, but then I got back muh grade an' it was a measly C! He must have been just a old plow horse, but he had horn rim glasses an' his own briefcase!" The technique of riding, for all its bravado, was alas only marginally successful. The athletes, using their own limited deductive abilities, figured that the best students were people who *looked* like good students. It never occurred to them that a well-muscled jock could pull an A. Neither did they figure a fat unattractive female could miss so much as a question or two, what with all the free time she had to devote to her studies. And so it was that the riders were regularly amazed when their nefarious practices netted them mostly C's, occasional B's, a few giddy A's and, oh the shock of it all, even some D's and E's (picture the sad irony of realizing you had superimposed someone else's failure upon your own!) To blunder in such a manner meant not only did you pass up a chance to perhaps guess your way to a better score, but that you couldn't even—hold onto your Stetsons, boys—*cheat right* for chrissakes!

And if that wasn't enough of a pisser, consider the possibility that one might just be unlucky enough to sit in front of some snit who would take umbrage at one's goggle-eyed yawns and turn one's tender ass in to the exam proctor, which would entail lord only knows what kind of unpasteurized shit; word had it that the so-called Honor Court even had the power to suspend rubber-necked scholars from school.

It was with considerable trepidation that Jack Nubbins ripped open the envelope whose return address clearly indicated that it issued directly from the Office of the Prosecuting Solicitor of the Southeastern University Honor Court. The letterhead bore not only the standard blindfolded Maiden of Justice, holding her delicate scales, but also somewhat incongruously displayed a smiling caricature of Daryl the Swamp Dawg, the school's unique and unswerving mascot, who seemed to be sniffing at Maid Justice's scales as if tracking down some Alpo.

If the comic impact of the letterhead was lost on Nubbins, the contents were not:

```
Mr. Jack Nubbins
Room 207, Hiram Doobey Memorial Hall
Kernsville, Florida  32601

Dear Mr. Nubbins:

This office has undertaken an investigation as a
result of certain reports made to this office
involving yourself and another student during a
recent Physical Science Progress examination in
Humbolt Hall on September 2nd.

Comparison of your paper with the other student
in question (whom we now believe innocent of any
wrong doing) resulted in a Wrong Answer Correla-
tion (WAC) of 98%. As you perhaps know, this office
makes its decision on whether or not to prosecute
a case based upon the number of wrong answers two
suspects have in common. Generally speaking, a
WAC of 60% is considered sufficient to indict.

Your arraignment, therefore, has been set for the
evening of October 12, at 7:30 p.m. in the Honor
Courtroom at the Steven C. Prigman Student Union.
You may be represented by counsel of your choice
or we will appoint a student attorney for you.
Please be prompt.

I feel I should inform you, Mr. Nubbins, that a
98% WAC is, to my knowledge anyway, a Southeastern
University record.

Sincerely yours,

A. William Duva, Esq.
Solicitor General, Honor Court
```

This last gratuitous paragraph was debated extensively and though he had reservations himself, Cassidy decided to include it, reasoning that by the time Nubbins got to the end of the letter, he would be more or less reduced to a lump of

quivering redneck paranoia and therefore quite unlikely to catch such a subtle clue.

Which was the case. Nubbins received the letter on a Friday morning. Cassidy, who had been running a varsity meet in Knoxville, returned Sunday night to find no less than three notes pinned to his door, all from Nubbins. Delighted, he put his bags down and read them right in the hall in the order he figured they arrived:

> *Dear Captin Cassady:*
> *Need to have a pow wow with you when you get back from Tennesee. Please come by my room, which is numbered 207.*
> *—Jack N.*

> *Capt.*
> *Since it is important that I speak with you right away, I thought I would say you can come by whether it is late or not (when you get back).*
> *—Jack*

> *Sir:*
> *This is you know who. I have decided to lay low awhile so if you call 392-1458 and ask for Betty Sue Applewhite, she will know where I am because it is still inportunt that I speak with you right away. I have told her what you're voice sounds like so there will be no funny business.*
> *—You Know Who*

On the last note there was a postscript: *P.S. I hope you're as good a mouthpiece as everyone says you are.*

"Who is it?"
"Cassidy."
"I'm sorry?"
"Cassidy."
Silence. Cassidy sighed, rolled his eyes to the back of his head. "Roll over Beethoven," he muttered to the ceiling.

The door opened a crack and he was inspected by tiny frightened eyes.

"Come on, Betty Sue," said Cassidy, brushing by her. Nubbins sat on her bed with a humorous resigned expression.

Cassidy thought: too good, Jack. No one would ever think of looking for you in your girlfriend's dorm room.

"Looks like I've really stepped in it this time, Captain," said Nubbins mournfully. Cassidy sat on the bed beside him and gave him a what's-this-all-about pat on the knee. Betty Sue flicked off the Dating Game and perched at the end of the bed with her feet drawn up under her.

Nubbins' ROTC bivouac gear lay in a heap in the corner. Cassidy knew that somewhere in the equipment was Nubbins' cherished purloined issue .45, which he kept loaded at all times. Why he had lugged all the stuff over here, Cassidy couldn't figure. Perhaps Nubbins was thinking along the lines of Ethan Allan and the Green Mountain Boys. Cassidy pictured him set up somewhere in the Ocala National Forest with a regulation latrine, rain gullies and perimeter warning devices. At night he would forage through the campgrounds, snatching limp hot dogs from vacationing Ohioans.

"Jack," Cassidy said, "you need to get a grip on yourself, son." He put down the letter unread. He didn't actually need to read it since he had typed it himself only three days earlier. But Nubbins' fidgeting was keeping him from even doing a good acting job.

"What do you think, Captain? They've got my ass nailed, don't they?" Nubbins, trying hard to buck up, had adopted a fatalistic outlook. It seemed to comfort him to defer, military style, to Cassidy's very unmilitary captaincy. This dorm room was his last stand before the bastards stormed the walls; his own personal Alamo. He envisioned perhaps a ballad about himself.

"Well Jack, I'll lay it on the line to ya. It does *look* pretty bad." Nubbins lowered his head and nodded.

"But I'll tell ya somethin' else," Cassidy continued, his voice quavering with emotion, "I've gotten some sons a bitches out of jams a helluva lot worse than this!" He gestured at the letter with the disdain of a man who saw paper threats for what they were, a man who dealt with his own crystalline brand of reality, using insight gained only where such knowledge is available: through hours in the breech, days on the firing line, weeks behind the eight ball. What's more, he was clearly a man who did not abandon his friends when, as the

Attorney General himself used to say (before *his* indictment), the going got tough.

"You no doubt have heard about my work on the defense side in the Honor Court?" Cassidy asked with a trace of pride. Nubbins became suddenly animated.

"Why they say that you're . . ."

Cassidy held up a hand; he was not a man who needed idle flattery.

"But you'll take my case?" Nubbins asked, wide-eyed.

"Godamn right I will!" Cassidy stuck his jaw out.

Nubbins peered up at his counsel with something like true love, brushed manfully at his glistening eyes and tried to clear his throat.

"And you think we can win?" he croaked.

"Does a pigeon walk funny?"

13. The Trial

Buoyed by his attorney's confidence, Nubbins returned warily to Doobey Hall. After all, hadn't he been hearing for weeks tales of Cassidy's remarkable courtroom prowess? Still, in those long hours between their numerous conferences, Nubbins' spirits faltered. He was in considerable and very real distress most of the time.

His thinking went like this: If worse came to worse and he found himself suspended from the university, it would cost him a year redshirting somewhere else, assuming that another school would take a convicted academic scoundrel. But he knew that even so he would have lost a great deal by not graduating from Southeastern (Coach Cornwall had gone out on a limb just to get him admitted on special status).

And there was the additional shame of facing the many members of the Nubbins tribe, all of whom were as proud as they were baffled that some fancy dan university would not only let one of their wretched clan in, but would actually pay him real money just for pursuing an activity many of them had cultivated involuntarily while eluding various game officials, marine patrolmen, and deputy sheriffs; namely, hightailing it on foot. That this brilliant progeny should be shipped home in disgrace for some academic indiscretion would, of course, be accepted with a degree of sympathy and fatalism (it *had* been too good to be true after all), but on the other hand there would be a lingering suspicion that somehow the scatterbrained young'un had blown his big chance to become president.

Such was the young runner's discomfiture that Cassidy considered calling the whole thing off, an All Time Classic in the making was one thing, but watching this central Florida palmetto tramper sitting mute and bug-eyed over his scrambled eggs every morning was a bit more than Cassidy really wanted in the way of humorous feedback. The kid was hooked, living out this awful fantasy all by himself while the

71

others looked on with growing alarm. They all just wanted to bring the scenario to its dramatic conclusion, have a good laugh, and then let the poor boob down (hoping to God he was unarmed at the Moment of Truth). But having set the trial date themselves, they were stuck with it. Cassidy told Nubbins cockily that he had filed a motion to move the case along quickly and that on the night in question they would ". . . wrap this turkey up once and for all."

For two more days Nubbins sweated out his future. The more frantic he became, the more unsure the plotters became. Mizner brought up the unpleasant thought that Jack might become so depressed he would decide to chew on the end of his own forty-five. Who would want to live with that?

Cassidy had no doubts who would be damned if that happened. But he knew Nubbins well. Cassidy figured anyone who would squat with his ass in freezing water for three hours before dawn just for the chance to blast the feathers off a hapless mallard could damned well keep a date with Maid Justice without cracking. Cassidy kept everyone as calm as he could.

But finally even Hosford, the most vindictive of the puppeteers, caught a case of nerves.

"Geez, do you think we maybe ought to tell him? He's getting a little flakey around the edges."

"I think he'll make it okay," said Cassidy, trying to memorize his lines. "He's only got until tomorrow night."

"Yeah, but let me tell you. He came up to me this morning and started talking real strange. In this real cocky way—you know how he is—he starts telling me what a great lawyer you are and how he had personally seen you get people off who were guiltier than hell . . ." He looked at Cassidy. "You've never tried any cases for real, have you?"

"Never been *in* a courtroom," Cassidy chirped, studying his script.

"Anyway, he told me you had pull with the chancellor, and that you and this Duva guy, the prosecutor, drink beer together all the . . ."

"Who is a figment, of course."

"A figment?"

"Of my own fevered mind."

"Yes, well, he's doing everything but hyperventilating. You really think he'll do all right?"

"I think he'll make an excellent defendant. However, I have grave doubts . . ."

"Doubts?"

". . . about counsel's ability to bring home the bacon."

They were all there. Mizner wearing his official blazer with the court seal over the pocket, Cassidy in an attorneyish double-breaster, the chancellor in his black robes and stern wire-rims, the prosecutor in a rather obnoxiously dashing sports jacket, and Betty Sue Whatsherface, whom Nubbins had timidly asked be allowed to sit in on the "proceedings." And then there was Nubbins himself. Cassidy had told him to dress conservatively, using his own judgment. The lad wore a plain white shirt and black knit tie, and for his jacket selected a smart suede cowboy job with rather short fringe on the sleeves. The effect was prairie/formal: Daniel Boone addressing a joint session of Congress. The various participants had been carefully screened by Cassidy and Mizner. There were a few others in the room who had simply heard about the affair—despite the harsh oath of secrecy—and had begged to watch. All in all, the courtroom, which was never used for real trials at night, was about half full.

The chancellor was a contradiction in terms: a law student with a sense of humor. He generously offered to lend his solemn presence to the occasion in exchange for a print of the eight-by-twelve glossy Cassidy was having taken of the Defendant and the various court officials. For this purpose a friend of Mizner's was introduced to Nubbins as the "court photographer" who was going to "photograph key points in the proceedings for the record." Nubbins nodded with the bland assent of a three-time loser being fingerprinted.

Selecting the prosecutor had been difficult. Surprisingly, several sadistic individuals had clamored for the job. There resulted some hilarious tryouts during which Cassidy found himself doing a reasonably bitchy director: "Look baby, you've got to give me some *hostility*, for chrissakes. This guy is a lousy cheater and you're a self-righteous asshole, so let's emote that to me, baby, eee-mote. Okay, let's take if from '. . . if this treachery goes unscathed, our very foundations of self-government etcetera etcetera . . ."

Eventually everyone got into the act. The rejects for the prosecutor's job got to be the bailiff and the stenographer. Everyone dressed for his part with uncanny professionalism. It looked like Divorce Court without commercials.

Cassidy thought the courtroom itself was the perfect backdrop. In the manner of all effective courtrooms (as well as legislative chambers and religious edifices) it was designed to impress upon the single blinking supplicant that there was a *power* out there, a force all around that was fierce and swift and terrible in its retribution, an ascendancy that would— should he so much as fart without permission—crush him like the vermin he knew in his heart he was.

How polished mahogany could have such a debilitating effect upon the individual spirit, Cassidy could not figure, but that it did there was no doubt, for here beside him sat this quaking leather-fringed buffoon, sweating like a field hand and looking for all the world like he would leap straight up and grab onto a light fixture if someone so much as said *boo*. In fact, when the chancellor's gavel went down with a THWACK Nubbins popped up like overdue toast. Cassidy reached over with a reassuring lawyerly hand.

"All right, next matter. What is this case?" said the Chancellor.

"Case number 72-3689, your honor. Student body versus Jack Nubbins. Three witnesses. WAC of 98%."

The judge looked up from the papers he was studying and made a low whistle, obviously impressed.

"Ninety eight percent, why that would be a . . ."

"That's right, your honor, a . . ."

". . . record, wouldn't it?"

"Record, yes sir. We checked."

They brought if off with such pristine sincerity, these volunteer Thespians, that Cassidy swelled with pride. He had written all the lines himself for this far off-broadway production and his people were doing him proud. They all (except Cassidy) had scripts in front of them in legal folders, but no one seemed to need them.

The script at this point called for the judge to request the prosecutor to approach the bench. This gave Cassidy a chance to lean over and inform Nubbins that this judge was not the one he usually dealt with. There was mention of illness. They would have to feel their way along but not to worry because...

"Mr. Cassidy," the chancellor was interrupting. "I think it only fair to inform you that I will not allow you to get away with the kind of monkeyshines that I understand are your very trademark."

"Judge, I'm just a simple country lawyer and I'm sure that the Court knows I would never stoop to . . ."

"You know precisely what I mean. Just watch it!"

"Yes sir!" Cassidy leaned over and whispered to Nubbins: "I was afraid of something like this."

As the hearing went on, Cassidy did not look at any of his confederates about the room. If their eyes locked for more than a split second, great uncontrollable quakes would start deep in his diaphragm and, if unchecked, very quickly the whole mad, delicately balanced facade would crumble in premature hilarity. To cover himself, a few times he feigned coughing spells. He needn't have gone to the trouble, actually, for Nubbins, sensing things were not going well for the home team, was staring straight ahead in a melancholy trance. He now knew his lawyer, brilliant though he might be, was out of favor with this particular judge. Even as Cassidy rose to voice his objections, he was being overruled. And Nubbins could not remember having stumbled upon a human being, a total stranger at that, who obviously felt such open and hostile loathing for him as the natty prosecutor. It was hard to imagine that the fellow did not have some grave mental problem, such was his rancor. It seemed as though he might at any moment leap across counsel table and come at Nubbins with a hidden dagger. But apparently his cruel and clever antagonist had no need for such weapons in this arena; his objections were universally taken under consideration and just as universally sustained by the smiling judge. With each such telling point the prosecutor would look over, resplendent in his ensemble, and openly sneer at Nubbins and his obviously overrated attorney. Nubbins was going deeper and deeper into a kind of shock. He had never been in a situation where the cards had been so obviously, so inexorably, so uniformly stacked against him. His attorney, he now realized, was fighting a holding action against implacable odds; he was simply outmanned by the same immutable stars that had brought Nubbins into this courtroom in the first place.

Everyone was due for an unmitigated shitstorm at some time in his life, Nubbins figured, and this was clearly his turn.

Attorney Cassidy, struggling valiantly in this lost cause, was making motions that the entranced Nubbins could not have possibly paid any attention to, else he would have detected the faint but unmistakable aroma of rotten halibut on the breeze.

"Your Honor, I would like to make a motion *E Pluribus Unum* . . ."

"I object! He can't move for *E Pluribus Unum* in this proceeding. There isn't even a jury empaneled!"

"Sustained."

"Well then judge, I would like to request a *quid pro quo* in order to . . ."

"Objection! Clearly improper before the Defendant takes the stand."

"Sustained. Mr. Cassidy, I must warn you, sir! Please sit down!"

This went on long enough for Nubbins to clearly get the drift. Then Cassidy requested a recess in order to discuss something important with his client. Even this request was only grudgingly granted. As a group, all the court personnel, the spectators, and even Nubbins' timid girlfriend (sensing somehow that it was the thing to do) rumbled out of the room leaving lawyer and client alone in the large chamber. Cassidy, his borrowed horn rims cocked up on his forehead, rubbed his weary lawyer eyes.

"Well Jack, I guess you can see things aren't going so hot."

"Yeah, that judge doesn't like you one *little* bit. And the prosecuting one! What's he got against me anyway? I don't know him from Adam's nephew."

"Just doing his job, Jack, doing his job. But the chancellor. I think we may have a chance with him. He seems to be perturbed that we're dragging this thing out with a full-blown trial. Another lawyer told me once he likes to see people come in and lay it on the line. Otherwise, if you go through a trial and he still finds you guilty, he really throws the book at you."

"What do you think we ought to do?"

"I'm thinking we ought to go ahead and plead guilty and throw ourselves on the mercy of the court." Steady, he thought, burst out laughing now and you'll blow the whole thing.

"Well, you're the boss, you know that. We've come this far . . ."

"Listen Jack, I want you to know . . ."

"Hey, I know. Listen, I thought you were doing a great job. Some of those motions, man . . ."

"Yeah. I should have won a couple of them at least. Anyway, let's give it a go. And Jack . . ."

"Yeah?"

"Remember no matter what happens, I was there when you needed me." They shook hands solemnly. Nubbins was still sure he had a fine lawyer. Cassidy notified the bailiff and everyone was called back in. Defense counsel advised the Court that his client wished to change his plea to guilty as charged, and to ask for the mercy of the Court. He could barely get the words out. He dared not look at anyone as he spoke; they were all holding it together with sheer will power.

The judge seemed relieved by this announcement and thanked Cassidy for sparing the Court a "long and arduous trial." He then thanked the court personnel for their patient efforts. He requested that Nubbins rise with his attorney while he pronounced sentence. Since Cassidy had put several hours of work into the sentencing speech, he was gratified to see it delivered with the loving attention of a fine performer.

"Mr. Nubbins," the chancellor began, removing his spectacles, "I must admit that I have often wondered why we so seldom see athletes in here, what with all the speculation that goes on about the ethics of those who reside in Farley Hall. I know I should not let my personal feelings become involved, but I've always sensed that you jocks think you run this institution. Now, I'm not a varsity athlete myself, Mr. Nubbins—oh, in high school I played a little basketball and was conference champion in the 200 butterfly, but I guess when they got around to handing out the scholarships . . . oh well, that's neither here nor there. What I'm here to tell you this evening, Mr. Nubbins, is that I am now a serious student here at Southeastern, and there are many of us serious students here, Mr. Nubbins, students who don't get their way paid by rich Uncle over in Farley Hall, read me? It's too bad that you have to bear the brunt for all the ones who have done the same thing you have and gotten away with it, but I don't know any other way to bring the message home that *you jocks don't run this campus!"*

He paused, as if regaining his composure somewhat, and added as an almost understood afterthought: "We politicos do."

"This is your sentence, Mr. Nubbins: You are hereby suspended from this university indefinitely."

There was a perfect silence in the courtroom.

Such was the demented sincerity of this last diatribe that many of the onwatchers, though they knew it was a farce, were actually a little mortified at the chancellor's rancor. There was much sullen gaping going on, as if no one knew exactly how to end the whole ordeal. Nubbins just stood quaking, his mouth a small, dark cave. He stared unbelieving at the still-bristling judge.

Suddenly the "court photographer" ran out of the spectator's section, snapped a flash picture of Cassidy and Nubbins and scurried back. Cassidy could no longer control himself. Weakly, he bent at the waist, held his stomach with both hands, and began making deep, resonant yelps not unlike the fierce mating call of the male peacock. Nubbins looked over at him; his own lawyer found the penalty so harsh he could not keep from laughing!

That broke the dam, of course, and the entire courtroom was quickly engulfed in a giant spasm of raucous laughter. With a wild clamor, the teary-eyed actors and half-paralyzed spectators began stumbling over feebly to shake hands with the Defendant and pound his back gleefully.

The little runner's wide eyes did not blink as his head swiveled back and forth, a berserk lighthouse. He thought: how can anyone be so cruel as to actually enjoy seeing me get booted out of school? And my own lawyer is still laughing; did he find it amusing too?

Even the judge, black robes flowing, came down and threw his arm around Nubbins' shoulders, barking all the while.

Betty Sue sat amidst the considerable confusion with a vague smile on her face, wondering what in the bejesus was going on. She knew one thing: Old Jack had done something wonderful and she was very proud.

14. *Indoors*

Winter arrived in the panhandle in its usual desultory fashion; a time of bright, cool days, chilly rains, fading landscapes. The harsh glare of those cloudless days muted the grass, the moss-draped oaks and sometimes the higher callings of the spirit.

"It is easier to train hard up north," Denton told them. "Snow is snow. You either run in it or you don't. It gives you something to go against, an irritant. But also a stimulus, if you know what I mean. Down here the freezing rain runs down your neck one day, next day you'd think spring had sprung in January."

"What's wrong with that?" Cassidy asked.

"Such a winter is always getting your hopes up."

But winter was the indoor season and for Cassidy it was a time of renewed hopes. He had had his cross-country drubbings; now he longed to turkey trot a victory lap.

"I've just had an odd thought," said Cassidy, looking out the oval porthole, enjoying immensely the crisp, heady vacuum of jet flight.

"Do tell," Denton looked up from his botany journal.

"Here we are flying several miles high across the eastern seaboard—look, that must be Savannah—flying across the eastern seaboard a couple of thousand miles at a cost of several hundreds of dollars so that we can take off our clothes, put on little kangaroo skin slippers that weigh about three ounces each, and shag ass around a little board track for exactly one mile—two in your case. And there are these people, thousands of them, who live in skyscrapers of block and glass, and who will pay money to come and watch us do it. This is the culmination of man's technology, zipping us along at 600 miles per hour . . ."

"Maybe it just means that civilization has progressed to the point where it can afford even the most esoteric of specialties, even in sports. We are the athletic equivalent of pickled bees knees in the gourmet section at the Winn Dixie."

"Hah." This last took Cassidy by surprise. He looked over and Denton smiled back sweetly, letting Cassidy know once more that there are some people you do not take for granted, even for a second.

Cross country had ended surprisingly. At the AAU National Championships in Chicago's Washington Park, Cassidy, to his own great surprise, kept the leaders in view almost the entire race, finishing with frozen slush halfway up his calves in 15th place, four ahead of Mizner. He had never beaten the younger runner at any distance over two miles. Denton won the race with such ease that the other top cross-country men, stacked up in the finish chute, simply shook their heads in discouragement even as they bent to their knees still gasping from the effort. Denton seemed more delighted with Cassidy's finish than he was to win yet another national title. He even did a little jig as Cassidy, sprinting through the mud to edge out an Oregon runner, sailed into the chute with a grimace. A few seconds later they were all standing around in the slush, laughing though still out of breath, kicking mud at each other. Even Mizner, disappointed as he was, seemed to have a good time, though Cassidy could see he was worried.

Cross country, to Cassidy's immense relief, was over for another year.

"In lane six, wearing number 278, from Southern California, the PAC champion . . . "

The announcer was going into the introduction for the two-mile, the longest running event in the Millrose Games in Madison Square Garden. Cassidy jogged out onto the track to take Denton's sweats from him. The other two-milers milled around with incredible nervousness; some trotted back and forth in their lanes, some bounced up and down. It was a time of cruel stress. One race represented months of training; each step the product of many miles of preparation. They would have thought of this race countless times, some of them running it in bits and pieces during interval training or overdistance. They would have thought of creeping up to Denton's shoulder with a lap to go; that sort of fantasy could get them through long hours on the roads at night. But with the starting gun only seconds away, their heads were roaring with anticipation and anguish. They wanted to be into it. They wanted to be *over* it. The race itself was bearable, for that they had trained. The waiting, however, was hell on square wheels. Denton handed Cassidy the navy blue sweat top with USA in red and white piping, a status symbol, the sign of a member of a national team. Two other runners in the field wore the same kind of sweats; this would not be a stroll.

"Hang in there," Cassidy said quietly.

"Yeah," Denton was glazed over in concentration, even for a race that he surely couldn't consider very important. He was not a classical indoor runner; both he and Cassidy were too tall to maneuver the banked turns as easily as the shorter runners. And Denton never, never took a race for granted. Though he said little to Cassidy, Cassidy knew he was appreciative of having someone there to offer small comforts.

"*In lane three, two-time AAU six-mile champion, one-time three-mile champion, twice a member of our Olympic team . . .*"

They were getting into the heavies, now. Cassidy took the sweats, swatted Denton on the rear and jogged to the infield to watch.

"*And in lane one . . .* "

The crowd was already beginning to rumble.

"*. . . representing Southeastern University Track Club and the United States . . .*" It was difficult to hear now. "*. . . ladies and gentlemen, the Olympic Gold Medalist in the 5000-meter run . . .*" Bruce Denton trotted forward in his lane with a serene little wave even though he had not heard his name. No one had. This was what that one perfectly executed race and the thousands of miles of training it required had earned him: the right to have his name lost in the uncontrolled frenzy of this crowd. Denton thought: *I only won by three yards.*

Such adulation had roared down for him many times since he first heard it sprinting down the straightaway in the Olympic stadium. He would surely hear it many times again in his life. But as Denton trotted out and wistfully accepted it once more, Quenton Cassidy thought his smile seemed sad indeed.

"*. . . and entering the final lap now ladies and gentlemen . . .*" The starter's gun went off with a loud crack: gun lap. "*. . . Gold*

Medalist Bruce Denton followed by . . . " It was all meaningless. The pack was a full half lap behind, running for places. Denton cavorted. He ran wide up on the banked turn and zipped back down onto the straightaway, playing roller coaster. Cassidy shook his head. Here he was running some of the best distance men in the country, and he was playing around. When Denton crossed the finish line, Cassidy trotted up alongside and handed him the sweats. Denton, despite the ease with which be had won, was in no condition to talk; he took the sweats, grinned at Cassidy, and jogged on. He occasionally waved as a section of the audience stood to cheer when he passed beneath them. Cassidy shook his head, ran slowly to the outer hallway to complete his warmup; his race was in 35 minutes, according to the almost universally unreliable schedule.

Cassidy had ripped the order of events out of the program and was careful to check his watch often. By listening to the announcer, he would be able to tell how far behind the meet was running and thus time his warmup accurately. The large cold hallway did not make a complete circuit, but it was roomy; brightly colored sweatsuits flashed by at various speeds. Cassidy had jogged the elliptical half-circle three times by the time Denton came out to find him. Even now his face was red, his voice hoarse from the harsh smokey air.

"Want company?" It was a rhetorical question. Here in this chilly, foreign environment, with so many talented athletes everywhere, it was easy to get psyched out. Cassidy knew no one here except Bruce. He was already beginning to ask himself the eternal self-doubt question: What Am I Doing Here? But now he wasn't just some nobody in a Southeastern University sweatsuit jogging back and forth, he was "the guy with Bruce Denton." His stride took on a proud bounce.

"Do you know any of these guys in the mile?" He asked Denton. The older runner took the list and studied it as they ran.

"Well, Marcel Phillipe you know. He's a Fordham guy, can't be in real good shape yet. O'Rork I'm sure you remember; Kerry Ellison, Texas El Paso: tough cookie. Those guys get in shape early like we do. I'd say he's the man to watch."

"I didn't think he . . ."

"He doesn't run on the cross-country team, is why you didn't see him at nationals. They have a bunch of true six-milers, so he doesn't have to. No, he'll be in shape. Wouldn't be here otherwise."

"Yeah, but what about old . . ."

"Liquori is scratched."

"Scratched? Jeez . . ."

"Breaks your heart doesn't it? I talked to him a few minutes ago. He is in pretty good shape but he sprained his ankle a few days ago. I hate to say this, but it looks like you might have a chance to take all the marbles."

"Bruce, I . . ." His forehead wrinkled with concern, "Bruce, the Wannamaker Mile . . ."

"Look. This is the way it happens. You keep at it hard, just like you've been doing. You hang around the fringes waiting for your chance. When it comes you go for it, hard. You do good, that gets you psyched. You go back, work even harder . . ." He stopped for a moment, reflected, then laughed. "Hell, I don't know. Who the hell knows?"

"The Milrose mile . . ."

"All I know is that you could win the thing. Your best races are the ones where you just relax and let it flow. You've got great speed, Cass. Jeez, I wish I had it. All you have to do is keep from fretting it away early. It doesn't do any good anyway, indoors especially. Avoid hassles; when you make a move, go around the problems and stay around them. You can run behind just fine so long as you don't get lulled into a bad place late in the race. If you're in a good spot, don't panic even if you're a little crowded. Hang in there and hum a little tune, talk to yourself, look at the girls, *anything* . . . just stay in contact and get yourself to a good position with two laps to go. Don't wait until it's too late to get to your spot. You just don't make up really big gaps indoors, especially on this track."

"Yeah, it's a little slow, isn't it?"

"It's pretty bad for the sprinters, but okay for us. A little spongy is all. I don't think it will affect you that much, but since you push off strongly from your calves you might try to get a little more float out of your stride, instead of trying to get oomph from the track. It doesn't have it to give."

"Got it. Want to do some striders with me?"

"Striders? Striders? Hell, I just did an 8:32 deuce and you want me to do striders with you just to keep you company?" He took off down the concrete hallway in a sprint, scattering runners in all directions. Cassidy smiled; it was always a great feeling to have it over with.

"*. . . four laps to go and it's O'Rork of East Tennessee, Phillipe of Fordham, Ellison, Cassidy, Wheeler, and Hector Ortiz of Western Kentucky . . .* "

Cassidy tried to make his mind work. Eleven laps to the mile, two and three quarters equals one regular lap. Unaccustomed to gauging fatigue-versus-distance-remaining on an indoor track, he had to make conversions as he went along. A runner is a miser, spending the pennies of his energy with great stinginess, constantly wanting to know how much he has spent and how much longer he will be expected to pay. He wants to be broke at precisely the moment he no longer needs his coin.

He calculated: outdoors it would be the third lap. For the time being he was content to tuck in with the middle of the pack and wait for something to happen. The pace had not been impressive; Cassidy felt comfortable with it. They had gone through the half in 2:02 in a bunch. Each time he went by the far turn, Bruce Denton, arch-fan, was one voice among 15,000 who called just for him. Denton yelled things that were not in the least irritating like most of the things you hear during a race (things like "pick it up, pick it up" or "faster, faster, don't let them get away"), things that make the runner think: If you think it's so damn slow, why don't you godamn well get out here and "pick it up" yourself.

Instead, Denton said: "Good pace, Cass, hang right there!" Or: "Good position, stay alert . . ." To the runner, traveling at a dizzying 15 miles per hour around a tiny oval track, entranced by pace concentration, the idea of staying alert seemed positively brilliant.

With no warning and but two laps to go, Kerry Ellison surged powerfully. His brown legs flashed smoothly as he let out a burst of brutal speed. Cassidy responded immediately by pulling out, but he had to wait for a straightaway to pass the two runners in front of him. Damn! Then he realized with a sinking heart what Denton had said to him on each of the last two laps: "Move up now. Move up now."

But he had not heeded. Now he was just where he didn't want to be, in a bad position late in the race.

The gun went off as they banked into the penultimate turn. By now Cassidy had pulled back to within ten yards of the flying Texan. With growing confidence he crept steadily up to Ellison's shoulder, using the entire far straight to do it, but feeling—though fatigued from the pace—that he had spirit left. He had gotten out of the jam by responding immediately to Ellison's bid and he seemed to have something left to throw into it. He was excited and just as curious as the spectators to find out what was going to happen. The crowd, on its feet since the crack of the gun, didn't seem to care who won. They just wanted a race.

The excitement of the approaching finish yarn, as always, caused a little prickly feeling at the back of his neck. Cassidy started to pass on the final turn, but just as he pulled up and began the effort, he heard Denton through the din: "NO!" That was all he said. This time Cassidy heard.

He hung on Ellison's shoulder all through the tiny turn and with a gasp flung himself out and into the final straight. Ellison was not finished either; he pumped smoothly and leaned into his final sprint. But Quenton Cassidy was by far the faster kicker. He easily gained seven yards on Ellison in the last straight. From the crowd came a subdued roar that signified the anti-climax. Denton jumped up onto the track and trotted up to where Cassidy was bent over in the familiar gasping position.

"Don't grab those knees, boy," he shouted above the din. "Here are your sweats, get 'em on. But don't you grab those knees though because you got to run a little of that off. You have just become the Wannamaker Mile champion and you got to let them *know* . . ."

Cassidy's face was the old fire engine color and his breathing still desperate.

"Know. What?" He tried to jog, but it felt as if his spine were made of bamboo. Nothing worked properly, lactic acid bound him into a solid block. He could not swing his arms.

"That it feels GOOOOD!" Denton seemed much happier at the moment than his young friend.

On the plane, Cassidy was a zombie again, smiling vaguely but apparently unable to assimilate what was going on around him. They had gone out to eat and hadn't gotten to bed until two in the morning. Denton insisted they take a token morning run, so they clomped around stiffly in the gray Manhattan morning. Denton assured him most muggers did not work early.

Cassidy barely made it to his seat. The stewardess woke him to ask if he wanted breakfast—he did—and woke him again a few minutes later when she brought it. When they arrived in Philadelphia, Denton woke him again.

"Hey champ, end of the line. All milers off." Cassidy mumbled something and then snoozed while the other passengers got off. He nodded off gently while Denton got a cab and then slept soundly all the way to the hotel as Denton sat in the front seat and chatted with the driver.

"Whatz wrong wid yer buddy?" the driver asked.

"Wannamaker's Syndrome," Denton said. "Sub-clinical. Real pity is the guy used to be a fine athlete."

"Too bad," clucked the driver.

"Hey Rip! Time for grub. Let's get it on." It was Denton again.

Cassidy thought: he's enjoying himself, there's no doubt about it.

"I don't think I'm going to live," he told Denton.

"They've got great clam chowder at this place only a couple of blocks away," said Denton, as he dressed. "Also a nice little rib-eye steak that I, for one, would not miss on a bet."

"What the hell is that?" Cassidy pointed out the window.

"That my boy is snow. White stuff that falls from God. It won't hurt you actually, as long as you don't swallow any or carry it in your pocket. Some people claim it has magical powers. Try to put on long wooden planks and slide on it. Personally I don't think it will catch on. Come ON! Get your ass in gear, I'm starving."

Despite himself, once they were out in the cold air walking to the restaurant Cassidy started to feel better. After he had some tea, he tried to snap out of it altogether.

"I don't understand how I can have jet lag in my own time zone. How do you do this all winter?"

"This?" Denton crumbled some crackers into his chowder. "This, my boy, is fine. This is your reward for getting into good shape early, cause these northern sharpies won't fly you in from the coast or Florida to run in their shows unless they know you can produce. Hell, they could get a fairly respectable field in the mile or deuce from the New York-Boston area if they had to. We furnish an element of the exotic. You'd best get used to the idea if you keep winning. A 4:01.3 is not a bad time, indoors. Especially on that sponge cake track in the Garden. That might be worth, oh . . ."

"Come on, Bruce . . ."

"That might be worth a three . . ."

"Cut it out, Bruce!"

"A 3:58 or so, Cass." He looked up seriously from his chowder.

Cassidy sipped his tea morosely. These things were not to be bantered about lightly. It was bad luck to put your mouth on times your feet couldn't reach. Denton got up to talk to someone paying his check.

"Who was that?" Cassidy asked.

"Someone who is going to make your evening interesting."

"Come on . . ."

"Just don't try any of that last straightaway kicking crap like last night or you'll hear someone behind you distinctly laughing his ass off."

"Bruce, who . . ."

"Sammy Bair."

"Shit."

The Philadelphia meet was a classic second-meet-of-the-weekend letdown. Denton won in 8:44 from an undistinguished field and Cassidy ran 4:05.2 for second. Sam Bair didn't laugh at him but he might as well have.

By the time they were seated on the plane the next morning, Cassidy was back in his walking coma.

"You gonna have breakfast?" chirped Denton as they strapped in. "I mean if you don't want her to wake you. . ."

"Bruce, you can have my godamned breakfast. Why don't you just try to cheer up a little?" He dropped off into a sleep that didn't abate in the slightest until they reached Atlanta where they changed planes.

He didn't dream.

15. Casualty

The splenetic fireplug of a nurse turned the page of her *Cosmo* juicily, saw it was going to get pretty good, and elected to take a pit stop before going on. The article was entitled: "Your S[exual] Q[uotient]: Rating Yourself in the Boudoir."

As soon as she toddled off, the vigilant Quenton Cassidy tossed aside his *National Geographic* ("I Lived With The Bagharack Mountain Apes" by Dr. Jane Tully-Wells, one for the neo-Freudians, he thought), grabbed the aromatic flat box and sprinted for the stairwell. This was past visiting hours. This was illegal. This was keeno neato fun.

He sashayed into Mizner's room with the box on his upturned fingers, singing in a lusty though muted voice: "Cara mia whaaay..."

Mizner: "Shhhh!"

Cassidy moaned: "There's a village called Surrentohhh..."

Mizner: "That godamned old bat of a..."

"In the can."

"Oh."

Mizner sat up in bed, pale in his old sweatshirt, a faded dusty purple job with the traditional winged foot and the nearly illegible legend: POMPANO BEACH TRACK. Cassidy scurried around setting up. He stuffed a towel in the crack under the door. He pulled up a chair and produced with considerable flourish the two cans of beer, one from each pocket. Mizner applauded quietly. Had Cassidy stood still for just a moment and really looked at his friend, real tears might have slid down over his fleshless cheekbones. Mizner was what they called a Hurtin' Swamp Dawg. But he told Cassidy: "You brang sich joy into mah hort." In a dreamy, nearly dopey voice this was.

They attacked the disk, which—although containing mostly squashed tomatoes and fermented animal parts—the Italians will scarcely claim. Even after Mizner threw in his napkin, Cassidy kept on eating, primarily because he wanted something to do. He was still unstable here.

"So tell me about Milrose, dammit. Every detail. Do not stint. Do not leave out a spike hole or a careless elbow," Mizner said impatiently.

"The *Kernsville Sun* captured it quite well actually," Cassidy said, "following their normal tradition of printing straight wire copy, despite the fact two local heroes did good. Let's see, Liquori scratched, bless his little heart. No furriners, for some reason—maybe immigration rounded 'em all up or something—just me and Ellison in the last lap. I kind of slipped up on him after the bell and when we got to the last straight I pulled the trigger. For a second I didn't think anything was going to happen. Then it caught and I blew by him. I actually ended up getting him by seven, but he probably eased off when he saw he wasn't going to come back. Bruce was beside himself. I think he has decided that he, you know, *discovered* me or something. Despite the fact that I had to run a 4:00.3 last year before he hardly said more than hello."

"How did his race go?"

"Oh, he just blew them right off the track. Art Dulong, Drayton, and that guy from Minnesota. They were never even in it. He ran 8:32 like it was a workout."

Mizner shook his head. "It would have been great to see. Both of you." But Cassidy knew what he was saying.

"So what is the word here? Is it confirmed?"

"Shit yes. They think maybe three, four months of no training. Even then it's touch and go because of the possibility of relapses. But at least I get out of here pretty soon."

"Well, hey, at least you didn't blow your eligibility. Except for cross country." Very quietly, this last.

"Hey, listen. I already have a complete list of the silver linings. It's the godamn cloud that's killing me."

"Yeah." Cassidy looked at his feet. There were no good words for this one, he thought. A runner who could not run was out of his element. He would not even think of himself as an athlete; ridiculously there would be a kind of guilt about it; that was the worst part. He would begin to feel uncomfortable around his training comrades and the feeling would be mutual, like a newly wounded soldier among the embarrassed whole ones, who would not wish to be reminded of certain

crap game aspects of life. Cassidy was not surprised when
Mizner told him he was going to move out of Doobey Hall
for the next quarter. This was getting them both down.
Mizner sensed it and changed the subject.

"What's happening with all the yelling and screaming on
the haircut rules?"

"Hmmm. I wish I knew. It seems they are really serious
about the thing. I hear they've been cracking down around
Farley Hall, measuring sideburns with little rulers, making
guys change shirts before they let them eat, stuff like that.
Real, you know, brilliant stuff from the football minds over
there. Even the football players are mad as hell. Nothing has
happened at Doobey yet, but everyone figures they just
haven't quite gotten around to us."

"Jeez. And me stuck in the infirmary."

"Consider yourself lucky. That godamned Hosford volun-
teered my room for some kind of rabble rousing meeting
tonight." He looked at his watch irritably.

"I guess I'd better go. They might set fire to my Kip Keino
poster or something." He tossed his beer can into the trash
can and winced as it clanged. He had forgotten.

"Is there anything I can . . ."

"Naw. I've got everything; the guys brought my books and
stuff. You better take off. Thanks for the pizza; I'd kiss you
but . . ."

Cassidy laughed. "Then I'd get the thing and we could be
roommates in here. Look you take care of yourself, yuh hear?
I know . . . I know this is a pretty rough deal . . ."

"Well, the tour was getting to me a little, you know? I
mean Akron one night, Utica the next. Now at least I can take
the time to work on my steps and followthrough."

"And coming over the ball, don't forget to come *over* the
ball . . ."

Mizner laughed. "No doubt. Hey Cass, really, congratulations on Milrose. I think it's just great. You should have heard
me when I read the paper Saturday morning. They thought
I had slipped and broken my ass on the way to the john or
something." Cassidy nodded, smiled at him, and turned for
the door just as it was shoved open bruskly. The white stock-
inged fireplug stood glaring at him.

"You!" she cried. Cassidy leaned over and solemnly kissed her on the forehead, then sprinted out the door dodging a relatively serious swat with her rolled up *Cosmo.*

On the way back to Doobey, walking along with his hands jammed in his pockets away from the chilly evening, he was filled with loss and an off-brand of nostalgia for events that were supposed to become part of his past but now wouldn't at all. In the mind's special processes, a ten-mile run takes far longer than the 60 minutes reported by a grandfather clock. Such time, in fact, hardly exists at all in the real world; it is all out on the trail somewhere, and you only go back to it when you are out there.

He and Mize had been through two solid years of such regular time-warp escapes together. There was something different about that, something beyond friendship; they had a way of transferring hurt back and forth, without the banality of words.

But now in the vague recesses of his mind, Cassidy detected deep and sinister rumblings; storm clouds that chilled the air but were not yet visible on the horizon.

And too, he did not do well with hospitals and infirmaries; repositories of laboratory smells, lethal looking silverware; launching pads for flagging hopes . . .

16. *New Territory*

Quenton Cassidy returned from his afternoon visit to Mizner and now sat in his darkening room feeling not so much despair as nerve-jangling emptiness. The scenery was closing in on him. Low blood ph, he thought; the trick is to keep from getting nervous in the pack, like Bruce says. Think of how anchovies must swim a thousand to a square yard with a perfect twin on either side and a tiny bung flitting up ahead.

The *Kernsville Sun* lay in a heap at the foot of the bed. He had stopped trying to read when the sun got too low and he realized he was too tired to get up and turn on the light. So he just sat, staring out the window. It was slim pickings in the limp little sheet anyway; warmed over wire stories, a hard-hitting editorial on sewage bonds, an irate letter from a lady complaining about a neighbor's dog shitting in her azaleas, and sports editor Jack Hairlepp's column urging full support for Dick Doobey's next season. There was a quote from the coach about ". . . some fine junior college transfers who are going to be a real great help to us out there next year." At that point Cassidy had tossed the paper, idly wondering if Hairlepp drew his salary from the newspaper or just picked up his check on Friday from the athletic department's publicity office.

Perhaps he was too hard on the local gazette. There was, after all, real news in the human interest vein on page 2A under the *Smile For The Day* logo. It seems that somewhere out in the great American night a felonious ebony hand had skillfully slid a flat piece of steel down a car window, allowing a hopped-up connoisseur of spot remover to become the temporary (if illegal) bailee of a Ford Fairlane with transmission problems; thrown into the deal were the contents of a dark green garbage bag in the back seat, which contents were exactly: someone's dead mother-in-law.

Cassidy had thought: *Oh, this is a fun-loving citizenry.*

"Hey, how come it's so dark in here?" Hosford wandered in, cracking his knee on the edge of the dresser.

"I'm afraid if I turn on a light I'll look in the mirror and see that I look as bad as I feel," Cassidy said, but not uncheerfully.

"Ah, well. Mind if I sit down? Hey, the *Sun*. Anything in here?"

"As usual the only important message is contained in Doonesbury."

"Well, as it happens, I bring news myself. I hope it's not bad. Western Union guy just brought it a few minutes ago. I thought you were asleep, so I signed for it."

"Telegram? Thanks, Hoss . . ."

"I'll mosey along, I guess. Hey, listen . . ."

"Hey, this is open . . ."

". . . congratulations, Cass, all the guys think it's just great."

"All the . . . Hosford! Come back here you nosey son of a bitch..."

"Bruce? Sorry to call during dinner, but you'll never guess..."

"You got invited to the Sunkist Games next weekend," Denton said. Cassidy slumped.

"How the hell did you know?"

"Talked to the meet director when we were at Milrose."

"What did he say?"

"He wanted to know if I thought you could go under four minutes on his track in San Diego."

"And?"

"I asked him did a fish hold his breath under water."

Cassidy yelped, then calmed himself.

"Wonderful, Bruce. I haven't even run that outdoors yet..."

"Life is short, life is hard."

"You're running the three?"

"Right."

"Good field?"

"I don't know what you call good. Just Shorter and a bunch of . . ."

"Shorter!"

"Mmmm. You'd think the little bastard of a marathoner would stick to the great outdoors. Unfortunately he seems to *like* the boards. And in case it slipped your mind, he once held the American record for two mile indoors. On that very track."

"How, uh, do you think you'll handle him, Bruce?" Was that concern in his voice? Denton rattled around on his end for a few seconds; Cassidy couldn't tell what he was doing.

"Why Quenton, *I'll break his back . . .* "

Braggadocio has little to do with it, however, when the really good boys clash and everyone is feeling chipper. The two gold medalists broke away from the field early and were soon circling the track at a distressing pace that quickly found most of the other runners lapped. Although Denton's credentials were in a race slightly longer than three miles and Shorter's in the marathon, their training was remarkably similar. The crowd was standing during the last half mile; the lead changed three times as they probed at each other. Denton's long powerful strides were matched by Shorter's clipped, silky ones. The marathoner was so smooth as to give the impression of gliding on wheels. The strain of the pace showed around the edges of their otherwise unemotional faces. Cassidy watched in awe as they threw surges at each other. *Sheeeitfire,* Cassidy thought, this is awful. We need some relief.

His shouts were lost in the general pandemonium as the two runners entered the final lap with Denton slightly in front and Shorter on his outside shoulder. Cassidy figured it was highly unlikely a marathoner would be able to outsprint a 5000-meter champion, but his joyous victory whoop came just a trifle too early. It was a doubly painful revelation to watch the all-too-clear demonstration of mortality that was the last lap of that race. Frank Shorter had to break an American indoor record for three miles, and his margin of victory was exactly one tenth of a second, but there was no doubt whatsoever that when Bruce Denton reached the finish line, he had the unique experience of finding the yarn already parted for him. Cassidy was stunned.

Despite the incredible effort of their contest, the two runners were soon coherent enough to be interviewed by a particularly irrelevant Howard Cosell. Cassidy waited outside the glow of hot television lights in a pale haze of his own confusion. He had never seen Denton lose a race and he wasn't sure yet how he felt. When the interview was over, Denton and Shorter left the infield together and sprinted through a veritable tidal wave of little kids waving programs and pens. Denton turned, spotted Cassidy, motioned for him to join them. When the miler caught up to the pair of distance men in the hallway, they were already lost in the numerical shorthand of training talk. Shorter was reserved, shy, yet with a sweetness that seemed positively contrary to the cruelty he could summon up for his competitors. His eyes reflected that irony. Cassidy wanted to ask him a hundred questions but bit his tongue. He was in truth a bit flabbergasted. First he had watched Denton outsprinted by a marathoner and now he and that marathoner were jogging along chatting about training like it was old home week. Denton had never mentioned that he even knew Shorter. Cassidy only half-listened to the mumble of mileage figures:

"... at altitude of course, and then 123, 132, 137 and 145, but with only two interval sessions a week ..." "... and a long one on Sunday, about 20, Louise goes the first 10 with us ..." "... step-down starting with a 4:12 mile and a 3:02 three quarters ..." "... then 35 times 220 all of them pretty quick for me, 28 to 30 or so ..." And so on. It was quiet for several seconds before he realized he had been spoken to.

"I'm sorry?" Cassidy said.

"I said Milrose. You won Milrose two weeks ago, didn't you?" Shorter was being polite, trying to include him in the conversation.

"Ah. Yes. The field wasn't that strong, you see ..."

"Well anyone who can run close to four on that track gets my respect. I think they made it out of pound cake dyed green."

"At least no one will get shin splints on the thing."

"I hate to interrupt a medical discussion," Denton said, pointing to a clock on the wall, "but I believe it's time for the stud milers among us to be doing some striders. This is one meet they generally manage to run on time. Mr. Shorter here finished the three so quickly he put them several minutes ahead."

Cassidy held out his hand to Shorter. "Hey, it was nice to meet you. Uh, do you have any parting words for an aspiring young runner?"

Shorter looked puzzled, amused. He looked over at Denton, then smiled back at Cassidy.

"Well, no, not actually. Except have a good time." Denton laughed and waved Cassidy off.

"That one," Denton said, tilting his head at the departing miler, "keep your eye on that one . . ."

Shorter nodded.

That night Quenton Cassidy ran the best mile of his life and thereby changed his position in the tiny universe of runners nearly imperceptibly. He ran 4:00.1 and of course would never be quite the same. But his race was also a different kind of revelation.

And although Denton tried several times on the flight back to put things into perspective for him, Cassidy knew he was on the fearful and nebulous border of new territory.

He finished fifth, and was lucky to get that.

17. Breaking Down

Cassidy had been through it before, every one of them had at one time or another, but it had never been quite this bad. Denton called it "breaking down," although Cassidy preferred the nomenclature of certain Caribbean quasi-religious groups; walking death was much closer to it. Quite a bit more, really, than the simple exhaustion of a single difficult workout, breaking down was a cumulative physical morbidity that usually built up over several weeks and left the runner struggling to recover from one session to the next.

The object, according to Denton, was to "run through" the thing, just as he maintained one should attempt to "run through" most of those other little hubcaps life rolls into your lane; everything from death in the family to cancer of the colon.

Breaking down was not a required checkpoint on the road to competitive fitness. In fact, many coaches warned against it. But Denton viewed it as an opportunity to leapfrog over months of safer, less strenuous training, thus tempering survival-hardened muscles. The alternative, total rest, was too much the other extreme, the easy way out. That wouldn't do.

The toll on the runner, however, was high if he chose not to slack off. Psychologically as well as physically, he paid the price. He became weak, depressed; he needed 12 to 14 hours of sleep a night. He was literally desperate for rest, spent his waking hours with his legs elevated, in a state of general irritability. He became asexual, rendered, in the words of the immortal limerick, really quite useless on dates. He was a thoroughly unpleasant person.

But then his life was most certainly focused on The Task. And hadn't he decided at one time that he would do whatever was necessary to become . . . whatever it was he could become? Perhaps. But at this juncture, many a runner begins to reexamine some of the previously unexamined premises. The question that plagues the runner undergoing breakdown training is: Why Am I Living Like This? The question eventually becomes: Is This Living?

From the crucible of such inner turmoil come the various metals, soft or brittle, flawed or pure, precious or common, that determine the good runners, the great runners, and perhaps the former runners; for those who cannot deal with successfully (or evade successfully) the consequences of their singular objective will simply fade away from it all and go on to less arduous pursuits. There has probably never been one yet who has done so, however, without leaving a part of himself there in the quiet tiled solace of the early afternoon locker room, knotting his loathsome smelling laces for yet another, jesus god, ten-miler with the boys. Once a runner...

Cassidy always felt that those who partook of the difficult pleasures of the highly competitive runner only when comfortable, when in a state of high energy, when rested, elated, or untroubled by previous exertions, such dilettantes missed the point. They were the ones who showed up at the beginning of the season, perhaps hung on for a few rough periods, maybe ran a race or two. But Cassidy noticed that their eyes always gave them away; the gloom, one could tell, was too much for them. It would soon engulf them. They would begin to ask themselves the questions too many times. Soon they would miss a workout. Then a few in a row. Then they would chicken out on themselves during the tough, stupid, endless middle of a bad race. And you don't easily hide such things from yourself, much less your teammates. Soon when the questions were posed, there would be no answers. The runner would begin to feel self-conscious around the others, knowing that he was no longer one of them; eventually he would drift off, and be a runner no more . . .

Quenton Cassidy's method of dealing with fundamental doubts was simple: He didn't think about them at all. These questions had been considered a long time ago, decisions were made, answers recorded, and the book closed. If it had to be re-opened every time the going got rough, he would spend more time rationalizing than training; his log would start to disclose embarrassing information, perhaps blank squares. Even a self-made obsessive-compulsive could not tolerate that. He was uninterested in the perspective of the fringe runners, the philosopher runners, the training rats;

those who sat around reading abstruse and meaningless articles in *Runner's World,* coining yet more phrases to describe the indescribable, waxing mystical over the various states of euphoria that the anointed were allegedly privy to.

On the track, the Cassidys of the world ate such specimens alive.

Cassidy sought no euphoric interludes. They came, when they did, quite naturally and he was content to enjoy them privately. He ran not for crypto-religious reasons, but to win races, to cover ground fast. Not only to be better than his fellows, but better than himself. To be faster by a tenth of a second, by an inch, by two feet or two yards than he had been the week or year before. He sought to conquer the physical limitations placed upon him by a three-dimensional world (and if Time is the fourth dimension, that too was his province). If he could conquer the weakness, the cowardice in himself, he would not worry about the rest; it would come. Training was a rite of purification; from it came speed, strength. Racing was a rite of death; from it came knowledge. Such rites demand, if they are to be meaningful at all, a certain amount of time spent precisely on the Red Line, where you can lean over the manicured putting green at the edge of the precipice and see exactly nothing.

Anything else that comes out of that process is by-product. Certain compliments and observations made Cassidy uneasy; he explained that he was a runner; just an athlete, really, with an absurdly difficult task. He was not a health nut, was not out to mold himself a stylishly slim body. He did not live on nuts and berries; if the furnace was hot enough, anything would burn, even Big Macs. He listened carefully to his body and heeded strange requests. Like a pregnant woman, he sometimes sought artichoke hearts, pickled beets, smoked oysters. His daily toil was arduous; satisfying on the whole, but not the bounding, joyous, nature romp described in the magazines. Other runners, *real* runners, understood it quite well.

Quenton Cassidy knew what the mystic-runners, the joggers, the runner-poets, the Zen runners and others of their ilk were saying. But he also knew that their euphoric selves were generally nowhere to be seen on dark, rainy mornings. They primarily wanted to talk it, not do it. Cassidy very early on understood that a true runner ran even when he didn't feel like it, and raced when he was supposed to, without excuses and with nothing held back. He ran to win, would die in the process if necessary, and was unimpressed by those who disavowed such a base motivation. You are not allowed to renounce that which you never possessed, he thought.

The true competitive runner, simmering in his own existential juices, endured his melancholia the only way he knew how: gently, together with those few others who also endured it; yet very much alone. He ran because it grounded him in basics. There was both life and death in it; it was unadulterated by media hype, trivial cares, political meddling. He suspected it kept him from that most real variety of schizophrenia that the republic is currently sprouting like mushrooms on a stump.

Running to him was real, the way he did it the realest thing he knew. It was all joy and woe, hard as diamond; it made him weary beyond comprehension. But it also made him free.

18. Meetings

Sitting quietly over his sandwiches, Cassidy chewed mechanically. He did not look happy. From the kitchen came metallic clatter and laughter; cooks, he thought, are a carefree lot after everyone has been fed.

This morning had been typical of the past two weeks. Cassidy wondered quite seriously if he could (should someone put a big gun to his head) go out on the track and run a 4:30 mile flat out. The morning seven had been sluggish and Mize wasn't there to commiserate with. While dressing for his first class he glanced at the mirror, shrugged, went back to bed. He slept soundly for five hours, woke grumpily and stumbled downstairs for a late lunch. In the three weeks since the Sunkist meet Denton had taken a special interest in his training. They now ran together in the afternoons, an arrangement approved by Cornwall since Cassidy's growing strength was beginning to dishearten the others in interval workouts.

Denton then insisted on raising mileage. Tired as he was after the Sunkist weekend, Monday was a 23 mile day. The week totalled 127 and it appeared they would not be slacking off any. He lived from workout to workout, hanging on like a crazed marsupial in a flash flood. Life was becoming, he admitted to himself, more than a little morbid.

Hosford wandered over with his tray.

"Sandwiches again," he said, sitting down heavily across from Cassidy.

"Fuel for the furnace, hardly makes any difference." To demonstrate his point, perhaps, he chewed as if it were an effort he could barely maintain.

"Are you going to run Boston Gardens this weekend? Cornwall says that if you want to double, he might take a two-mile relay."

"I'm not even sure I can run the mile. The way I've been drag-assing around here for two weeks, I may have to take up triple jumping or something."

"Well, just a thought. I suppose you heard about Pospicil?"

"Hosford, I've been underwater for two weeks. What about Pospicil?"

"That asshole Slattery gave him a pretty hard time yesterday. Came up to him at the training table at Farley and started flipping at his hair, you know, real nasty-like, saying stuff like 'Don't you know this is the training table, deary? Where the athletes eat—men athletes honey, not girls . . .' That kind of stuff. About as bad as it could be."

"Aw, Christ. Poss is such a nice guy. He probably didn't understand their idiot rules in the first place. He doesn't even speak much regular English, much less grit English."

"I don't think he knew anything about it. How would you like to be the number three player in your country, get a big recruiting come-on, show up in the wonderful United States of America with your tennis racket and a big smile and then run into an asshole like Slattery with his haircut rules? I bet Poss has never even seen a redneck before. Jeez, poor guy."

"When you think of the crap that Slattery pulled when he was an undergraduate here . . ." Cassidy shook his head.

"Uh, look, what I really wanted to tell you was that some of the tennis guys got pretty hot about the whole thing. And they got some of the track guys stirred up again. I mean, they all respect your opinion and all, especially that stuff about living well being the best revenge, but I think maybe it's gone too far now."

"And?"

"Bottom line is there's another meeting in your room tonight."

"My room?"

"I guess that was my fault. I told them you probably wouldn't mind. Plus everyone knows that you're planning to go to law school and all that. They listen to you, Cass.."

Cassidy said nothing, rubbed his eyes painfully.

"Cass, somebody has got to do something. This Pospicil thing is not the first. People are starting to get pretty upset, even a bunch of football guys. I mean, you being a team captain and all, it's really kind of your job . . ."

"Okay, okay, Hos*ford!* Christ, 132 miles last week, Mize flat on his ass, Andrea in some kind of snit, Denton's intervals got me walking around bumping into walls, and now suddenly the entire football staff experiences a collective brain fade." He rubbed his eyes again, and Hosford for a horrifying moment thought he was going to blubber.

"Look, Hos, I'll come and listen. Maybe there is some reasonable course of action to take. But I get this gut feeling..."

"Not too hopeful, huh?"

"Hosford, you're talking southern football mentality now. People who covered 5000 square yards of beautiful cool stadium grass with a green plastic death mat that scrapes big hunks of skin off your ass if you so much as sit down on it wrong. People who think Joe Paterno is a dangerous intellectual. People who think Vietnam is a . . . an *opportunity.* I mean, how are you gonna . . ." This was just making him tired. Hosford didn't really understand what they were dealing with yet. Cassidy tossed his sandwich on the tray like a blackjack dealer disinterestedly busting himself.

Hosford would have liked to have snickered at the death mat stuff, but knew it was not the right time. Cassidy picked up his tray, deposited it on the cart with a clatter and wandered out of the dining room feeling perhaps as bleak a child of America as the tots on the Appalachia posters. Quenton Cassidy reflected that at least he was well-fed.

He knew though, that had a single germ strolled up and surveyed the premises, he could have set up shop without even a damage deposit. This is definitely a low ebb, he thought. He stood at the bottom of the stairs, looking tiredly out through the living room to the front yard where two dogs fought without enthusiasm for a small patch of shade. At times like this he felt weary and land bound, and soothed himself by thinking of the ocean. He pictured translucent pink anemones, floating like ladies with deadly long skirts. Then: a sero mackerel somewhere on the pale turquoise of the Bahama Bank, working a school of greenies with unemotional fervor; a guide poles the flats soundlessly, turns wrinkled black cheeks to the burning sun and smiles to visions of Canadian school teachers "on holiday."

Cassidy did not look forward to this gathering of irate citizens in his room, but tomorrow night he was taking Andrea to the Windjammer and that, along with his sea thoughts, would get him through another day. Still, it became in the end a little difficult making it up the three flights of stairs back to the musky womb of his bed.

19. The Awesome Midnight Raid

The Windjammer would have at one time been called "camp," with musty colored lights and unlikely looking plastic fruit hanging about. There was a pleasant little trio that sounded not unlike the Pozo Seco Singers, but for Cassidy the real allure was the raw Appalachicola oysters, offered at $1.50 per dozen and, of course, the draft beer, which was very cold.

They were due for a "talk" of some kind, he and Andrea, but Cassidy was not very good at "talks" and could not remember one that did not end in some kind of confusing nastiness; abstract dialogue from a Woody Allen screenplay without enough detachment to make it funny.

Instead, he made much over the oysters, mixing horseradish in his cocktail sauce and adding a dash of tabasco. And he told her of the dire rumblings around Doobey Hall.

"It seems I have become the official draftsman. It was my own fault, of course. I told them that all their petition would really demonstrate was that they are nearly illiterate. Very shortly I found myself at the typewriter and everyone was talking at once."

"So what happens now?"

"Well, nothing maybe. We got something whipped into shape, but we sat around talking for a while and everyone agreed to hold off again and see if maybe the thing won't just blow over. Hell, we're athletes; we don't need this kind of aggravation. But if things keep up, they will take the petitions around and see how many signatures they can get on them. If we have enough support among the rest of the teams, they will take them to the Athletic Department and then it's their move."

"Do you think it will do any good?"

"Oh, yes, petitioning Dick Doobey and the Athletic Department will be like going down to the Kissimmee Zoo and formally debating the cottontop marmoset. It will win the day, I'm sure of it."

"Quenton."

"Wanta dance?"

"If you do."

Cassidy had a helpless affinity for places like the Windjammer. In a room off to the side, two longhaired construction workers clomped around the pool table in their heavy boots, obviously stoned into yesterday, laughing at each other's ineptness.

"Godamn, Harlan," said one as a ball jumped the rail and hit the wall with a crack, "put some power to it. You ain't got a black hair on your ass 'less you dent some paneling." They both keeled over, helpless in the face of each other's wit.

Cassidy thought: Oh, to be blue collar in the seventies. Real life, such as it is, is being committed here.

"Andrea, do you realize this is the first time I have touched your body with any sort of lust in mind in four days?"

"I know." Of course she knew, Cassidy thought, such timetables are a lady's tea and scones.

"I wonder why that might be."

"Well, there was the organic test on Monday, there was that awful computer program that wouldn't run, there is the fact that you are becoming a very difficult person to get along with . . ."

"Ah . . ."

"Quenton, I'm trying very hard to understand, really, but what can possibly justify what you are doing to yourself? You've started cutting classes, you can't eat dinner because you're still tied up in knots, you fall asleep over your books after 15 minutes of studying . . ."

"Andrea, this is not a permanent condition you are seeing here. Bruce says . . ."

"Bruce says, Bruce says."

"Isn't this getting a little obvious now?"

"Oh Quenton, I wonder sometimes if you know how I really feel about you. How much I'd like for it to work out. If there was only some compromise, some . . ."

"Well, there you have touched upon something, Andrea, because that's it right there: The thing itself is the absence of compromise. There are no . . . deals available. I wish there was someway to explain that. The thing . . . doesn't dilute."

He shrugged and held her closer. Just trying to explain was tiring. You can either do it or not do it, he thought, but you can't talk about it worth a damn. "Let's not discuss it anymore," she said. "The more we talk the more it slips." The music stopped but they lingered, still holding each other closely. It was true; he did not have the ability to give that which she most needed, and she did not have the ability to understand that eerie dimension to him that even he did not know well. These fundamental imbalances led them into concentric circles of ever decreasing size: a nautilus shell of their discontent.

The Awesome Midnight Raid took place that night. It started as a low rumble on the first floor, as if a group of rowdies was just getting in from their rounds. But instead of gradually calming down, the rumble soon became a roar. Cassidy awoke dream-like to the racket. There seemed to be loud arguments, much scuffling about, objects hitting walls, random bellows in the night. When he was finally completely awake, he sat up and listened carefully. There was no laughter or mirth of any kind in the tumult, but there were definite traces of panic and anger. The resident counselor had gone early for the weekend, leaving the three team captains technically in charge, so Cassidy jumped up and pulled on some clothes.

What was happening below was that Harold Slattery and two other assistant football coaches were, very simply, raiding the dormitory. They were aware that members of the opposite sex occasionally spent the night at Doobey, and it was their intent to ferret out the transgressors and perhaps have some fun in the bargain. They were going through the rooms, one by one, knocking once loudly and then barging in with their flashlights, invoking their unassailable authority:

"Coaches! Coming in!" Then they rushed in the room. Those athletes who fortuitously found themselves sleeping alone heard them say something like: "This one's clean. Mark 'im off." Then they tromped off to the next room, hoping for some kind of action. Soon they had an entourage of irate athletes following along behind them, grumbling, shouting, and perhaps on the verge of forming a lynching party, authority or no.

Cassidy was almost out the door when he heard the tumult come to a sudden halt below. The coaches had reached room 207 and, self-righteousness and bravado running high, had decided to forgo the knock as being too polite and simply barged in. When they got inside, they found themselves staring into the small, dark, and very genuine looking hole which was the muzzle of Jack Nubbins' forty-five. In the dim light it barked deafeningly and the door knob, only a few inches from Harold Slattery's hand, disappeared with a sharp metallic clang.

Nubbins switched on the light sleepily, the gun still trained on the wide-eyed Slattery. Betty Sue huddled up under the blanket, her tiny frightened green eyes peering out. "I'm not that good a shot," Nubbins said, yawning. "I might have blowed your dinner away!" Slattery stood still as a snapshot, his upper lip white with that most absolute brand of fear you get right before your life flashes in front of your eyes. It was probably the yawn that made the little fuzzy hairs stand up on the back of his thick neck.

"Now I will generally hit a shot like that, mind, but right about now I am sleepy-eyed. Lot of good shots will wake up from a sound sleep and not be able to hit a blessed thing . . ."

"We're uh . . ."

"Yeah, I know what you are," Nubbins said calmly. "But be godamned if I didn't think you was a ordinary burglar. Didn't you think so Betty Sue?" He looked over at the frightened girl, who didn't so much as blink. "Yeah, I did too, honey. Matter of fact he might still be a burglar for all I know. I can't see real well in this here light."

"Now look here, Nubbins . . ." Slattery was regaining some of his composure and did not like the idea of this anecdote getting around. It was time to recoup himself a little dignity and he took one nearly imperceptible step forward as he spoke. The gun exploded again and the molding on the opposite side of the door frame splattered.

"There I go again," said Nubbins. "I was actually aiming about three inches higher than that." By the time the plaster and wood chips had settled, Slattery and his gang had formally abandoned the hunt.

When Cassidy got to the second floor it was all over. Everyone was talking at once and no one was making any sense. Once he got the story pieced together it occurred to him that some truly dark forces, ignorant of their own madness, were at work.

And fate, of course, swings to and fro on tiny hinges; a cable is misplaced and a king assassinated; a vacuum tube blinks and a ship is lost with all hands; a general fails to get laid and thousands are firebombed . . .

20. Night Run

Cassidy raced along to a night rhythm, pocketa pocketa, a steady tatoo of pleasant solitary effort that starred him under many streetlights, rendered him anonymous in dark neighborhoods, sent him smoothly up and down the gentle hills of Kernsville while dogs howled and Mom and Pop passed the mashed potatoes.

A passerby might have thought him in a trance, but he missed nothing in his darkling backdrop: the smells of winter blooming flowers, clean coolness of blackjack oak, damp pepper of Spanish moss. The sounds were of early evening teevee silliness, dinner, children's squabbles. He was a shaded meteor plumbing a twinkling universe. The night made even more acute the runner's senses, lent more poignancy to his aloneness, made his fast pace seem even faster, generated an urgency, a subdued excitement in the act of solitary motion.

The seamless sphere of his reverie was occasionally marred by some missing link in a Chevrolet who would yell: "Hey Runner Runner!" Cassidy would flip a finger reflexively and otherwise indicate his considerable displeasure by some base epithet. For years he had tried ignoring them to no effect. Now his policy was to lash back. They were surprised when the runner (a gentle creature, no?) would exhibit such aggressiveness. What it was in human nature that generated this irresistible urge to bait the runner, he did not know. But he knew by now that it was deep, formidable, and nearly universal. An English writer of a different era recorded the taunts of street urchins: "Hey, looke at the runner, ee's got nae clothes on!" At Cassidy some would yell "hut, two, three, four . . ." and laugh at their own preposterous wit, in some cretinous confusion unable to disassociate running from the military experience.

Cassidy resented the ignorance of their intrusion. And, too, he had had things thrown at him. Too many people seemed to think the runner would have no spunk (after all, running itself is the act of a coward, is it not?), thus he found automatic belligerence a healthy and effective response: They shut their sorry yaps up in an almost hurt shock. Once, by sprinting nearly 200 yards, he caught up to a particularly obnoxious carload of rowdies who, panic stricken now, were halted at an uncooperative redlight. Thinking themselves safe after rolling up the windows and locking the doors, they watched in horror as Cassidy ran up the trunk and over the top of the car without breaking stride.

In training he was fearless, felt himself too easily capable of violence. He often contemplated what he would do if someone stopped and challenged him. He figured he would put them through a little of what his life was all about first; taunt them into giving chase. He would stay just a little out of their grasp, egg them on and on. Perhaps they would make half a mile or so, depending on how well he could lead them on, perhaps their own sense of pride might surface, a by-product of a terrible misconception about what was actually happening. Shorter had once run the legs off an entire gang of hooligans in the hills of New Mexico, despite already being tired from a 15-mile run. You would watch for the signs, Cassidy thought, the ones you knew so very well; the pain, the bewilderment, the blankness that would eventually come close to despair. He would make it a challenge, so they would forget their original purpose and keep on going just to show this bastard, this . . . this . . . (then it would dawn) *runner.*

Then he would simply turn and face them. He would take on anyone like that, he thought. He would take on Muhammad Ali, so long as he could direct the preliminaries.

Cassidy knew very well that he could take men, otherwise strong and brave men, to places they had never been before. Places where life and death overlapped in surreal valleys of muscle gloom and heart despair, where one begins to realize once more that nothing really matters at all and that stopping (death?) is all; where all men can finally get the slick skin of civilization off and see that soft pink glow inside that tells you—in both cunnilingus and bullet wounds—*that there are no secrets.*

A visitor's taste, in short, of the distance runner's daily fare. He would fight them then, if they still wanted to, after they knew. But they wouldn't want to, he was sure of that.

They would walk away with nothing more than a hard-won understanding.

This night no one stopped. No one gave form to verbal menace. No one did any more than add his simple-minded bleating to the dark background of the runner's ritual.

Cassidy flew through the night.

"Bruce," he said into the telephone, "I need to talk to you. I'm at Doobey now but I can't talk on this hall phone. Can you meet me at the Nineties or something."

"Sure. Where have you been? I thought you were going to do quarters with me this afternoon. Did you run?"

"Of course, I ran. I just did ten hard. Listen, I had to go see Dick Doobey in his office this afternoon. Something's up. Can you meet me there in 15 minutes or so?"

"Okay. But I'm not going to sit there drinking beer all night like you guys. I'll have a couple and . . ."

"Okay, okay. No problem. I gotta take a shower, just got in. See you there."

The Nineties was not crowded during the middle of the week; Fat Fred, the owner, was so exultant having Bruce Denton in his place that he bought him a pitcher of beer. It was an enthusiasm he felt he could afford, there being a relative dearth of gold medal winners in Kernsville. The two runners retreated to a corner booth.

"So what is the crisis?" Denton was pouring as the jukebox maintained: ". . .*and time . . . washes clean . . . lu-huv's wounds unseen . . .*"

"You've seen the stuff in the papers this morning?"

"Who hasn't?"

"Well, they have decided that since I was the one who typed up the petition and also the one who delivered the signatures to the A.D., that this whole little number was conceived and, uh, '*per*petrated' as they say, by myself and one or two other unnamed conspirators."

"How do they figure? Every jock in this school is so pissed off . . ."

"Basically I'm convinced they really are as fucking stupid as they make out. When they couldn't find themselves an outside agitator . . ."

"I noticed you carefully disassociated yourselves from the Yippie element."

"Lot of good it did. Bruce, do you know that Doobey sat there and told me he didn't really blame me for all this fuss, he figures the real blame should be levelled at all the communist and left-leaning professors on the other side of the campus who have been working on my poor little brain all these years."

"Good god. Do you suppose he's serious?"

"Oh he's serious all right. He isn't a humorous man. He kept coming up with all these military analogies. 'In the Army, by God, you did what you were told, or they broke your plate—over your head.' That kind of thing. And then he goes into this stuff about my professors. Christ! Here I've been taught by fuel-injected right-wing loonies and closet Nazis for three years and that idiot thinks I've been brainwashed by some leftist academic conspiracy. My godamned econ teacher thinks Milton Friedman is a liberal! Hell, if this campus got a decent teacher, they'd have the son of a bitch re-binding books behind the stacks somewhere . . ."

"All right, calm down. What happened exactly?"

Cassidy finished his second glass with a grimace. He was still dehydrated from the run.

"They're taking a hard line. Apparently what's got everyone all stirred up is the fact that a bunch of football players signed the damned thing. Apparently Doobey was called on the carpet by Prigman himself about it. I guess if it weren't for the football players involved, they could probably just write the thing off by saying the spring sports guys have gone commie on us. You know, we're all in individual events anyway, not part of, you know, a team effort . . . "

"Oh say, that makes sense . . ."

"And I think I'm beginning to get wind of a little gambit that smells something like the bottom of somebody's locker."

"Lively analogy." The jukebox played: ". . . *has anybody here seen sweet thang . . .* "

"Doobey said something to the effect that he figured something like this was going on during the season, otherwise with the talent they had, they would have never gone four and six. Get the drift?"

"What!" Denton was incredulous. "They're gonna try and pin . . ."

Cassidy let the air out of his lungs. Physically he was keen, immensely strong at this point in his life; he could run a hundred miles. Yet he was starting to feel some smothering weight descending over him, a pale shroud he was helpless to evade.

I feel old, he thought. I have been dead once, I guess you can't get any older than that. But that was long ago, in the salt salt sea.

To Denton, still sitting looking unbelieving at the ceiling, he said: "Bruce, I'm so close. It seems so stupid to have something like this . . ."

"Yes. I know. Hang tough, don't get nervous in the pack . . ."

Three days later, a befuddled Coach Cornwall called Cassidy into his office and told him that due to circumstances over which he, as track coach, had no control, Quenton Cassidy would be henceforth suspended from participation in intercollegiate athletics.

21. Steven C. Prigman

Southeastern University President Steven C. Prigman had once sat on the Florida Supreme Court bench and during his seven-year tenure had taken part in several illustrious decisions that stood as landmarks in jurisprudential comedy.

The most famous of these much-read cases involved a young black man who had the audacity to request admission to Southeastern University's law school. He wasn't exactly turned down, they just lost his application. The third time they lost it, he filed suit and was quickly hooted out of circuit court. From there he took his appeal to the august tribunal upon which sat his Honor Justice Prigman and six of his cronies. Taking scant time to deliberate after oral arguments, they came down with a decision that said, in so many words, that if God Almighty had wanted all races to go to white law schools, Negroes would have been born with perfect LSAT scores and calfskin briefcases. Some months later, the United States Supreme Court, ignoring entirely the interesting logic used to arrive at the lower court decision, overturned the case at the same time it issued its *Brown vs. Board of Education* ruling, and sent it back to Justice Prigman and company without so much as a "nice try."

At this point the justices showed some real imagination. Declaring that the U.S. Supreme Court had made its determination on "constitutional grounds" alone, they decided that if there were other considerations for keeping the black out, then the decision wouldn't apply. Therefore, they decided to appoint a local circuit judge to be a "special master" to make a study of the situation and find out what would happen were a black man to enter the law school. The "special master" quickly found out that all hell would, of course, break loose; this would take the form of mass student withdrawals and attendant financial collapse. There would be great pandemonium in the school itself: riots, vandalism, even food fights. The "special master" was able to determine these dire consequences by the tried and true interview method ("Are you going to riot?" "Of course!" "Okay.").

And so it was that the Honorable Florida Supreme Court was able, in all good conscience, to blatantly disobey a direct mandate of the United States Supreme Court by saying that their new ruling denied admission to the black not on constitutional grounds, but on the inherent police power of the government to prevent violence. That the said violence would be caused by law breaking (and perhaps imaginary) whites, concerned them not a whit. The young black man, out of money and patience, disgustedly threw in the towel and went North to procure his degree.

Steven C. Prigman had always been a charter member of the Florida Panhandle good old boy school. Sipping 15-year-old bourbon, his handsome ruddy face aglow with good humor, he could and did charm the fangs off water moccasins. Although Sidecar Doobey often referred to him as a "snub-nose little twerp," the two men understood each other very well. Doobey was very influential in helping Prigman relocate to an academic setting when the jurist decided to step down from the bench.

And when he finally did so, he left Tallahassee with no small measure of pride that he and his associates had been able, for even a short period of time, to staunch the flow of the 20th Century. Their golden moment still preserved in Volume 93 of the second Southern Reporter series, to this day provides many fascinating hours of comic relief for law students all across the country.

Dick Doobey had felt a trifle ill at ease the day before on his way to Prigman's office. His squishy, rippled-soled coaching shoes squeaked embarrassingly as he walked up the marble steps to the president's office.

"Hello, Roberta," he winked at the middle-aged and not unattractive brunette, wondering if the old man was getting any. She looked up pleasantly, greeted him and then ushered him into the quiet office. She was a charming woman, but Doobey knew she did not like him. Her smile was that of a head waiter.

"Well, Coach!" said the old man heartily, rising to shake hands. "Have a seat, my boy. Make yourself comfortable." In the battle of the giant offices, Prigman had it all over Dick Doobey, even though his carpet did not bear a giant Daryl the Swamp Dawg. It was decorated much more in the taste of a former state supreme court justice. Dick Doobey envied the dignified brown and tan hues that commanded the respect that his colorful mishmash of caricatures and trophies never seemed to elicit. The aura of the office was, in a word, impressive, and Dick Doobey never sat in that chair without feeling he was near the very top.

"Well, what kind of spring practice are we going to have this year?" Prigman asked. Doobey had not expected this kind of question, so frenzied had been his other problems of late. He started to launch into his routine about some junior college transfers and redshirts that were going to be "of real great help to us out there next year," but he didn't get very far before Prigman cut him off.

"Fine, fine. I know what some of our detractors are saying about last year's record, but I know you're going to pull the program together once you get your feet on the ground here."

"Well, yes sir, I feel that I'm just now getting to the point where I can . . ."

"Fine, fine. Coach, what I wanted to ask you about . . ." he reached over to a corner of his huge polished desk and held up a legal-sized Xeroxed page ". . . is this. Do you know anything about it?"

Dick Doobey took the sheet, held it away from his face as if it were a small serpent, and studied it carefully. He tried to act as though he had never seen the likes before. Prigman knew better. At the top of the page was a paragraph that began: "We, the athletes of Southeastern University, hereby wish to make known certain grievances . . ." The page Doobey held contained 38 signatures. There were other sheets as well, and Doobey knew that all in all, about 125 varsity athletes, including many of his own football players, had signed the petition.

"Well, sir, I do happen to know something about this particular matter."

"Perhaps you'd like to fill me in." There was the faintest hint of menace in the old man's voice.

"Well, sir, this morning an athlete from the track team dropped by a stack of these, uh, petitions. It seems that quite a few of the athletes have signed them and . . ."

"How many?"

"Well, sir, I don't know exactly but somewhere I would say, oh, around 100 or so, sir, and . . ."

"A hundred!" He practically shouted it. Dick Doobey felt himself pressing backwards in the soft chair.

"Well, yes sir, more or less, sir . . ."

"Any football men among 'em?"

"Oh, I don't know, sir, I didn't check the lists out very carefully or any . . ."

"I *asked* . . . if there were any football men . . . *on the lists?*" Very quietly, this last.

"Yes sir! There were, oh forty or so, I would say offhand, sir."

"Forty!" Prigman rested his chin on the steeple of his hands, turning his chair to the side, either deep in thought or too angry to speak. Doobey prayed to God it was the former.

The old man swung the chair back around and leaned forward, skewering Doobey against the chair with a stare that seemed a physical force. It was the kind of gesture Prigman had developed to a high art, and he noted with satisfaction Doobey's bobbing Adam's apple.

"Well, *Coach* Doobey, perhaps you can explain to me what in the devil all this is about?" Doobey started to say something but the old man continued.

"I mean, just for instance what is this stuff about 'unwarranted neo-gestapo raids upon athletes' rooms . . .' and 'militaristic hair and dress regulations . . .' Perhaps you could explain just what in the hell is happening on *my* campus, *Coach* Doobey!" He was half standing in front of his chair, but slowly forced himself to sit back down, giving the impression of rage brought under control only with great effort. Doobey had been thinking all morning what he would say at this particular time, and though he thought he had it worked out several times, it all left him now. He stared at the petition as if it would provide him with some clue.

"Well, Mr. President, it seems that some of the athletes are a little upset over our new hair and dress code, sir, and then there was an incident at the track dormitory the other night which was not authorized on my part and which perhaps was a little, uh, unwarranted, I mean, trying to be subjective about the whole thing and all . . ."

"What in the hell are you babbling about, man? What hair and dress code? What incident?"

"Well sir, the code was a little idea of mine to try to boost morale a little, sir . . ." Doobey told the old man, in the best way he could, what had been going on during the past few weeks. When he finished, the elder man sat sideways again, in deep thought. After a while, Doobey thought he had been forgotten such was the length of the old man's meditation. Finally, Prigman swung around to face Doobey, but he spoke so softly the coach had to lean forward to hear.

"I had a call from Walter Davis this morning, you know Walt?"

"Well sir, I . . ."

"He's the UPI man out of Miami, Coach Doobey. But I couldn't talk to him right away because I had Norman Johnson on the other line. You know Norm?" Still very quiet.

"Yes sir, I . . ."

"He's the AP man out of Miami. Well, it seems these representatives of our nation's wire services were pretty much interested in the same thing . . ." He held up the petition with one hand, tapping it briskly with the back of his other hand.

". . .the same thing as the fellow from *Sports Illustrated*— I've never had the pleasure of talking to those folks before— and the sports editors of about twelve or so major newspapers around the Southeast. Roberta has been real good about that. Anything with a circulation below 50,000 and the call gets diverted to a vice president or a dean. Now, of course, I don't know how many calls they had . . ."

"I talked to quite a few myself and . . ."

"I'm not *interested!*"

"Yes *sir!*"

"What I am interested in," calmly now, "is exactly what in the name of all that's holy are we going to do about this thing now that you have so blithely gotten it rolling for us, *Coach* Doobey?"

"Well I . . ."

"I mean, do you realize the implications, sir, of an athletes' revolt? Do you know, can you appreciate the fact that we've

just gone through several years of strife and violence on our
campuses because of our country's selfless efforts in Vietnam?
And that throughout that time of crisis our athletes have been
our mainstay, our rock? No matter what kind of crap was
going on everywhere else, our boys were out there every
Saturday, hitting hard, blocking clean, going at it like there
was no tomorrow, giving it the old guts-balls *college try*. Why,
those boys have been carrying on, in our darkest hour, our
very American traditions!"

Doobey perked up. "Why yes sir, that's exactly why . . ."

"I'm not *through*. And now, Coach Doobey, now just as
our athletes had come to symbolize all that was good and loyal
and patriotic about our country, now we find them running
around and . . . and . . . *signing petitions!*"

"I'm as surprised as you are sir!"

"Surprised *batshit!*" He picked up another sheet of paper.
"'Sideburns not to be lower than a line extending perpendic-
ular from the bottom tip of the earlobe . . .' Where did you
get such . . . such *notions?*" His contempt was barely contained.

"Well, sir, some of them I picked up from my military
training . . ."

"Mmmmmm."

". . . some of them were suggested by assistant coach
Slattery, uh, he came up with the one about shirts with no
collars . . ."

"Collars," said Prigman, miserably.

". . . and some of them I just sort of made up myself, sir."

"Somehow I might have guessed that one all by myself,"
said Prigman very softly to the ceiling.

Their conference went on into the afternoon. Prigman,
his rage somewhat mollified, now concentrated on the prag-
matics of solving the problem at hand. He pretty much knew
what Doobey was going to tell him anyway, but was not about
to forgo the pleasure of his pound of flesh. He would deal
further with this dodo son of Sidecar's later; for the time
being he was content to watch the involuntary quiver of fear
that ran through the portly body every time he emphasized
the word *coach*. But this was a time for action; policy had to
be formulated, the media had to be dealt with. It called for

swift, clear, imminently intelligent decision-making. It required, in short, the kind of grit that Prigman proudly reflected was precisely the reason he was where he was. Secretly, he relished the prospects.

"Who brought the petitions to your office?"

"It was a track man. A Quenton Cassidy, sir. He just dropped them off."

"Did he say anything when he left them?"

"Yes. He told Mary Lou, that's my secretary, that he would be glad to talk the situation over with me at our mutual convenience."

"At your . . ."

"Mutual convenience, that's what he said, sir."

"Jesus H. Christ."

22. Brady Grapehouse

Over the whirlpool in the large training room a hand-lettered sign read:

You can't make the CLUB
Sitting in the TUB

Brady Grapehouse presided here and since he knew that healing waters sometimes had not so much to do with real physical injuries as with providing a good place to hide from a hurtful world, the sign—like everything else in this domain—was his idea.

He had been the head trainer at Southeastern for 10 years before Dick Doobey arrived as football coach. Many generations of athletes felt a single emotion for Brady: love, pure and unabashed. If an interrogator were to corner the toughest, meanest son of a bitch of a lineman from among Brady's former customers and ask him point blank if he loved Brady Grapehouse, the lineman would say: "Godamn right I love Brady Grapehouse. *Everybody* loves Brady Grapehouse." Everybody except Dick Doobey, who hated Brady Grapehouse.

It was probably the love he generated among his athletes that did Brady in; everyone knew that Dick Doobey had told him his contract would not be renewed in order to bring in Zip Simmons, a sycophantic dolt Doobey knew from the Army, who he liked having around because he was one of the few grownups Doobey had ever been around who didn't make him feel at least a little dim-witted.

Like many men who found competence puzzling, Doobey did not like to have much of it around him at any one time.

Brady was nearly a caricature of himself. Short and round, he always had a cold stump of a cigar in his mouth (there was speculation he bought them that way from some furtive supplier). He had short wavy black hair flecked with gray; he gave the impression not so much of age as of having been around. He moved around the training room gracefully on the balls of his feet like the old boxer he was. Had he been in the service, he would have been the tough old top sergeant

124

whom everyone would admit, when cross-eyed drunk, was a pretty good son of a bitch.

Brady had seen them all. Hot shot All-American quarterbacks, hostile giant linemen, seven-foot basketball freaks, flashy tennis stars, future pro golfers—most of whom would make hundreds of thousands of dollars with their incredible legs, hands and eyes. All of these were mixed in with the myriad ranks of steady performers, who were (though they didn't realize it at all) at the pinnacle of a life destined to peak so early that the remaining long slide is not so much a career as a wistful reminiscence of days when poetic deeds were the order of the day.

Brady ministered to them all with the same gruff efficiency. They would come to him, at times when they were physically quite well, tapping on the glass partition of his fishbowl office in the training room, usually in the morning when there was no taping going on and the place was a cool, tiled chapel.

"Uh, Brade," they would say, a little hangdog, "Brade, you gotta secont?"

"Gotta secont? Gotta secont? Now what else would I have better to do than sit around here jaw-boning with one of you jacklegs all mornin'?" The door would close and he would take it on. He was an uncle, priest, medical advisor, psychiatrist. They came to him with things they couldn't discuss with their closest friends. The married ones, cut off from the rough intimacy of the athletic bachelorhood, came in to talk about problems of the hearth: children, sex, fidelity, money. He took them all, listened to them with the stub of cigar going round and round, still gruff and impatient, but with a look in his eyes that clearly intimated a deep understanding, forgiving and nonjudgmental, a look of someone who could not be shocked, who had his own agonies and wasn't ashamed. When he heard enough he cut them off and told them whatever it was he had to offer. Sometimes he picked up a phone and in a few whispers a medical specialist was enlisted. Many times his counsel was no more complicated than: "Hey Jimbo you got to stop mewing and stand on your hind legs to her. Don't you think she expects that? Why else would she be workin' so hard at it?" Or he might simply listen and console, offering only the comfort of one who saw life in all perspectives at once, the pigeon droppings as well as the statue, and who could make others see it too. They almost always left feeling better, not infrequently laughing, glad to have found solace in someone so wise, so knowing, a man who also found humor in the leavings of incontinent wildlife.

Cassidy had been in the main training room the day Jolie Benson came in, a brilliant athlete from south Florida who could play very nearly any position on the football field; Jolie, who had in his junior year in high school walked into his father's study to find the old man in his leather chair, thirty-eight in hand and a lap full of gristle that Jolie could never quite forget and which now reduced his voice to a most horrible stutter, a problem so debilitating at times he could not communicate.

Brady had been taping yet another anonymous ankle, muttering as usual to himself, when Jolie burst in and commenced with his routine: "Bray . . . Bray . . . Bray . . . Bray-dee, I . . . I . . . I . . ." and so on. Brady watched for a few seconds, fingering a roll of tape, his great sad eyes studying Jolie intently. Then finally he snapped:

"Jolie! Cut it out! What the hell do you want?" And Jolie just jumped back in shock and suddenly started talking almost normally, telling Brady whatever it was he had come in to say. This was no screenwriter's permanent cure, of course, and Brady did not for a moment believe he could work such miracles. He knew the soul could sustain far deeper wounds than he could reach with his ultra-sound machines, his muscle balm, ice-packs, and gruff humanity. But Brady could, by god, get a man to talk straight to him, even one whose teenage eyes had beheld the infinite sorrow of sudden resignation from the human race; that was the way you talked to him. You weren't allowed to hide behind your own illusions because Brady did not hide behind his. It was little wonder that generations of athletes departed Southeastern with such a wry and honest love for Brady Grapehouse.

One day when Danny Ingram wandered into the main training room to get some tape for the track team, he saw Brady stalking briskly to the water fountain. Jolie Benson was sitting inside the glass enclosure, staring at the far wall, desolate tears falling unnoticed onto his incredible hands. Danny stopped his fiddling to ask Brady what was wrong and only then saw (he would swear) large tears also rolling down the round impish cheeks of the head trainer.

"What the hell do you want?" Brady croaked.

"Nothin' Brade," Danny mumbled, grabbing the tube of tape rolls and scrambling for the door.

Brady was not exactly transparent, but most people figured him out sooner or later. That is probably why Brady was Brady.

It seemed like the natural thing to do after wandering aimlessly around the campus all afternoon, but by the time he got to the training room, it was three o'clock and the basketball team was straggling in for their taping. Cassidy was still in shock. How could they do this? He was a star. He was captain of his team. Like the death of a close friend, this was a shock his mind wouldn't accept.

Brady and two of his adoring student assistants were holding forth, working quickly, efficiently, tearing the white strips with quick little rips. Normally it would have been a boisterous time, but since they were again bitterly discussing Brady's imminent departure, there was only pious anger. Jim Quillain, a 6-6 starting forward who was generally unemotional and soft spoken, demanded that someone come up with a plan to fight Brady's unjust dismissal. The others were in general agreement. Yeah, Brade, why don't you do something?

Cassidy, realizing he had hit the rush hour, leaned in the doorway and watched. Some of the players nodded or gave a little wave, but most were engrossed in the discussion.

Finally, Brady stopped and stepped back from the ankle he was working on, hands on hips, cold cigar stump going round and round.

"Hey," he said impatiently, "let me tell you birds something. I mean some day you're going to be leaving this place and you'll have to go out there in that big shooting gallery your own selves. And you're gonna find there's a big . . . *monster* waiting for you. You're gonna find wonderful little surprises like this waiting for you all the time. It ain't all gettin' patted on the ass and 'hey nice game Jimbo fella' and 'hey, you look so pretty in your jock, let us give you a free ride.' No siree. That ain't the way she goes at all. But if you want to spend all your time fretting and sputtering about it, then that's what you'll do. But you won't get a hell of a lot else done, dollars to donuts. You better pay attention to that, boys, cause it's the straight scooby-doo. Old Brady's gonna do all right, but there ain't no law says you ain't gonna get a royal screwing 'stead of a round of applause, so if you want to bellyache, you can bellyache, but you could put your efforts into somethin' lot more productive, like sendin' Care packages to the Rockefellers or somethin'."

"But Brade, they promised you . . ." Quillain's young, sincere face clearly showed the strain of trying to deal with something so patently unjust he couldn't accept it. *No one promised you there would be universal justice, you know,* Cassidy thought.

"Promises," Brady scoffed, taking his cigar out, "With a basketful of promises and your right hand you could probably jerk off, Quillain. But then, you're a lefty, aren't you?" They all roared, even Quillain, though he colored quickly. It was Brady at his finest, even here in his own pot of stew, trying to give them something that would work, something that—no matter how hard to face—was at least real and useful as opposed to the embroidered half-baked platitudes peddled elsewhere on campus. The straight scooby-doo was all they carried in Brady's training room whether a brisk pronouncement that you were out for the season or a simple observation that life is sometimes a bitch; and nothing, not even the demise of Brady's own reign, was going to change that.

Brady had seen Cassidy standing by the door and knew exactly why he was there. He had heard two assistant football coaches talking about it at the Farley training table. He hoped the miler would stay around until he was through with the basketball team, but as the group was laughing at his last remark, he saw Cassidy turn with a smile and leave. Then he heard him chuckling down the hall. Maybe he will come back, Brady thought, as least I hope he does. He's one of the foxes and I'd like to see him uncaught until he hits his stride.

When he got to the field house, Denton was already dressing. Some of the others were there early and they quickly gathered around his locker, all talking at once.

"All right, all right," he raised his hands, asking for room. "There's nothing we can do about it now, so let's just leave it. I gotta get my run in. But I appreciate it, guys, really. I do appreciate it." They went reluctantly back to their routines. *Gotta get my run in?* he thought.

Cecil, the equipment room man, hobbled over and started mumbling something about how equipment privileges were to be shut off that day and locker privileges at the end of the week.

"Cecil," Cassidy was exasperated. "What kind of equipment do you think a distance man needs? I get from you every day a fresh towel and a pair of shorts. I don't even trouble you for a jock, for Chrissakes. And the shoes are mine, the gift of a generous manufacturer. I got a spare towel and shorts, though they aren't real clean. They can take their godamn equipment and . . ." He took a deep breath, as Cecil stood there wide-eyed, staring up at the miler. It wasn't Cecil's fault, Cassidy knew, so he just waved his hand at the old man and smiled wearily. It was apology enough and Cecil limped sadly back to the equipment cage, back to his niche among the hanging gloves, the spiked and cleated shoes, the balls and bats, vaulting poles, racket stringing post, busted hurdles; back to the brassy clean male smell of sweat-stained leather from several generations of boys who played with such earnestness and abandon in the spring sunshine.

Denton watched the whole thing quietly, already dressed, arms crossed on his bare chest.

"Let's run," he said.

Denton selected, for some reason, an obnoxious in-town course. Zip zip they eclipsed spatters of neon clutter that is franchised America. Krispy Kreme, What-A-Burger, Pizza Hut, Pizza Inn, Pizza 'n Brew, Pic 'n Save, Pic 'n Pay, Pic 'n Scratch; and close at hand, always, the noxious spewing fuming chrome and rust serpent of the roaring two-laned variety that is America at quittin' time. This country at times stinks in the nostrils of the runner.

They had already passed their cul-de-sac, their sliver of serenity in the middle of town, an old part of Kernsville, a taste of a slower, bygone era, a small park area known as the Duck Pond. As they passed, Chief City Engineer Homer Windenberry had ceremoniously given the signal to his foreman, who pulled the lever and with an inch and a quarter of high grade Type S-1 molten asphalt, paved over a mama and seven itty bitty ducklings.

Make no mistake about it, Kernsville was on the go.

"I am speaking of countrified air," Denton was saying, "where the body is not rattled apart by the insane pounding of heel against concrete. I am speaking of connective tissue given a fair shot . . ."

"I don't want . . ."

"A change, basically, of pace is what I am actually getting at . . ."

"I don't want to sound like a crybaby, but I honestly never thought those clowns would actually go so far as to . . ."

"Cut their own throats? Don't kid yourself, Cass, they don't give a flying you know what about spring sports, just so long as they're respectable. The pigskin is the only thing that cuts any ice down here in grit country. Do you know in Europe I get people coming up to me on the street? You think that kind of thing happens around here? No, Doobey may not be right, but this is his ball park and he knows it."

"But old man Prigman . . ."

"Was the fire marshall on the Hindenburg."

Cassidy giggled.

"He and Doobey were joint lookouts at Pearl Harbor. Architects of the Walls of Jericho. Night watch on the Titanic..."

"Stop, I can't run." Cassidy was trying to run slightly bent over, making his little peacock noises. Finally he calmed down and they ran along in silence for a few moments.

"Rodent control officers during the Black Plague," said Denton and they nearly had to stop altogether.

By the time they got back to the track Cassidy had not the slightest idea about what to do with his sorry life. But they had blown out the tubes on a 1:15 13-miler and if the truth were known, he felt fine. Just fine.

23. More Horse
than Rider

The same schedule that didn't allow much time for fretting about trivia likewise had no room for major catastrophes; Cassidy was content to follow the routine numbly. It was painful to no longer have a woman in his life, and soon he wouldn't have his team, either.

Bruce Denton, who now saw himself as a man with a mission, came by to run *very* early. The varsity wasn't even moving around yet and they started at 6:30 a.m.

The sun was nowhere near dawning and a thick fog was hung up in the rolling hills around Kernsville, turning it into a damp and quiet void inhabited by milkmen and sleepy policemen, where the whir and click of stoplights seemed inordinately loud in the chilled air. Soon Denton and Cassidy were outside the city limits, sliding quietly by acres of quiet pastures, occasionally leaving the fog below as they crested a hill. There was no sign of daylight yet and had they been less familiar with the course they would have had the impression they had already come a very long way, a notion that they suppressed neatly and automatically. Little tricks of the mind were important to them. They knew, for instance, that it was psychologically easier to run a familiar course than a new one, so contrary to the advice in the magazines and jogger manuals, they seldom went exploring for changes of scenery. Because they were covering a good deal of ground at uniform, reasonably efficient traveling speeds, on any given training run they might run into and out of rainstorms, into or out of cities or counties, and into one geographically unique area and out of an altogether different one. To them the sensation was not unlike riding on some kind of very minimalist vehicle, one that traveled at a steady though unspectacular pace, and that would take them, they felt, just about anywhere they wanted to go. It was that feeling, perhaps, that inspired members of certain subspecies of their breed to embark on cross-continent excursions, 100-mile trail runs, and other such madness.

Though the toil was arduous, they rarely spoke of the discomfort of training or racing in terms of pain; they knew that what gave pain its truly fearful dimension was a certain lack of familiarity. And these were sensations they were intimately familiar with.

That morning Denton was not talkative so Cassidy locked into a steady pace, allowing his mind to slip into the pleasant half-conscious neutral state that all runners develop; he was soon lost in the cool gray isolation of the fog.

The rumbling brought him out of it. He was tensing for the shock of big cold drops when he saw them and realized this was not a storm at all but a herd of horses and ponies charging towards the fence in a pasture across from them. Denton said nothing.

The herd reached the fence, turned sharply to the right and proceeded parallel to the runners at the same pace, looking straight ahead and running at a slow gallop with what appeared to be considerable pleasure. When they reached the corner of their pasture, they turned again and galloped off in a straight line directly away from the runners, disappearing as quickly as they had come. In a few seconds even the pounding of the hooves was gone.

Cassidy tottered. Could he have seen that?

"Was that an actual occurrence?" he asked.

"Damned if I know," said Denton.

"Do you suppose it was a coincidence?"

"Not a chance. Happens every time I run this course early. They always match my pace exactly. They were running with us."

"Riderless horses in the fog," Cassidy said mysteriously. "Do you suppose it's an omen of some kind?"

"Mountless riders in the mist," Denton said just as mysteriously. "That's what we are to them. Do you suppose *we* are omens?"

Cassidy sucked on his lower lip and said nothing. There are times, he thought, when you can't get away with anything.

Denton drove out State Road 26 towards Newberry. It was a beautiful day, a crystal day with a shocking blue sky; a day for mock heroics and knowing smiles.

"I can't wait to hear The Plan," Cassidy said.

"And I can't wait to tell you. Meanwhile let's not look to horsies and moo-cows for auguries. Let us, as they say, keep our eye on the ball."

"Okay."

"And I have a little story to tell you," he gave a little Uncle Remus kind of chuckle, "that I think you will find real entertaining." Cassidy clapped his hands stiffly, child-like.

"But first, I'd like to know some things. Like, has anyone around campus called to offer help of any kind?"

"Oh, sure, I guess so. Hosford said there have been calls from a bunch of student government honchos, Father Granely at the Catholic Student Center, the ACLU guy in town, Feldman. And, of course, all the guys want to march, boycott, demonstrate, etcetera, etcetera. Hell, for all I know, they're getting up another petition."

"Well, at least they're on your side."

"Hell *everyone* seems to be on my side. Even old Doobey said he was doing it for my own good. I get a few more people on my side and my side is going to sink."

Denton said nothing.

"And the worst is not even out yet. They have this statement—Prigman and Doobey—I mean, that they are releasing to the press this afternoon. It accuses certain spring sports athletes, of which I am singled out as the quote ringleader unquote of fomenting a veritable rebellion among the various athletes and of infecting the football team with radical-type thinking. They claim this process has been going on right under their unsuspecting noses since football and they casually mention those close games with Tennessee and Auburn right there at the end of the season. Jesus!"

Denton rolled his window all the way down, letting the air blast in, forcing him to talk above the roar.

"Well, let me tell you my little story before you get all worked up. We had a black half-miler at my college in Ohio, a very talented kid who managed to run 1:47.5 as a junior. And that looked like he was just warming up. Beautiful runner. This kid was a writer also; took it seriously and all, and actually he wasn't too bad. I read some of his stuff in the school quarterly—don't give me that look, I know what you think of my literary judgment. Anyway, this guy had a story in the magazine that had the word 'fuck' in it. It wasn't a particularly dirty story. Matter of fact, it was about some athletes and the word was used in some locker room dialogue. It wasn't even his best story. But anyway, the administration got a collective heart flutter; they confiscated all the issues of the thing right off the presses and fired everybody they could think of who didn't have their asses covered. As you can gather, our school was not exactly a bastion of libertarian thinking.

"Our 880 man was a whale of a celebrity," Denton continued. "A suit was filed and some federal judge informed the administration that as far as he knew the First Amendment was still on the books. It was a fine day for the good guys."

They rode in silence for awhile. Cassidy turned to Denton. "And?"

"And the kid ran 1:56 that year and then disappeared altogether."

The little A-frame cabin was back up in a thicket of tall straight pines and waist-thick live oak and looked like it belonged. There were stacks of paneling and other wood lying around inside along with other signs of on-going construction; the whole place had the clean, chewing gum sweet smell of cut wood. Cassidy kicked and poked around, trying to act like a man who knew his way around a construction site.

"It's great," Cassidy said, taking the mug of coffee Denton held out, "Whose is it?"

"It's mine."

"Yours?"

"Right. Come on over here and sit down where it's not so dusty. I guess this will be a day of revelations, in a manner of speaking, and I'm telling you right now, it's all in the strictest of confidence. Also I don't want you to go drawing any conclusions or moralizing on me until you have heard me out."

"All right," Cassidy said. What next, he wondered.

"The place is mine, along with 15 acres, lock, stock and septic tank. I've had my brother-in-law working on it for nearly a year, but now he's gone back to school in Boston. We've done it all ourselves. It's still a little rough around the edges, but when I finish my doctorate, I plan to move Jeannie and myself out here and grow some of the godamndest exotic plants you have ever laid eyes on. There are two greenhouses in skeletal stages in the back right now . . ."

"Yes, but . . ."

"Let me tell you and then you can handle it any way you want to. This is partly about money, as you probably guessed. I don't know how much you know about this kind of thing, but here it is: I was paid $25,000 in cash to wear blank brand of track shoes in the Olympic 5000 meter final. I have no personal knowledge, but I suspect that everyone in that race had some kind of deal. Myself, I had a signed and witnessed contract that probably would have stood up in a court of law, though I would have never run again as an amateur if it had ever gone that far."

"They gave you $25,000 . . ."

"Cashier's check. Negotiated in a bank in Luxembourg."

"But what if . . ."

"*They* found out? *They* don't want to know. I suppose if they had their noses rubbed in it, they would go huffing and puffing around and start suspending people. But, if you haven't figured it out yet, the guys that run sports are light-weights; old jocks that didn't make it or couldn't leave it behind. They don't want any trouble, they just want their blazer patches and their freebie trips. And see, all the shoe contracts have a clause guaranteeing a legal defense against any attack on an athlete's amateur status caused by the payment. But like I say, the federations don't want to know about it. The communist bloc countries have been supporting their athletes completely, the Europeans have blatantly been getting paid for years, even the American sprinters have been raking it in when they go over there. Only in the past few years have our distance runners been, uh, taken care of."

"Twenty five *grand* . . ."

"Oh, that's not all, of course. There were bonus clauses built in for various highly unlikely potentialities, such as my winning the race or setting a world record. The amounts rather reflected the startling odds against me, of course, and big numbers are just so much fun for businessmen to throw around when they're just so many paper zeroes."

Denton looked at Cassidy, who seem a little shocked.

"So, I don't want to bore you with the details, but to make a long story short, I find myself quite pleasantly, uh, *situated.* Remember, now, this is still in the strictest of confidence."

Cassidy nodded, solemn.

"And something else, Quenton, this is not to be considered the view from the top of the mountain, either. I am not trying to get you pumped up for that great bonanza waiting behind door number three . . ."

"What is this to be considered, Bruce?"

"In the first place, I don't appreciate that tone. But I guess it is probably to be expected, at least until you get used to the idea. But let us just call this a modest proposal. I want you to understand a little bit of what it's all about out there, I suppose, before you go making any big decisions about your future. In a way, what has happened to you *is* a part of what it's like out there."

Denton stretched his legs out on a stack of paneling, leaned back against the wall, and gestured to Cassidy to make himself comfortable before continuing.

"I was pretty much like you at one time—and I'm going to do my best to avoid melodramatics here—I busted my hump for six years for a chance to stand on that platform and have some old fart in a blazer and straw hat put that medal around my neck. That's really all I was up to, Quenton. I wanted to stand up there and let a little tear toll down my cheek while they played the Mouseketeer Club song and the old glad rag climbed the pole. I wanted to look into the camera while old Howard interviewed me and say: Hey Ma! Look at me! I'm the King Bee!"

"And?"

"And that's what I did. It was just great, Quenton, greatest experience of my life, no question about it. But then I found out that everything in the land of the free is not exactly free, but negotiable. Which doesn't mean much really, unless you let it."

"I'm not sure exactly that I follow."

"Oh, it's an all-weather loonie bin out there, Quenton, you know that. They're up to their assholes in fried chicken and non-dairy creamer; they're running around selling each other life insurance and trading wives at Tupperware parties. Their children are slack-jawed and aspire to drive stereophonic vans, and everyone expects their stars—of whatever category—to be modest and well-paid."

"I don't believe I am as naive as . . ."

"And before they got around to finding out I *was* a star, I couldn't get myself a bus ticket to the Kansas Relays, much less make a fortune for running a race. Would you like to know how I got to the Drake Relays that first year when I ran that 27:22?"

"They didn't invite you?"

"Hell no, they didn't invite me. Cornwall called them and said he had a graduate runner doing 28 minutes in time trials and they laughed and asked him did he time the guy with an alarm clock. So I called them back myself and asked if they would enter me if I got there on my own. They said sure. Good old American business, right? Never turn down the freebie. So I went out and borrowed enough from a small loan company for a one-way ticket. This is how your basic free enterprise system develops its Olympic champions of tomorrow."

"One way?"

"And Frank Shorter sent me an unused portion of a ticket he had from San Francisco to Atlanta; I had it changed and got back on that."

"Shorter did that? So you could go out and run against him?"

"Not for that. He just wanted me to have a chance. He had been through the same thing himself. Right after he got out of Yale and was just bumming around, training and trying to get into meets, he lived on the floor of my dorm room. This was before Jeannie and I got married. Frank and I trained, slept, cooked on a hot plate and dreamed about becoming stars. I tell you, I would have done well in that race if I had had to crawl across the finish line on my hands and knees. So that's it. Beforehand I had these people more or less laughing at me. But after that race, it was oh Bruce this and gosh Bruce that. I told Shorter I couldn't believe it. He just laughed; he knew. He had been through it all himself."

"I recall a song about too many TV dinners, about how everyone loves a winner . . ."

Denton smiled. "You're getting the picture." He stood, stretched mightily, sat again.

"But more to the point," Denton said, "What I'm getting at is, I'm advising that you practice a certain amount of discretion. I am advising regrouping, getting some country air, thumping some soft trails . . ."

"Out here?" Cassidy looked around. "What about school, the Athletic Department thing. What about *girls*, for crying out . . ."

"The vertical smile? The old furry bivalve? Well, the prospects are limited. Also graduate-level bull sessions, extended beer swilling, elaborate practical, uh, jokes of a legal nature. All limited."

"I see your point."

"All of this may be, you understand, a form of whacking off. I don't know for sure, I just . . ." Denton looked Cassidy in the eye.

"For a long time I didn't believe you could make it, Quenton. I still don't know, really. You seemed to have almost too much going for you, if you know what I mean. It's a very intangible thing that allows maybe a boxing champion from the ghetto to express himself quite nicely with a left cross. But in your case, to put it very simply, you never seemed quite hungry enough." Denton stood, walked back to refill his coffee mug.

"To be brutally honest with you, Quenton," he said, "I always figured that once you did four minutes, that would have been about it for you." He said this very quietly, almost sadly.

It was deadly quiet in the little house. Cassidy swallowed. Denton just looked at him, waiting for some kind of response. But all Cassidy could think was, *My god, you're right, you're right! How could I have not known?*

Finally, Cassidy said very softly: "I seem to have solved that problem. I don't exactly have anything going for me now. They've taken away . . ."

Denton slammed his mug down. *"They* have taken away *nothing! THEY* are irrelevant! That's what I want you to understand!"

"I must be slow or something . . ."

"Move out here, Quenton, and train. Train your guts out. Drop out of school, forget that mess for a while, it's nothing but trouble. They are all a bunch of small men with weak minds and tiny little goals for themselves; they'll cause you nothing but grief. There are great trails out here and a little grassy field for intervals. You can run barefoot on it the way you like to. It'd be ideal, a runner's paradise."

"Drop out of school?"

"You're a bright boy, you can do that diploma business any time. But I've been watching you since last year, Quenton, watching you very closely. Ever since you ran that four flat..."

"Four flat point three."

"All right, four flat point three. I've been watching you, your training, the way you handled breakdowns, everything. I've been watching, Quenton, and I can tell you that physically you are getting close. Very close. Do you know what I mean?" He didn't wait for an answer, but strode to the big picture window that took up most of the front of the structure.

"People conceptualize conditioning in different ways," he said. "Some think it's a ladder straight up. Others see plateaus, blockages, ceilings. I see it as a geometric spiraling upwards, with each spin of the circle taking you a different distance upwards. Some spins may even take you *downwards*, just gathering momentum for the next upswing. Sometimes you will work your fanny off and see very little gain; other times you will amaze yourself and not really know why. Training is training, it all seems to blend together after a while. What is going on inside is just a big puzzle. But my little spiral theory kind of gives it a perspective, don't you think?"

"Yes, but I don't see . . ."

"You've been in that momentum-gathering phase, Cass, is what I'm telling you. You've been in it for quite a while now and I think that—physically again—you're due. That four flat in San Diego was only the tip of the iceberg . . ."

"Four flat point one."

"All right, four flat point one. But your sights have been too low, Cass. You've always wanted to break four minutes so you could be a respected college miler. You wanted the other guys to look at you and say, hey, there goes Cassidy, the guy from Southeastern that runs four minutes."

"I'm not so sure that's such a . . ."

"Hell, forget about all that. *Go* for it, Quenton, is what I'm telling you, go for the big time, right now, at this precise point of your life, make up your mind to do it and do it. *Take your shot.*"

"But dropping out of school, Bruce. I'd feel like a quitter, like I was running away . . ."

For the second time this morning Cassidy thought Denton looked really irritated, impatient with him.

"Let me tell you something about winners and losers and quitters and other mythical fauna in these parts," Denton said. "That quarter mile oval may be one of the few places in the world where the bastards can't screw you over, Quenton. That's because there's no place to hide out there. No way to fake it or charm your way through, no deals to be made. You know all about that stuff. You've talked about it. It's why you *became* a miler. The question now is whether you are prepared to live by it or whether it was just a bunch of words."

Quenton Cassidy thought about it a few moments, and then very quietly asked Denton exactly what his personal stake was in the whole affair.

"Let's say I am chronically attached to the underdog . . ."

"Bruce . . ."

"Let's say I am an ardent fan of that classical footrace, the mile run, that I have never had enough speed myself to . . ."

"Bruce . . ."

"Let's say I'm angling for a percentage of the take and..."

"Naw." Cassidy waved that off as well.

Denton sat beside Cassidy, removed his shoes and socks and sat looking at his boney feet. Then he took a deep breath, and leaned over and pressed into the swollen skin of his bulbous red heels with his thumb. The surface remained indented, as if in modeling clay.

"They're full of lymph!"

"Yeah. They aren't as bad today as usual. Doc Stavius says the achilles sheath will become involved shoitly and then it will be just a matter of time . . ."

"Bruce, I'm real sorry, I . . ."

"The hell with it. I would have liked another couple of seasons, I suppose, before hanging 'em up for good, but the hell with it. Connective tissue, Quenton, that's what gets everybody in the end. Pound around asphalt America long enough and you're going to wear something out for real. We can mold the muscles, you see . . ." He looked down at his knees sadly.

"We can strengthen the mind, temper the spirit, make the heart a godamn turbine. But then a strand of gristle goes pop and presto you're a pedestrian."

"Can't they do anything?"

"Oh, you know how those things go. With a football player you can drill a hole in a bone and tie the godamned things all over the place; but a distance runner gets so much as a stone bruise, he limps a thousand miles . . ."

"Bruce?"

"I'll probably hang around at meets . . ."

"Bruce?"

". . .wearing my old USA sweats, pretending to be warming up for a deuce or a 5000. What?"

"You tell me win one for the Gipper, I quit immediately."

"Deal!"

24. Moving Out

There was nothing special about the room, but it was said that even a prisoner in the Bastille would wax sentimental over his cell after languishing in it many years. Leaving the third floor of Doobey Hall filled Quenton Cassidy with both nostalgia and foreboding.

Mike Mobley came by and watched for awhile, occupying nearly the whole door frame sadly as Cassidy puttered around with cardboard boxes and suitcases. Finally the weight man took a deep breath and held out his huge paw.

"Well, Captain Cassidy," he said. "I want you to know, I've always appreciated your . . . I mean, it's always been great the way you . . ." His big shoulders slumped wearily.

"Yes indeed, Captain Mobley. I appreciate it, really I do. You take good care of that heaving arm, you hear?"

Mobley lumbered out shaking his head. Cassidy smiled. He would miss the harmless rituals. Soon others began dropping by and finally it got so distracting Cassidy closed the door and put up the little sign that said: The King is not RECEIVING. No one really had anything to say anyway, they just sat around shaking their heads and trying to make small talk.

When Cassidy had nearly finished packing, he sat down on a trunk and looked out the window at the leaves that glistened with the dusty orange glow of sundown. But even as the room grew dim he did not bother to get up to switch on the light. Most of the others were soon downstairs at dinner, but he didn't feel like joining them. He decided he would take his posters with him. One showed Jim Ryun in agonizing full color running his world record mile at Bakersfield in 1966; another was a black and white blow-up that Cassidy had specially made, showing the classic moment in 1954 when Roger Bannister, his long hair flying straight against a gray August sky, passed John Landy as Landy looked to the inside to see how far back the Englishman might be, thereby losing in the final straight. I wonder how often Landy thinks about that moment, Cassidy mused. Maybe once a day?

The third poster had a sunflower on one side and a flowery message down the other: "War is Harmful to Children and Other Living Things." By asterisk it contained a typical Cassidy addendum: *Not to mention Young Draft-Aged Males.*

There was a slim profile shot of Kip Keino at full stride somewhere in his native Kenya, looking right into the camera and just grinning outrageously. Cassidy loved that one.

On the floor were various cardboard boxes and suitcases containing the effluvia of several years spent in a type of vortex; one box contained several fright wigs, a rubber chicken named Cletus, an Ella Fitzgerald mask, and a disappearing cane. A mesh bag held a diver's mask and snorkel, heavy jet fins, Hawaiian sling handle (the stainless steel shaft leaned in a corner) and several large conch shells with the hinges knocked out. There was a rolled up Wanted Dead Or Alive poster containing mug shots of the former President and Attorney General of these United States; there was an eight-by-twelve glossy of seer Jeanne Dixon, a speaker on campus during his sophomore year, that contained in suspicious-looking handwriting the message: "Quenton, someday you will meet a tall, rich, and well-dressed stranger. He will put on a lab coat and replace your blood with embalming fluid. I practically guarantee it. Love, Jeanne."

There was a cigar box full of cards, letters, and mementos of his time with Andrea, a box he did not have the gumption right now to go poking through. There was a brace of frisbees and a collection of various sized noses. One box held his record collection, which included the *Original Buttoned-Down Mind of Bob Newhart*, some early Shelley Berman, Mort Sahl, Vaughn Meader, et al. There was a sound-effects record offering exploding dynamite, grinding winches, breaking dishes and assorted animals in varying stages of distress (a popular cut was the turkey section). There were anti-war crooners, and Kingston Trios gone cloudy with the scratches of time. A scrapbook was fat and sloppy with plane tickets, pages ripped out of meet programs, newspaper clippings. The photographs were mostly of Denton or some California sprinter or vaulter; Cassidy's appearances were generally in agate type. Though there were two large cardboard boxes filled with trophies, medals and meet watches that did not run well, most of his booty was quickly sent home. There were stacks of paperbacks by Vonnegut, Mailer, Roth and the little-known Richard Stein. There was a collection of columns by one Ron Wiggins entitled The *X-Rated Hen Suit*. A shoebox held the entire output of Harry Crews in paper.

One suitcase contained practically nothing but t-shirts: DRAKE RELAYS, Run For Fun, PUMA, Speed Kills, I'm With Stupid, and Thin power.

There were two large boxes full of track shoes of every description; there were Adidas Gazelles in varying stages of decomposition, Puma interval trainers, several pairs of Tiger Cortez, one pair of indoor pin spikes, an old pair of long spikes still dark with vaseline and the mud of Chicago, road racing flats, nylon mesh Tigers for the steeple (still brand new) and beach hack-arounds with no real mileage left in them. He thought: I have measured out my life in worn out rubber.

He sat for a long time studying a pair of Adidas 9.9's that he had worn winning the conference mile the year before. Denton had given them to him one day in the locker room. He had tossed them over casually and said: "You might like to have these, seeing as how we're the same size and all. But I want you to know these shoes have never been second." Then he had winked at Cassidy.

Three days later at the exact moment of truth, Cassidy had thrown up his fingers in the victory sign and made himself grin right at Denton, who was standing by the finish line. Not at all like himself, Denton had jumped in the air and whooped. The shoes still had not been second.

Cassidy sighed, tossed the 9.9's into the box with the others. They had all seen a lot, had their own decrepit personalities. He sighed; the Trial of Miles, Miles of Trials. Sometimes it seemed sad to him and he really didn't know why.

A timid little tap at the door turned out mercifully to be Mizner, who was now living on campus. He plopped down on the bed and quietly helped observe the sentimentality of the moment. It finally made Cassidy nervous.

"How do you like civilian dorm life," Cassidy asked.

"Three major water fights in four days if that tells you anything. I try to stay away as much as possible."

Cassidy nodded. He was sitting in his usual chair, feet propped up in the window sill. Finally Mizner spoke.

"Are you really going to do this hermit thing?"

"I suppose. You know how we were always saying, what if a guy were to really shut everything out . . ."

"Yeah, well, when the nearest civilization is the town of Newberry, I don't think you have to worry about shutting out much of anything, except watermelon farmers, and I understand they're not all that rowdy. The question is, is this some kind of big push, for Pan Am, or maybe the, uh, Games?"

"Who the hell knows? It sounds silly to even talk about, doesn't it? You might as well say you're building a rocket ship to go to Mars but it won't be ready for a few years."

"And when it is, it may not fly."

"Right now I'm selecting the upholstery. Say, how have you been feeling anyway? Will they let you do anything yet?"

Mizner gave him chapter and verse of his medical situation. They talked on until it was nearly dark in the room and both of them began to realize it wasn't going to get any better. Mizner stood and held out his fine brown hand. Cassidy took it self-consciously.

"It has all turned out so differently," Mizner said. Cassidy lowered his eyes.

"Really something, isn't it? Last summer we were talking about going to Drake this year and how maybe we'd both try to learn to hurdle so we could run the steeple together, and then later in the summer for the hell of it we'd jump in a marathon somewhere . . ."

Mizner took a deep breath, slowly let it out. "I guess I'd better be going. Listen you hang in there. And you better be tough next cross-country season because I believe we have some old business."

"I knew it! I knew Chicago really got to you, but you didn't want to let it show!"

"Nah," Mizner said, laughing. "Well, I guess I'd been due for that one for a long time. You don't know how many bad dreams I've had about Quenton Cassidy being with me with a quarter to go." He shook his head, smiling sadly.

"Yeah, well . . ."

"Hey listen, Quenton—I never call you that, do I?—anyway, Cass, there's something I was to say that I guess I wouldn't get around to except for a deal like this . . ."

"Hey Mize, you don't need to . . ."

"Oh, yes I do. What I want to say is that, well, I know we joke around a lot, what with Bruce the way he is and all. But we both know that when you get right down to it, the guy is pretty damned intimidating. It's only because we *know* him that . . ." Mizner swallowed.

". . .and Cass, we've been friends for a long time now . . ." He lowered his head, as if too weary to go on. Cassidy looked out the window.

"Listen Mize," he said.

"Quenton, you know how sometimes on a really bad one when you realize how it's going to be real early, like the second lap, and there's just nothing you can do about it except tuck in and gut it out? And how hard it is for the other two who are not running to sit and watch and know what is happening and not be able to do anything about it? Christ, Cass, I've seen you go through it so many times and every time just when I think it has finally gotten to you for once and you are going to slack off on yourself a little bit, you . . . just come blowing out of that last turn like some godamned maniac and I just . . ." His voice cracked and he turned away slightly. Cassidy was distressed.

"Jerry, it's the same with you. You know how it's been. The same for all three of us. Bruce, too."

"Yeah, Mizner said, "but with him there's no mystery left in it."

Cassidy considered that.

"Not as much," he admitted.

"And it's gotten so there's not much left with you either, Cass, is what I'm trying to say. I guess I've gotten so I'm not really afraid for you that much anymore."

Cassidy studied his bare feet. He never in his life expected to hear such a confession and he couldn't think of anything to say.

"Aw, who the hell knows?" Mizner laughed. "I just wanted you to know I've become kind of a fan, that's all. Hey, don't let it get to you out in the boonies. One of these days this mess will settle down and it will be just like it always was." He had almost closed the door when he stuck his head in and gave Cassidy the old smile, white teeth flashing against the dark background of his face.

"Miles of Trials," he said.

"Yes," Cassidy smiled back, "Yes, indeed."

The door closed softly. Cassidy sat alone on the sheetless mattress in the eerie gloom, staring at the barren room which was even now growing cold to his mind. Finally he heard the horn of Denton's car down below. He exhaled deeply and stood up. Quenton Cassidy was a believer in all manner of Comebacks and Second Chances, but whatever happened, it would *not* be like it always was.

Never, ever again.

25. The Woods

Life in the cabin had an unusual effect on Cassidy. The runners had always leavened the unavoidable solitude of their sport with the social atmosphere of the team, but now that Cassidy's isolation was geographical as well as physical, he slipped towards goofiness. He read massively. When that didn't do it and his natural gregariousness boiled over, he began to carry on conversations with inanimate objects.

"Why do you do this to me?" he would ask of a broken shoelace.

"Getting a little grubby, aren't we?" he suggested to the coffee pot one morning.

These one-sided conversations had begun, naturally enough, during the first few days when he had tried watching television (Denton brought a little portable, thinking the diversion might help).

"Oh, let's the fuck not!" he had cried to the silver-haired uncle type who had implored: "Let's talk for just a moment about constipation." And when the prim and proper lard ass Aunt Nell walked into the young bride's new house, turned up her little snoot and made a just barely overheard remark about "house-i-tosis," Cassidy got up from his chair, muttering softly: that, really will not do. He unplugged the set, wrapped the cord around the handle and placed it in the oven (which he used only for heating the kitchen.)

"You're going to stay in there until you godamn well learn some manners," he informed Aunt Nell, and then promptly forgot about her. And not just her. He also forgot about all the rest, all the legions of thrombosed bridge partners, impotent husbands, adorably precocious children and finicky pets. Cassidy thought: descendants of spelling bee champions and fellers of giant trees are cooed to by pill-crazed thespians acting out the slings and arrows of lower tract distress; a monk sets himself afire in the street and folks run for the marshmallows. Or am I being picky?

After that when he wasn't running or sleeping, he read. When his eyes tired, he tried just sitting. He began to feel like the lama on a mountaintop who is so finely tuned he senses the very food moving through his body, the air molecules penetrating lung sacs and being dispersed to the far flung cells. He treated such newfound sensitivity not with pride but suspicion; Eastern religious gimmickry was endorsed enthusiastically by any number of dorm-bound adolescents and Quenton Cassidy had always treated such trends with the same respectful distance he might a ripe mule carcass.

He quickly settled into a mesmerizing pattern of hard training, reading, eating simple fare, sleeping like a wintering bear, and talking to the pots and pans.

"I'm going nuts," he informed himself happily in the mirror one morning.

Denton came out on weekends and after training together they worked on the greenhouses in back. Once he had the idea, Cassidy was able to hammer away by himself during the week, but when the February rains started, he was deprived even of this activity for the most part.

Denton however was crafty and understood all too well the logistics of single-minded effort. He often brought fresh reading material for the hermit, books that zeroed in on a subject of a mutual interest. Cassidy devoured them all: Sillitoe's *Loneliness of a Long Distance Runner*, Roger Bannister's urbane *The Four Minute Mile*, Peter Snell's *No Bugles, No Drums*, a novel called *The Olympian* by Brian Granville (not bad at all), another called *The Games* by Hugh Atkinson (pretty awful). Soon Cassidy felt he had read everything ever written about running. He poured over Fred Wilt's *How They Train*, a compilation of the bare training schedules of the elite and near-elite. It was helpful to him, this little library, for it kept him focused on his task. The novels, while generally flawed technically in one way or another (sometimes tragically so) occasionally clumsily captured certain elements of his own striving; he found them comforting. The biographies were more esoteric, suffered no attempt at art, and delighted him no end. From them he learned he was not really alone in many ways. He especially loved *A Clean Pair of Heels*, the story of the great New Zealand distance man, Murray Halberg.

Often after a late-night reading jag, he took to the country roads and wooded trails with renewed energy, comparing his impressions to his historical or fictional counterparts. He decided that no one had quite captured the strained satisfaction of tooling through the middle miles of a hard fifteen mile run; but then he thought some experiences do not easily lend themselves to descriptions of mere word butchers. It was a good thing, he decided, not to have everything available in capsule form. Few others mentioned how wonderful, delicious and life-giving it was just to *stop* sometimes, at the end of a run, with such a pitiful thirst (with swollen tongue and all) that the runner is convinced he knows what it would be like to die of thirst in the desert; when the first beer is not like liquid at all but just a kind of wonderful fire burning down a viscous throat.

But all the books helped him in some way or another. Quenton Cassidy was not enthusiastically going about the heady business of breaking world records or capturing some coveted prize; such ideas would have been laughable to him in the bland grind of his daily routine. He was merely trying to slip into a lifestyle that he could live with, strenuous but not unendurable by any means, out of which if the corpuscles and the capillaries and the electrolytes were properly aligned in their own mysterious configurations, he might do even better something that he had already done quite well.

He was trying to switch gears; at least that is how he thought of it. And though it was a somewhat frightful thing to contemplate for very long, he really *was* pulling out all the stops. After this he would have no excuses, ever again. This here train, he thought, *she's boun' for glory.*

Ain't she?

26. Recon Work

Forays; he liked the sound of the word, implying as it did woodsy recon work. Illicit after-hours excitement for the young rogue about town. What the hell, he thought, I'm getting 23 blooming miles a day.

Thus he found himself for the first time in Newberry's only bar, which was thankfully not called the Dew Drop Inn, being more or less alternately ignored and scowled at by any number of local good old boys who figured this bird was looking for trouble.

But then they also noticed that he looked a little on the, well, *wiry*, side. They kept their distance.

The juke box twanged away in the corner, evoking the bucolic muse. Cassidy picked up a napkin and began a soggy composition, a sure-fire country song sensation entitled: *Don't Send No Form Letter To Your Sweetheart After You Done Mass-Mailed Your Love All Over Town*. About halfway through, right after a line that said: "This is where the teardrops dry up for me, *buster* . . ." he tired of the theme, started a new one with more appeal perhaps for the short-term credit community called: *Go Put Your Love On Master Card, You Got No Credit Line With Me.*

Down at the end of the bar, an obvious regular engaged the proprietor in a loud, showy mock-argument in order to demonstrate his status:

"Leroy, I swear if you don't cut this Wild Turkey . . ."

"Now James Lee I'll run you ass right on outa here . . ."

I am back in real life again, Cassidy thought, in the dank ambience of a panhandle bar amidst a group of drivers of real pick-up trucks. And that barmaid has got herself a fairly decent chassis packed in them Levis.

"Real pretty hair," he told her with what he still thought of as his impish grin, as she brought his third dizzy Pearl beer.

"You barkin' up the wrong sleeve, honey," she told him.

27. A Too Early Death

The rains of February came, bloating the pine forests and capturing all of life in the gray rumble of its clouds and the wetness of its seepage; all life except the unsmiling hermit who reluctantly left his dry nest in the same manner twice a day: standing on the small porch, savoring the last vestige of the eave's shelter, he surveyed the swollen clouds, the drenched colorless trees, the red mud seeping up through the pine needles like thin dirty blood, and with a sigh stepped gingerly into the first puddle like a cautious water bird. Then he struck out.

He had four pairs of training shoes, each of which remained wet all the time. If he could, by propping a pair up against the small electric heater, get them to a stage you might call "damp," he slipped them on with the greatest of pleasure. At one time there was a good deal of confusion about the use of spiked shoes. Cassidy rarely wore them in training; thin on the bottom and affording little protection to the heel and arch, he considered them risky for nearly all training. He had suffered for years wearing shoes made of kangaroo leather. He was grateful for the recent switch to nylon, but his thick-bottomed trainers still seemed to soak up a great deal of water; after a time he felt as if he were running with soggy pillows on the feet.

Some mornings he rose to find the huge mass of clouds rolled back, exposing a most brilliant, newly-washed blue sky. He would pull on his slick shoes without a grumble and lope off along the soggy trail with his bounciest stride, wondering how he could have ever gotten himself into such a state. This, now *this*, he thought, was wonderful. All color and life had merely been disguised by a film of water. Birdies sang, moo-cows mooed, and Quenton Cassidy, a man with only the vaguest sort of plan, would sometimes laugh right out loud.

By the next afternoon, however, the clouds would have resumed their sentry and it would be pouring or sprinkling or at least threatening.

Such a winter, Cassidy thought bitterly, *is* always getting your hopes up. And he would resolve then to scowl through the next sunny day just by way of not being taken in. But it was a resolution quickly forgotten, such are the surges of a young heart given promise.

Were he completely honest with himself, he would have perhaps admitted that he didn't mind it so much, this rain that furnished the same kind of isolation as the dark of night. Snell used to say he didn't mind running in the rain because he always felt his opponents would have to be quite insane to be out in such weather, and while they were somewhere dry and cozy, he was gaining yet another few tenths of a second on them.

But occasionally at night Cassidy would sit over his training calendar and the full weight of it would descend on him as he stared at the figures. At those times he dared to wonder if it really was too much. He would think of the comradeship of Doobey Hall, the horseplay, the unpredictable silliness. His world now had too many sharp corners; he craved the soft contours of the feminine. Surely such longings were natural enough, he thought. Even the buffoonery of Jack Nubbins seemed a far-off entertainment that he had too lightly regarded in happier times.

But out on the trails he slipped along in the soggy warm envelope of his own fierce body heat and needed precisely nothing. At these times, moving silently against the washed-out backdrop of countryside, his mind unfettered except for monitoring the steady 6:00 pace, he went back to his childhood, back to the time of his too early death. He pondered what it meant, if anything; if anything at all.

Such a significant event as dying in childhood must take some meaning in the end, he reasoned, if only a simple safety message, grade school style: This is the Watch Bird saying look both ways before crossing the Santa Monica Freeway. But his death seemed to mean nothing.

On one of those rain-lashed afternoon runs, Cassidy finally decided that there was a great deal of vanity tied up in his demise, and in this respect perhaps Andrea had been right

about his obsession. Perhaps it was *not* excellence he sought
at all, but something else entirely. That part he would work
on later. It had taken him a long time to arrive at the vanity
part.

I used to frolic in the salt salt sea, he thought, and now
my toes wrinkle white in this hillbilly mud.

When he was very young he learned to slip into the sea
and plummet like a stone to fifty, sixty feet, there to look
around leisurely before floating back, calm and haughty in
his control of the pale green waters. On rough, sunny days
he would ride his bicycle across the Singer Island bridge and
out to the inlet and scamper among the giant slippery boul-
ders, at ease among the skittering crabs.

"What's he doing?" the white-kneed tourists would ask,
seeing the waves crashing against jagged rocks so slick they
could not even walk on them.

"Where are his parents? He'll be drowned!"

The child would spit into his mask, lean over and rinse it
out in the sea, then grip the spear and wait for the right wave
to come bashing frothily among the deadly crags and barna-
cles. Then, like a spirit, he would slip easily into the receding
swell and with a shiver, be gone.

Below, in the sudden quiet, he felt at once peaceful and
serene in a terrain he knew better than his own room. The
formation of rocks below was home for a school of big red
snapper, skittish and crafty, which might let you get off one
shot from a distance before disappearing for the day. At the
cable crossing there would be sheepshead (easy marks—he
ignored them) and schoolmaster snapper. Out towards the
tip, closer to the open ocean, the real ocean, one could find
just about anything; some days the sea would be literally alive.
Quenton Cassidy had cavorted there like a young seal, sometimes actually feeling an illogical resentment at his addiction
to air, a dependence that forced him regularly to make his
way wanly to the top where he endured poorly the noise and
neon of an altogether different kind of world.

The fishermen, wrinkled cigar-chomping retirees, cursed
him for "scaring the fish" as they dangled their silly bait

randomly in the sea. He felt the hunter's ancient disdain for the trapper. They almost never knew where he was.

The other kids were fascinated; they knew the waters too, but that Quentie was known to go places they would never try and bring back a handful of sand, a rusty nail, a little lump of coral and show them, laughing, the simple evidence of his prowess. Quenton Cassidy at ten already had his lungs.

The others wanted to know the secret. "Vitamin Z," he told them laughing. He suspected even then that there *was* no secret, but didn't exactly know how to tell them.

One time though his best friend had pleaded until, when they were alone on the end of the jetty late one afternoon, he told him: "You've got to make yourself calm, right down to the little blood veins in your fingertips, and when you are as calm as you can make yourself, then you make yourself like a rock and start sinking, and the most important thing is that you've got to not care. That's the hard part, the not caring part. And the deeper you go and the colder it gets the more you have got to not care. And then when you start back up, back towards real life . . . then you've got to start caring again. A *lot*."

His father had a 22-foot open fisherman that they took to the islands every summer and it was Quenton's job to fetch the anchor when it got stuck, silent and unmoving, on some ramp or drop-off far below.

"Now, Quentie, it's deep, you'd best put on a tank this time," the old man would say. The old man wore a pipe. He worked in photo-engraving at the newspaper.

"It's okay, Pop," this as he flipped out of the boat with his mask and snorkel. If his heart raced with excitement of the challenge he would have to make it slow again, like he always did, calming himself, making himself into a rock and then slipping, slowly at first, then more rapidly as he went along, down into the darkening green, down to the cold depths where all the mysteries were. When he reached the bottom he would quickly work the anchor loose, then plant his feet in the sand and shoot upwards, streaming bubbles all the way, wondering if he would make it this time.

One time he didn't make it and died there in the cool green waters.

There was a man from another boat on this trip, a lawyer his father knew and a good diver who had a grouper speared and holed up about forty feet down. The fellow was too tired to get down and pull him out.

"Hey, Mr. C," he had called, "Shame to waste those filets. Whyn't you send that boy of yours down for a try?" They had all heard as much as they wanted to about this little twerp, this little Quentie-fish and there was a distinct challenge in the invitation. His father looked at him resting there on the front platform and said: "Now Quenton you're very tired. You've been up and down in thirty feet all day long so if you don't feel like doing it, you don't have to." But he was poking around for his gear already; the idea of leaving a dying fish tucked up under a coral head to suffer for days nearly made him weep. And he had always made it before no matter how bad it seemed, and the worse it seemed the sweeter the air was at the top when he finally broke through and got at it. As he floated on the top, though, looking down to the coral head miniaturized below, he absent-mindedly hyperventilated, thinking how far down it was, how tired he had become; by the time he took his last big gulp of air his system was all oxygen. He was still peering around under the coral head and taking his time when he realized something was wrong. But by then it was too late; he just barely managed to trip the spring buckle on his weight belt and let the seven pounds of lead fall to the sandy bottom as he streaked towards the top. He was still 20 feet under when the blackness thundered in. The limp body floated serenely to the top, and there bobbed gaily in the wind chop, looking for all the world like a lazy snorkeler, tracking his game. It took awhile before the elder Cassidy noticed how remarkably corpse-like little Quenton looked, before he noticed the absence of any motion whatsoever; no little flips for forward motion, no play of the hands to turn or stop.

He was saying Jesus Jesus Jesus as he slashed the anchor rope with the filet knife (and cut his own thumb down to white bone at the same time) and then roared over to pull the little gray body from the water, draining sea water from every orifice. There was seaweed in the teeth.

It was too much for the old man, it was too final-looking. The bottom of the boat was becoming slick with his own blood as he slid down onto the deck mumbling. But the others were more efficient. They had seen drownings before and were not so overcome with grief. They began blowing into the fouled little mouth and crushing the rib cage with strong hands. After half an hour there was some vomiting. He vomited and then they vomited. But color was coming back, and there was a faint pulse; finally some wild thrashing.

He had been floating around on the top for perhaps ten minutes, possibly more, and they had not held out a great deal of hope even as they frantically worked over him. Then as he started coming back, although no one said anything, the big fear was that they were rejuvenating a mindless blob that would henceforth sit in some white-walled institution and drool contentedly.

But they did not know, could not know that the cardio-vascular system they were priming with their frenzied efforts was capable of withstanding even greater shocks than it had that day. The lungs, the veins and vessels, the resilient throbbing heart; he had them all, even back then.

The next day they flew him back across the deep purple Gulf Stream at an altitude of one hundred feet; his blood was still so blue they feared to go higher. When he awoke finally in Good Samaritan Hospital in West Palm Beach he wanted to know what had happened to him. His father told him the story again. But every time Quenton went to sleep, he would forget it completely.

"Don't you remember, son? Don't you remember diving and . . ."

"I remember one time. I remember this day I was in the inlet working my way along the rocks at about thirty feet. And this little bull shark about four feet long was coming in from the real ocean; he was right in my path but I didn't move over, just kept swimming straight ahead. When he saw me he acted like he didn't care but he moved over a little to let me pass by. I was so ferocious with my sling, Dad, I wasn't afraid. I laughed because he was going so far in and I knew the hunting was better out near the tip."

Then he held his father, grabbed him and buried his head in the old man's chest and cried. His father had not seen him do anything like that for a long time.

This one, he thought, what is it with this one?

Nearly ten years later a land-bound Quenton Cassidy flew along on the soggy February trails and wondered the same thing.

28. Time . . .

Outside the afternoon rained on.

Cassidy leaned forward and placed all four legs of his chair on the floor carefully. He sighed heavily. The books were stacked up all around, finished and bleak-looking. He was tired of reading. He set his mug down on the table with a grunt. He was tired of tea.

He hauled himself to his feet, walked stiffly over to the picture window, a fogged square of chilled gray. He was tired of walking around with his joints creaking like an old man. He had a sudden passing desire for broccoli.

Afternoon workout was an hour and a half away; time to begin thinking about it. He was tired of psyching himself for workouts.

He was tired of being tired.

In reverse mirror script he wrote on the pane of cold glass: HELP! IMPRISONED IN FEBRUARY.

Little drops of excess moisture cried down from his letters as he looked out through them and waited for time to pass.

He stared out for a long time . . .

29. Twenty Four in the Rain

It had not been so awfully hard on Andrea Cleland, as she was beginning to tell herself lately. She had ended a few difficult relationships in the past but she was a very mature young lady and she managed. It was her maturity in fact that probably caused some of the distress. She was often a little too far ahead of the game to really take it seriously; though she had believed herself in love several times, it did not take her long to assay the true metal of the relationship. Before Cassidy she had begun to have some confidence in her ability to judge that most complex and shifty element in human dealings: motive.

It was not as if she had not had experience with ambitious men (or more accurately, ambitious boys); she knew very well when she was being sized up as a future charming hostess by the president of some fraternity, some bright, good-looking fellow who was easy to like and whose father owned an office supply outfit in Orlando. She chafed a little, but played the role. It was her sensitivity that made her more mature, gave her an edge over her hapless pursuers, and allowed her to set the boundaries. When it was over, she knew it first. And though she might grieve truly, it was a bittersweet emotion because though sorry, she was always sure of herself. She played hearts like fiddles.

And now this had to happen. She realized finally that she had never really understood Quenton Cassidy very well, that she had tried to use her past experience to take his measure and it didn't work. "His *cir*cuitry is all different," she told her twin sister. His ambition differed in essence as well as degree. Whereas with others she could tell the point at which she might assert certain proprietary rights (the very first hints of nesting behavior), with this runner there was never any question about her rearranging his priorities. This rankled her from the start. She might have the ability to make him miserable, perhaps, but she swayed him not an inch from his path. He told her as much, and she found out quickly he meant it. There was something in the ferocity of his dedication that challenged the formula of her femininity. She responded to the challenge without even realizing she was doing so.

To Quenton Cassidy, who knew nothing about women in general and less about Andrea in particular, their meandering, halfhearted breakup was a thing without reason. It would not abate with discussion, not be cured by soul-searching, not be resolved by agreement. They both recognized certain deep feelings that couldn't be denied, so why, Cassidy asked again and again, all these problems? She found it impossible to tell him that this simply wasn't the way she had imagined it would be. Though she was mature for her age, she was not experienced enough to know that it rarely is.

Cassidy thought that it was entirely fitting that all the underpinnings of his world should collapse at one time. When he took to the woods and his first nearly total solitude, it was almost with relief. At first it was.

The huge oak in front of Andrea's sorority house was over 300 years old, had been an arm's thickness when Seminole Indians camped in the spot where the sorority house now stood, had shaded weary Spanish cowboys who kept herds on Payne's Prairie not five miles from there. This was at a time when a muddy, mosquito-infested fort named St. Augustine was a fledgling mission.

Now this old tree kept the steady rain off Quenton Cassidy, standing there in the night, heat-mist rising from his body, feeling anything but historic. He loved this old tree, and as he leaned against the incredibly gnarled trunk he thought: What does this old fellow care about it all? The strength of the ancient tree somehow soothed his misery.

The body heat from his run would keep him warm for a while longer, then he would start to get chilled and have to get moving again to stay warm. His bright nylon shorts and yellow t-shirt hung on him like colorful mud. He was drenched clear through to his childhood. At last he saw them drive up. They were laughing about something as they shared an umbrella to the porch. When the guy kissed her, Cassidy felt a stab of pain that was close to physical, and therefore within the penumbra of hurts he told himself he could bear. As she turned to go inside, Cassidy called to her. The fellow, peering out from under his umbrella, stopped halfway down the sidewalk and squinted towards Cassidy in the shadows of the old tree. The umbrella man looked grim. It appeared his duty was not yet finished; at first unsure of himself, he finally opted to return to the porch. Cassidy stepped out of the gloom and the porch light fell on him, gleaming in the rain. He called again.

"Quenton!" she was afraid she sounded a little too excited to see him. Then she remembered umbrella man, who was still coming. "It's all right, George. I'll see you Saturday." Still looking grim, he stalked back to his car and drove off. He had seen the way she ran out there in the rain like that, up to that crazy galoot in the gym shorts. And he was *supposed* to be out of the picture.

"Cass, what in the world are you doing?" she gestured in a general manner, taking in the rain, the night, the silliness of it all. She seemed amused.

"Thought I would come to see you."

"But, you're drenched. You've been standing . . ."

"I saw your light wasn't on, so I decided to wait for a while, at least until I got too cold." She tilted her head in amusement, like she used to all the time, and finally put her arms around him. He seemed not to know what to do. She was getting wet now, too, but seemed not to notice. She thought: He's harder now, even than before, all cartilage and bone and skin. She wondered if he was eating right; perhaps he would make himself sick. Something moved deep inside her and she had to stifle it willfully.

"I, uh, guess I was missing you," he said with his chin on her wet forehead, "and I suppose I got sick and tired of it all and just bolted on in here . . ." Something occurred to her and she leaned back away from him.

"You ran here!" It sounded like an accusation. He was puzzled.

"Yeah, I . . ."

"You ran into town from out there, twelve miles. And it's been raining like crazy all . . ."

"I don't have a car out there and . . ."

"Cass, you ran twelve miles in the rain to get here and you're going to have to run twelve miles back unless you call a cab or something . . ." He appeared unconcerned.

"It's my overdistance day anyway. Listen Andrea, I wanted to talk to you because . . . are you listening?" She was shaking her head.

"Yes," she said softly.

"The last time we seemed to be like strangers. I've been feeling so horrible about the whole thing, I just get so frustrated that we can't seem to get anything straight . . ."

"Cass, I thought we had been all through that."

"I just keep thinking there must be some way to put it, some way that would allow you to understand."

"I think I understand." She looked into his eyes and thought that though once they seemed to balance the hardness of the rest of him, now they added to it.

"I think I've always understood," she said. "I just don't think I can live with it. Sometimes it seems too much for you, too." He looked down, shook the rain from his forehead. She was nearly drenched now too.

"Don't you want to come in?" she asked.

"No. I'll be going, I guess. I'm starting to get chilled."

"Cass," she said, pulling him to her again. "What is this all going to get you? You've dropped out of school, you're not going to graduate with your class, you . . ."

"I ran a 3:58.6 mile the other night."

"What?"

"No race or anything. Just Bruce out there with a stopwatch and me, at ten o'clock at night. I had to go around the joggers even. Funny, I always dreamed how it would be going under four the first time, lining up, the pace, how the crowd would get excited when we came through the three quarters under three minutes . . ." He looked at her with a sad little smile. "But there it was, just me and Bruce—and a bunch of joggers wondering what in the hell was going on. Just another godamned workout . . ." There was something that sounded vaguely like satisfaction in his voice.

"Quenton, why don't you come back into town? Where does it say you have to live like this, make yourself miserable like this?"

"It will all be over soon anyway. I'll be running Walton next month."

"And then what? You've already said you can't win. Even your exalted Bruce Denton says that. So then what do you do? Go back to your little cave and keep driving yourself until you are the one they talk about, the one they are afraid of like you're afraid of Walton? Is that what's important to you? Or maybe you'd be content to just go crazy trying? Then no one could say you compromised, could they? If something inside you just snapped?"

He looked down. She knew then he would not fight with her.

Then she did something that was not quite her and that did not work very well. It was a mistake and she knew it right away but it was such a precisely feminine gesture that it was perhaps dictated by some ancient genetic pattern she was helpless to control. With a pained little toss of the head she wrenched free and ran towards the porch; it was one of those shabby you'd-better-come-after-me-now gestures and she knew by the time she got to the porch that it was a bad show all the way around.

She turned to call, to try to take it back, perhaps.

But the runner had disappeared in the darkening rain.

30. Whirlpool

Mary Lou Hunsinger sat in the gurgling whirlpool, her beehive slumping somewhat; outside it still rained like a bitch. At that very moment somewhere out in the glistening night, a homeward bound Quenton Cassidy came upon, was startled by, and hopped over a poor black snake trying to keep from drowning by crawling up to the high ground represented by State Road 26. Cassidy was just about halfway home.

Mary Lou's frown, of late an almost permanent fixture on her otherwise attractive face, was now a pouty badge of impatience at Dick Doobey, whom she thought rather a clod. On the home front her mother would be getting dinner for her two slope-headed sons, which meant that by the time she finally arrived, they would be as mean as a pack of starving blue jays (Mary Lou knew very well that as evil as the boys were, her mother was a shrew in her own right; she didn't even mean well).

She considered these bubbly interludes more or less in the line of duty. Not that she didn't take some basic carnal pleasure in them, but they required massive revetting of her expensively maintained hairdo. For all of its architectural integrity her beehive tended to sag in this steamy sanctum in much the same way as Mary Lou's own flagging hopes.

In this surreal chamber he brought her all manner of world weariness, from his cold, church-crazed wife to the latest technical esoterica of his chosen profession. She bore it all with good will and no small effort to comfort and counsel. But what, after all was she supposed to know about the weakside linebacker's responsibility in defensing the quarterback roll-out option out of the wishbone? As to the other, she had no difficulty whatever in flatly recommending that Doobey drop his "dry-hole little bitch" in order to take up with Mary Lou herself in some kind of more widely sanctioned arrangement. It was a scenario she had come to think

165

of as the only non-felonious way she would ever get out from under those killing monthly payments to five trusting department and clothing stores, two "friendly" small loan companies, and "the Mastercharge," all of which her former mate—a two-fisted, bourbon-crazed paint and body man—had been so thoughtless as to leave as his only enduring legacy.

"Paint and body men's like a nationwide brotherhood, hon," he would warn ominously, "I could be in Tucson on Wednesday pulling down a hunnert and fifty dollars a day like that!" He would snap his stained fingers cockily. "Like doctors," he would say, "always in demand." When he finally did take off, he had sense enough not to go to Tucson.

The powdery pink flamingo on the front lawn now seemed a mocking reminder of more opulent days when she had nothing better to do than to hop in the station wagon and go shoppin' to her heart's content. She never looked at the sun-faded little plaster bird standing forlornly on its rusting pipestem leg without wondering where it was exactly she had gone so wrong. They never mentioned this in Home Ec.

Wrestling with the viscous mathematical intricacies of 18% per annum interest, compounded monthly in accordance with federal statutes, she was driven first to secretarial work (she hated waitressing) and thence to Dick Doobey's private whirlpool.

The head coach finally arrived and let himself in with his own key. The strain of his staff meeting was still on his face. He apologized with the profuse sincerity of a man unquestionably willing to debase himself in order to maintain a good thing.

"That's all right, honey," she said. "I got nothin' better to do but sit here and get my little love button parboiled."

A flash of uncomplicated lust shot through Dick Doobey's loins as she giggled at her own line. Doobey noticed that she had brought a quart bottle of Southern Comfort, which now sat on the moist floor beside an open can of ginger ale. He made a grimace.

She watched him undress with contained distaste. He had long ago lost the trimness that was a by-product of his athletic days; his arms and neck were unattractively sunburned to the edges of his short-sleeved shirt, much in the manner of a gas station attendant.

His stomach rolled around loosely, the result of his long afternoons on the high pyramidal coaching tower, looking stern while drinking Budweiser (hidden in a styrofoam Gatorade holder!), ostensibly surveying his minions scattered about the 25 acre practice fields—a general watching his field commanders through powerful binoculars—but in actuality keeping a rather dutiful eye on Simmons Hall, the nursing school dormitory, where one could (were one extremely diligent) catch an occasional flash of nubile young breast or mouth watering young thigh.

Dick Doobey loved his work.

He simply couldn't understand why some critics would wish to cause him anguish by suggesting that he was not doing a good job and should go away. He sincerely suspected communist influence of some kind.

When he had finally shed his damp garments and was settling his white bottom slowly into the scalding water opposite Mary Lou, he had managed to put out of his mind the distress of his latest staff meeting, where he had unhappily discovered once more that his staff was almost as much in the dark as he was. Football was becoming a damned complicated game and Doobey figured there was probably some foreign influence behind that as well.

"How did it go, hon?" she asked, shifting around to allow room for his considerable bulk. He was almost settled now, leaning back and heaving a sigh of relief.

"Aw shit honey, I don't know. I wanted that stumpfucker Erickson to read up some on this new wishbone formation—'member the one I tole you about where they can shift from weakside to strongside and run a option off the . . . no? Honey I just tole you about it last week."

"Well godamn angel you know I don't remember that kinda stuff very well."

"Oh, well, it don't matter anyway," he said, sinking now to his neck in the roiling water, "I'll just have to do it myself, like everything else." He smiled at that, and began probing for her with his big toe.

"Now honey don't you want a drink or somethin'?" she asked.

"Of that sweet horse piss?" He continued probing. She dodged with precision, as her sex learns to do at an early age in the republic. A thought struck her.

"Hon, I finished typing that talk for tomorrow, it's on your desk if you want to take it home tonight."

"Christamighty. I forgot about that altogether." The misery he had almost shed now settled on him again and Mary Lou was sorry she said anything.

"I wish I had some way to get outa that thing," he said mournfully.

"Why do you have to do it?"

"Old Man Prigman, uh, required it. Told me I'd never make conductor until I could face my own music. But lord, standing up there in the Plaza while a bunch of them snippy long-haired twats ask a bunch of asshole questions. Most of 'em *don't even go to football games!*"

"I thought that stuff was over."

"Over hell. They still got that whatever they call it, Conscription of Athletes or whatever the hell they call themselves. Prigman said it wasn't a godamn thing we could do about it except ignore it. Can you beat that? Here in America, and you can't do anything about people getting together to bad-mouth football!"

"Why can't you get rid of 'em?"

"Prigman said if we didn't nip it in the bud with that damn track guy, we would have to learn to live with it. Said we couldn't start throwing all of 'em out, it'd look too bad in the press. But boy, if I was runnin' the show . . ."

He rubbed his hands over his bristly head as if in some deep pain. "They keep issuing these mother lovin' press releases, Jeezus!"

"Aw honey," she said, taking his left foot, massaging gently. Slowly she worked her way up the hairy calf.

"There's gotta be something to do. I cain't keep up with all this stuff and operate a godamn ass-kicking football team at the same time. That's more'n a full time job by itself! More'n full time!"

"Now come on honey," she said softly, still working upwards, "We don't have to talk about that stuff all evenin', do we? Let's talk about somethin' else." Dick Doobey loos-

ened with a moan under the onslaught of her simple minis-
trations. The toe probed feverishly.

"What do you want to do, hon," he murmured softly.

"What do *you* want to do, angel?" she cooed back, as he
began sinking lower and lower until finally his mouth was
almost awash in the swirling water.

"Play alligator," he smiled evilly as his hot beady eyes
slowly disappeared beneath the surface.

31. Irish Highs

When no one answered his knock, Bruce Denton wiped his muddy feet on the filthy welcome mat and went into the cabin. He was accustomed to the disarray, but surprised to see a bottle of Bushmills Irish Whiskey open on the big cable spool that served as a kitchen table. He walked over, placed the cap back on the bottle and picked up the book lying beside it; it was a soft cover copy of *In Our Time*. He smiled.

"Hey, Nick," he called, "You in here, Nick?"

"Very funny," Quenton Cassidy croaked from behind a stack of paneling. He lay just under the front window, parallel to it, almost completely obscured by the lumber. Denton walked over and sat down on the wood. Cassidy smiled up at him, a coffee mug rising and falling on his chest (it contained several nearly melted ice cubes and probably no coffee, Denton surmised).

"So . . ." Denton let the word hang.

"I thought you were coming out here yesterday, jerk," Cassidy said, pleasantly.

"Ah yes, well sorry about that. Jeannie got to feeling bad and I ran her by the infirmary. We are, uh, waiting for word on the rabbit or whatever it is they do these days. When I got back it was dark, so I decided to come today."

"Oh. Pitter patter of little spikes around the house . . ." Cassidy yawned, did not appear very interested.

"So. What's the occasion? Or am I being too personal?"

"Occasion? Since when does a fellow have to have an occasion to bend an elbow?" Cassidy asked. Denton knew that Cassidy drank a lot of beer, but had never seen him take anything harder. He was partially amused, partially alarmed, but only the amusement showed.

"Doing a little reading, eh? What's this?" He picked up the paperback folded open beside Cassidy and turned it over to look at the cover.

It showed a young man sitting on a bench in a locker room putting on Tiger training flats; behind him an older man stood, towel around his waist as if he were about to yank it off with a cry of Lookey here! Cassidy giggled at him.

"That, my friend, is a book that explores a much overlooked and steadily growing athletic minority, the homosexual distance runner."

"Oh yeah?" Denton was leafing through the book. "What's the main . . . I mean, what do they, uh, you know . . . do?"

"I can see, sir, that you are a man of little sophistication. These fellows train themselves to a fine edge while maintaining dalliances with their ex-marine coaches, they fatten themselves up on yogurt and walnuts, and then they go out and run fantastic races despite the overwhelming social pressures brought to bear. Oh yes, they also 'rip off' 57-second quarters in morning workouts. But mostly . . ." He got up on his elbows so he could look Denton in the eyes. ". . . mostly they kind of lay around the locker room admiring each other's tawny hamstrings." He giggled again.

"Hmmm. Is this some latent prejudice of yours finally making its way out of the closet? I thought you were one of those put-it-into-whatever-you-want-or-whoever-you-want kind of fellows."

"Look, my view of sexual matters is that consenting adults should be allowed to run over each other with haybailers, if that's their fondest desire. So long, of course, as they don't do it in front of children. Or lovers of harvesting equipment."

Denton nodded, but he seemed engrossed in a passage in the book. His forehead wrinkled as he read for a few moments. Finally he tossed the book back on the floor.

"Whew!" he said.

"See what I mean? Now really, what does how you get your rocks off have to do with anything? So what if I'm out here whipping my wire 15 times a day? Who cares?"

"Yes, well, I see you're a little overwrought about this . . ."

"Overwrought hell. I'm drunk as a skunk." He giggled again. "I'm so fine tuned I get blipped from a tumbler of Dr. Pepper." Denton laughed.

"How about The Hem's Michigan stories I brought?" he gestured back towards the spool table.

"Yes, I liked them pretty much. Except for all the stiff upper lip crap. But the guy went out and did things, you know, I mean you could tell he really did those things, *knew* about them before going out and shooting his mouth off. He just sat down and tried to tell it as honestly as he could. That's a shit load better than sitting around New York with a bunch of other artistes diddling each other and writing about the state of being Jewish, or how anguishing it is to be an anguished writer. But then again . . ." His elbows were tiring, he flattened out on the floor again.

"Who cares?"

". . .who cares indeed?" Cassidy sighed. Denton thought: Here is a man who's been thinking by himself a lot lately.

"Christ, Bruce, I've got to get out of this hole. Take me to some food, to a place with people I can snarl at, waitresses in pantyhose, a place with that hallmark of civilization, a salad bar with fake bacon bits . . ."

"Just what I had in mind, assuming you can walk, steady there," Denton said. Cassidy was struggling stiffly to his feet.

"Did you run today?" Denton asked, helping him up.

"Can a fish tread water? Hell yes, I ran today, you think I'm out here to taunt the farmers? I'm going to take a shower."

Denton saw the training calendar on the floor where Cassidy had been lying. He picked it up and studied it for a moment, finally letting out a low whistle.

"What in the hell were you doing running 34 godamned miles yesterday? Are you going bonkers or what?"

Cassidy stuck his head out of the bathroom. "I ran into town last night. See, I thought my good friend and coach was going to be coming out to do a workout with me and he didn't show up, see? Oh hell. I went in to see Andrea. It was a mistake . . ."

"Okay. Fair enough. I won't stand you up anymore. I know this is rough out here sometimes, but I thought the Andrea business was all over with, wasn't it?"

But the bathroom door was closed. In the shower Cassidy crooned off-key: *"an' all of us here are just more than contented. . . to be livin' and dyin' in three-quarter time . . ."*

Cassidy was still in a good mood as they drove into town. Denton switched on the windshield wipers as they hit a mild shower. The intensity of the rains had waned lately.

"Now, if you'll settle back," Denton said, "I'll give you a rundown on the news. It's short, and not very pleasant."

Denton began telling Cassidy about the organization formed by campus athletes called Coalition of Southeastern University Athletes.

Its expressed purpose was talking, negotiating and otherwise "dealing" with the Athletic Association, Denton told him. When the group announced its formation, the media blitz that had so disrupted Dick Doobey's life at the time of the Awesome Midnight Raid returned with a vengeance. Sports writers rankled at the idea of an athlete's "union" and wanted to know how conditions could be so bad as to necessitate collective bargaining in jockdom. No one, least of all Dick Doobey, was able to provide a satisfactory answer. The athletes simply told reporters that as the writers did not live in the regime, they could hardly understand the current *zeitgeist.* More meetings were held, statements were released, Quenton Cassidy (who had apparently disappeared altogether) was eulogized as a martyred saint or damned as a self-serving rabble rouser. There had been editorial comment on some sports pages, Denton told Cassidy, "that would boggle your noodle." A progressive commentator at the *Pensacola News-Journal* suggested capital punishment for ungrateful student athletes.

While all of this was going on, Dick Doobey schemed in the heady fog of his whirlpool, aided and abetted by a bitter beehived trollop who counseled sweet revenge and moaned in false ecstasy.

"What it boils down to," Denton said, flipping the wipers off, "is they have scratched you from the list of competitors at the Southeastern Relays."

"*What?*"

"That's it. Now, please don't ask me to make any sense out of it. I am simply reporting the facts. Apparently there is no rationale behind it except, uh, you know, getting back at you."

"Are you serious about this?"

"Very."

"They are not going to let me run?"

"Nope."

"Did they say why, *for jesus godamn christ's sake?*"

"Now don't go taking it out on me. I'm just telling you what Cornwall told me. For what it's worth, he doesn't like it any more than you. He didn't even know at first how they found out you were running in the thing. Then he figured Hairlepp or one of the guys at the *Sun* went running to Doobey when they got the advance lists of competitors. You know how objective the old fourth estate is when it comes to sports. Anyway, Prigman himself apparently has authorized a policy that says Quenton Cassidy will not be permitted to compete on the Southeastern University tartan 'come hell or high water."

"My lord in heaven." Cassidy sat looking miserable out the window at the wet fields. "Can they *do* this?"

"Who knows? They're doing it. I asked my lawyer friend, Jerry Schackow, what he thought about it, but he said he couldn't tell without doing some research. He said it presents an interesting question."

"Swell."

"Meanwhile, not to worry. Training goes full bore. I'm going to start coming out in the afternoons more often to keep tabs on your interval work. You concentrate on the running and let me worry about getting you onto the track."

But Cassidy was despondent. He sat with arms folded, shaking his head in disbelief as he watched the fields and scrub forests pass. They finally reached Art's Steakhouse at the edge of town. Denton slapped him on the knee jovially.

"All right now, let's get us some dinner and try to think pleasant thoughts. I might even have an Irish whiskey myself."

"I wouldn't recommend it," Cassidy said glumly. "It seems to conjure up evil humors."

Bruce Denton rarely disclosed all he knew at one time. With Cassidy he preferred to let important information come in dribbles, as if by accident, counting on the act of discovery to serve as sauce for the meat of knowledge. He knew intuitively that such intelligence, invested with self-discovery, retained hard lines in a sometimes blurry world.

But as to his courageous attempt to intervene with higher authority—no less than Old Man Prigman himself—he chose to say nothing at all. Not that he was embarrassed by the comic futility of his effort; but he now realized the true nature of his adversary and decided to keep his own counsel while considering new tactics. He schemed with the controlled joy and abandon of a supposedly reformed street fighter suddenly finding himself in a brawl not of his own making.

He had gained his audience with Prigman in a very practical manner: He made himself an extremely good-natured pest. He sat around the waiting room reading old copies of *Florida Rancher*, grinning cheerfully at Roberta, cracking his gum like a blissful field hand. The secretary, who liked her office uncluttered could not handle it; when she typed three errors in the same sentence in an obsequious letter to the governor, she calmly got up from her desk, marched into the inner sanctum and pleasantly demanded action. Once in the door, Denton (had he not known better) might have thought Steven C. Prigman had been sitting around for hours in delightfully sweaty anticipation of his arrival.

"Bruce Denton!" Prigman wrung his hand heartily, "Now this is a surprise!"

"How do you do, sir?" Denton smiled despite himself. Why can't they deal with this man, he thought.

"I hope you received my telegram after your wonderful victory."

"Oh, yes sir, it was one of the first to arrive," Denton lied happily. This was going to be easier than he thought.

"Fine, fine. You know, I've been meaning to have you and Jennifer over for dinner one night, but . . . this job!" He tossed his hands, a man who could only hope those folks he truly liked could understand why he had such scant time for them. Denton wondered who the hell Jennifer was.

"Of course, sir, I know how terribly busy you must be, so I wouldn't presume upon your time unless . . ."

"No problem! No problem at all, my boy. I have all the time you need." To prove as much, he glanced nervously at his watch. "So, what is it I can do for you?"

"Well sir, it concerns a young man named Quenton Cassidy . . ."

Prigman's faced drooped so noticeably that Denton stopped, surprised. So Prigman was in on it.

"Oh," said the old man quietly, settling back in his chair.

"Yes sir. I understand that he is not being allowed to participate in the Southeastern Relays next month and . . ." Prigman squirmed in his chair, an adolescent movement, full of irritation and not at all in character.

"Might I inquire," he interrupted Denton, "As to the reason for your personal concern in this matter?" He had shifted, in the subtle manner of southerners of his species, from diplomacy to advocacy, disguising the maneuver with such sincerity and deference as to leave the object of his charm, whether hostile witness or cautious subordinate, unsuspecting until it was too late.

"Well sir, Mr. Cassidy is a friend of mine. I have been helping him with his training for some time now, and I feel he might be an outstanding competitor, perhaps even of Olympic caliber, given the right opportunities. I can't understand what possible reason there might be—and I know about the recent, uh, difficulties—possible reason that is, for keeping him out of the upcoming . . ."

"Now Bruce—may I call you Bruce?—this whole affair has been extremely unfortunate for everyone concerned. Extremely unfortunate. But I'm sure that you, being an athlete yourself, must understand that insubordination must be dealt with firmly. Now I know some mistakes have been made—on both sides—but in the final analysis, rules are rules. Perhaps your sport is somewhat different, being individual and all, but on the playing field there must be a supreme commander, a man who must make life or death decisions right on the spot. A game can be won or lost on a split second's hesitation. There is no other way to function, my boy. If you had to gather a football team together to take a vote on every play, why there would be chaos! Anarchy! Pretty soon the cheerleaders would want a vote, too! This democracy stuff just won't cut it on the gridiron, my boy. Now in track and field, I don't know . . ."

"Sir, respectfully, I don't think anyone has suggested anything different. If someone had taken the time to talk with Mr. Cassidy, they would have seen he was not advocating, nor anyone else who signed the petitions, anything other than stopping petty harassment and invasion of privacy of the athletes . . ."

"It's all a matter of discipline! Following orders! Dick Doobey may not have been right all the time, but he was still Dick Doobey! The general. He gave orders. And then what happened? *Petitions!*" He said it as if pronouncing the name of some loathsome disease that had just claimed a loved one.

"I suppose," said Denton very quietly, "that I just don't happen to subscribe to the militaristic sports metaphor. I don't believe that a football field or a basketball court are battlefields, except to the most simplistic and unenlightened observers. Even granting the analogy, I don't think a general at war would go out and order his army to eat shit just for the hell of it. Sir."

Denton had a vague notion he was no longer being listened to. *Sports and religion in the deep South,* he thought. When his last remark got no discernible response, he knew his time was up. Prigman was concerning himself with the lighting of a huge cigar.

"Well," the old man said at last, turning slightly to the side so as to look out his window across the windswept plaza, "at any rate, such insubordination and dissension cannot be tolerated among athletes. You have no idea the damage this whole affair has caused, not just to team morale, but to this university. I'm speaking in terms of our image among the people of the state of Florida. No idea."

Denton stood before the giant desk top, looking across at the gray, dapper old politico behind the desk. He had thought that surely sweet reason could be brought to bear, that somewhere an appeal might be fairly heard. But then, Denton was unencumbered by the knowledge of Steven C. Prigman's illustrious career as a jurist, and therefore was not prepared to meet an intellect capable of operating almost wholly in a bygone century.

"Sir, Quenton Cassidy has represented this institution honorably and well. He has been the Southeastern Conference mile champion for two years and the captain of his team. He holds numerous school records. He has a chance to truly excel now, and keeping him out of this track meet can serve no reasonable purpose whatsoever except . . ."

"I take issue with that," said Prigman, exhaling aromatic blue smoke. "You say that the boy might become a real blue chipper, eh?"

"Well, we don't use that term in running, but yes, he might very well become . . ."

"Well, *he shall not do so using the facilities of this university.*" Very final sounding, this last.

"I was going to say: 'except possibly for revenge of some kind,'" Denton said sadly.

"Mmmm." Prigman was shuffling papers on his desk, impatiently. Denton started for the door. "Your committee chairman, Dr. Branum," Prigman said suddenly.

"Yes sir?" Prigman was looking away from him, as if distracted by something out the window.

"Dr. Branum is very anxious for you to finish that dissertation quarter after next. You wouldn't want to get too involved in other matters and let that work slide, would you?" Denton considered simply walking out, but decided to stop. *All right little man, have it your way. But I'm going to go to school on you now,* he thought. With a crooked smile he turned back to Prigman.

"No sir! I guess I'd better keep my nose to the old salt mine."

"Fine, fine." Prigman was re-lighting his cigar, his mind obviously already on other treachery.

Denton thought: My lord in heaven.

32. The Interval Workout

An interval workout," Cassidy once explained to a sports writer, "is the modern distance runner's equivalent of the once popular Iron Maiden, a device as you know used by ancient Truth Seekers."

Although overdistance laid the foundation, intervals made the runner racing mean. Quenton Cassidy liked them. Others preferred bamboo splinters under their nails. Cassidy figured that a natural affinity for interval work was the difference between those who liked to race and those who liked to train. And there is a difference. Racers express little enchantment with training.

An interval workout is simply a series of fast runs of a specified distance in a specified time with a specified rest. The variables are limited only by the imagination of the coach and the physical limitations quickly apparent in his athletes (it is one thing to write "10 quarters in 58 seconds with a 220 jog" and quite another to carry out those instructions). While a ten-mile overdistance run might be generally thought of as a pleasant diversion, very few of Cassidy's teammates thought of intervals as anything but a grueling ordeal, satisfying at best, horrifying at worst. It was precisely the kind of training, he knew, that tempered the body for racing. Though the distance runner is constantly striving for aerobic efficiency, the race itself is primarily an anaerobic experience. Everyone, the winner in his painful glory as well as the loser many seconds behind in his equally painful anonymity, suffers the physical bankruptcy of total oxygen debt. And since interval training is usually sharp enough to bring the runner to grips with oxygen debt very quickly in the workout, he learns to deal with the debilitating fatigue from the first repetition on. Other sports use an abbreviated form of interval training

called "wind sprints," but where football and basketball players run 30 or 40 yards and take several minutes rest between
each, the miler will run 220 yards, 440 yards, a half-mile or
even three-quarters of a mile at a time. Each second of his
minute or two-minute rest period is sweeter than life.

It was little wonder Bruce Denton took more interest in
Cassidy's interval training than in anything else that made up
his 140 miles a week. In the beginning of March, Denton
began to come to the cabin on interval days, many times
spending the night; after running early with Cassidy in the
morning, he would drive directly to his lab. If such a program
had a deleterious effect on his marriage, he never mentioned
it to Cassidy.

"I hope you listened to me and took an easy day yesterday," Denton said as they jogged to the field.

"Okay, consider me psyched out. What's the program?"

"Twenty quarters in sets of five, 110 jog between the
quarters, 440 jog between the sets, 62 to 63 second effort but
no watch as usual. That's it. For now."

Cassidy was surprised. It was a tough workout, but nothing he had not done many times before. Denton had been
talking ominously about this one for days, and now the
runner actually felt a little let down. With Denton he never
knew what to expect. When, weeks earlier he had instructed
Cassidy to let his hair grow and not to shave, Cassidy made it
a point not to act surprised. He knew it had something to do
with getting into the meet, but he also knew that Denton was
not about to tell him any more. If he had wanted Cassidy to
know, he would have told him already. Now the sunbleached
curls were around his ears and his chin had sprouted, of all
things, a reddish beard which Cassidy was now becoming
rather fond of. He pictured himself a gaunt viking.

When they got to the field, Cassidy removed his shoes and
joined Denton in some striders to loosen up. It was a glori-
ously clear, warm day and soon the shirtless runners were
wringing wet with perspiration. Although he knew few runners who did so, Cassidy loved training barefooted. Denton
considered it an aberration, but since it seemed to cause no
complications, he tolerated the practice.

There had been, in fact, a few world class runners who competed barefoot on the track and seemed no worse for it; and then there was Abebe Bikila who, incredibly, ran the 26-plus miles of the marathon barefooted at the Rome Olympics, winning easily. There were arguments pro and con about whether it could be helpful in training or racing, but Cassidy just did it because he liked it. It allowed him to be closer to the grass, the soil, closer to the deepest hidden yearning of the runner: *to fly naked through the primal forest, to run through the jungle.*

They began. The first two or three always seemed somehow especially bad. Actually that was misleading. They seemed sluggish because the body was shocked by such a sudden demand for sustained speed. The heart rate shot up to the hummingbird levels it would have to maintain for a long time. The legs became prematurely heavy, and the central nervous system sent up the message that such punishment could not be endured much longer. But the central nervous system is overridden, of course, the runner knowing far better by now than his own synapses what his body can and cannot be expected to do. The runner deals nearly daily in such absolutes of physical limitations that the non-runner confronts only in dire situations. Fleeing from an armed killer or deadly animal, a layman will soon find the frightening limits that even stark terror will not compromise. The runner knows such boundaries like he knows the sidewalks of his hometown.

After the shock of the first several quarters, Cassidy settled into the pleasant, nearly comfortable rhythm of the workout, where each interval, though difficult, felt very much like the one before and the one to follow. After they finished the first set of five, the quarter-mile jog prescribed by Denton seemed almost too luxuriously long. During this time, once he had recovered his breath somewhat, Cassidy made a few remarks and generally tried to engage Denton in conversation; the older runner demurred, jogged on in what Cassidy thought a rather grim manner. They began the second set.

Round and round the field they went, each repetition so much like the one before they had to count out loud lest they forget how many they had done; Denton, the true obsessive compulsive, would assume they had done three rather than four and they would take a chance on doing an extra one. Cassidy, therefore, paid close attention to the tally. The only difference between one and the next was the slight increase in lactic acid in the lifting muscles on the top of the thigh that made each a little more difficult and started hurting earlier in the sprint. Otherwise, it was almost as easy to drift into the near neutral mental state as it was on their long distance runs. Denton was a perfect training partner; the pace did not vary more than a half a second from one to the next.

In the third set Cassidy felt as though Denton were picking up the pace, though it was unlikely. Becoming tired now, it simply required more effort to keep up the same speed. A miler, whose pace in a race was quite a bit faster than 63 seconds, could get a lot out of such a workout. The key was not how fast he could run, but how fast he could run while tired.

Cassidy did not allow himself to think of racing pace, for these 63 second quarter miles required so much effort it would have been heartbreaking to think how much faster a pace was required in an actual race. There were too many other factors: rest, a faster surface, and more importantly the incredible psych he would build up prior to running. Such comparisons were not helpful and were dismissed quickly. In training it was best to think about training. Circling this little field 12 miles from Kernsville on a Saturday afternoon, a race seemed an exotic and glamorous prospect indeed.

Number 14 was especially poignant. Finishing it, Cassidy rasped: "Eeeow, that one hurt!"

"Little. Fast." Denton gasped the words. Occasionally during a repetition one of them would let his mind wander to a race, long since run, and as the old memories seeped in, the pace would inch up as adrenalin began surging involuntarily through the system. The other runner would respond and soon they would be flying around the worn path, racing different phantoms from the past. The price for such a lapse was steep. They would begin the next repetition still out of breath.

As badly as he felt at the end of the third set, by the time they finished jogging their quarter, he was recovered. Denton's training usually called for very short recovery periods and Cassidy had been amazed how he responded to the tiny snippets of rest. Recovery was the key; the faster one recovered, the faster he could race. "A race," Denton would say, is all go and no blow. So why practice resting?"

The last set felt very much like the one before and when, at last, they finished number 20, Cassidy let out a whoop. They had been running very hard for an hour. He looked over at Denton, expecting to see the happy relief that follows a hard workout, but Denton jogged on grimly.

"What now?" Cassidy asked cheerfully, thinking they would perhaps finish with some striders or a mile warmdown.

"Another twenty." Even though he said it seriously, Cassidy had to smile. After they did a few more strides and Denton did not dispel the grimness of his pronouncement, Cassidy knew he was serious. This, he thought, is a dirty trick.

And they began it all again. In their minds they took up each set separately, as if it were all they had to do. Five little quarter mile circuits to be conquered, a mile and a quarter of hard running interspersed with those nearly cruel bits of rest, each quarter becoming in its own way a milestone, a feared and adamant obstacle that had to be dominated and put away so that its brother, now looming, could be faced. The sun was soon at tree level, splashing much of the field with dark cool shadows from the surrounding oaks. But for the desperate nature of their struggle, it would have been a remarkably pleasant scene; to the runners, however, it might just as well have been sleeting, so fierce was their attention to their toil.

Although as they finished the second set his legs were merely numb, Cassidy's arms and shoulders ached. When on occasion he slipped out of the trance to look at Denton, he saw no sign of unusual fatigue at all. This is how he puts the fear of god into them, he thought, he just keeps going and going like this.

They had both long since stopped speaking except to call out the number of the repetition as they finished, both of them gasping finally: "Twenty!"

The trees were now steeping in the beautiful dusty pink orange glow of sundown, the color of ripe mangoes filling the sky behind dark oaks. They jogged on, saying nothing; their deep hearty gasps echoed across the field. It did not really dawn on Cassidy until they were halfway around the field. By this time their breathing was getting back to normal, but they were still in considerable distress.

"Bruce, you're not going to . . . I mean, this is . . ." His voice faltered, weak with self-pity and resignation.

"Twenty more, Cass."

They jogged on quietly. Cassidy felt close to tears, and with no shame about it.

"Bruce. Sixty quarters, Bruce. You can't be serious. Nobody recommends that kind of stuff anymore. Arthur Lydiard..."

"Screw Arthur Lydiard. Quenton, this is where you find out. This is the time and place. All the rest is window dressing."

"I don't know if I can do it."

"Quenton," he smiled for the first time all day, "you can do very nearly anything. Haven't you figured that out yet?"

"Yeah."

"Look, runners deal in discomfort. After you get past a certain point, that's all there really is. There is no finesse here. I know you can do this thing because I once did it myself; when it was over I knew some very important things."

"That you're a lunatic?"

"Maybe. Maybe we all are. But I expect you'll find out in your own way. That's why I'm going to let you do them by yourself, just the way people do everything that's important. You can sluff off if you want, but by god, you'll sure as hell know when you're doing it, won't you?"

"I suppose," he said glumly.

"I'm going back to the cabin. I'll be back about the time you're finishing up."

"Swell."

He began the melancholy ritual as night was falling. After the first five he was running by the soft glow of a huge clear moon. Cassidy thought: Bruce thinks of everything.

Then he sought out the mental neutrality that is the refuge, the contained wan comfort of the runner. He grooved his mind upon the thin platinum rail of his task, a line that stretched out in front of him and disappeared into the gloom, further than he could contemplate all at once, even if he had the desire to, which he did not. When his trance broke and a word or phrase popped into his mind, his dizzy mind played with it like seals with a beach ball, in a disturbing, jibberishly mad way, the way your mind acts in the druggy twilight before sleep. In a very controlled, systematic way, he knew how much he was suffering; a break in his concentration would inevitably end in a welling up of self-pity.

He was, in a manner of speaking, accustomed to this distress. In the same manner a boxer is "accustomed" to being struck; but the familiarity of experience in no way lessens the blow or mitigates its physiological effects, it merely provides the competitor with a backdrop against which his current trial may be played, gives him a certain serenity and coolness in the face of otherwise staggeringly overwhelming stimuli, allows dispassionate insight where otherwise there would be only a rush of panic. In a hail of killing blows, the fighter's quiet center of logic, schooled in brutality, will be calmly theorizing: We are hurt pretty badly. If we do not cover up and take up the slack we will soon be unconscious.

Not that this quiet center of logic particularly fears unconsciousness (indeed, how welcome it might seem at times!), but it knows that one does not win while unconscious. In the same way, no highly trained runner slacks off because he fears the pain, but because the quiet center of logic tells him he will win nothing if he runs himself to a standstill.

All of this availed Quenton Cassidy not at all. His deeply ingrained conditioning and his mahogany hard legs merely allowed him to push himself that much more. He had the mental ability to literally run himself right into the ground like Black Sambo's tiger. He knew that Bruce Denton expected him to do exactly that, and, just as each repetition made the next seem more and more impossible, he knew that without question he *would* do it. There was no refuge in injury, his body could not be injured in this way. There was no refuge in mercy, there was nothing to forgive and no one to issue dispensation. And at last he saw: There was no refuge in cowardice, because he was not afraid. There was no alternative, it just had to be *done*.

He finished number seven, somehow running it too hard, which caused him to take deep and painful gasps and to spend a few seconds bent over grasping his knees before beginning his weak jog on to number eight (in his mind number three, and after that only two to go—beyond that he did not think). It was becoming harder and harder to get his breathing anywhere near normal in the 110 yard rest jog; he was starting the next interval gasping as if he had not stopped at all. Into the next he charged, down the straight, around the turn, by a pine tree slashed in half by lightning (that to him meant only the halfway point), into the last turn and then the last fifty yards of straightaway, legs, arms, shoulders, jawbone, ears, chest, fingers, all battling the strained numb pain of the lactic acid, all striving for that normality of motion that would preserve—should heaven and hell fall into each other in a cosmic swirl—the integrity of the stride. Let others flail; the runner runs truly to the end.

He finished and rasped: Eight. You. Bastard.

But the ninth took special revenge, reduced him to such a level that he had to spend several seconds holding his knees and sucking in sweet but maddeningly unsatisfying air. When he finally trotted on, he looked up at the bright clear stars and his eyes welled, mixed with the hot sweat of his face, tears ran down to the spittle around his mouth and chin, and he felt quite literally that he was melting, turning to human slush as he jogged along. Only when he started a repetition did he become hard, solid once more.

His mind had now taken up a melody, *Für Elise*, and played it constantly without apparent pattern except that as each new quarter mile began, so did his fragment of Beethoven; whereas the stars were cold specks of illuminated space dust to him, those haunting notes reassured that there were at least others in the universe capable of understanding. Each new quarter now began in a kind of physical sorrow and ended in nothing less than spiritual despair. He remembered suddenly the one marathon he had run. On the 23rd mile he had looked around and discovered that everything looked unfamiliar.

Convinced he was lost, he ran on like a forlorn child, blubbering and wailing. When he finished the race in 2:33 he saw he had been on the right course after all. But he still couldn't keep from weeping; he just didn't know why any longer.

After his fifteenth quarter he would have had to think for a moment to recall his own name. But now he had his full quarter mile of rest, that he took in mincing little steps, savoring every instant. His mind came out of neutral, reveled in giddiness. He was incredibly thirsty; his tongue was stuck to the roof of his mouth and he no longer had to spit out the thick white fluffs of congealed saliva; there was none. He dared not think of water, or of the first beer. Parched to the marrow, wobbly, near mad, he took his tiny jogging steps and waxed (so he thought) poetic:

> *Somewhere they fox trot madly*
> *While in lunar shadows sadly*
> *I keep pace with crickets gladly*
> *And Moon rises with my bile*

Lord godamighty he told himself, launching into number sixteen (in his mind number one). *Für Elise* cranked up again and he wished it would go away. He hardly felt anything at all now. He hardly cared. As he was putting seventeen away, *Für Elise* degenerated into a kind of steam calliope gone haywire. Misplaced notes made what had been haunting ugly, what had been precise and logical mad and horrifying. As if to keep pace with the crumbling music, his form occasionally broke and an elbow would flap out wildly, a knee would catch its brother instead of sliding by. Poor Elise, he thought. Poor everyone.

Eighteen was a shambles. Nineteen required all his effort to keep the pace from slipping down to a stumble. It had fallen off badly during the last few sets, but there was nothing to be done about it. When he finished the nineteenth, he let out a slight, wild, but oddly unjoyous whoop. He was vaguely aware that Denton had returned, but it quickly slipped his mind. His mind was devoid of any thought save finishing the last one.

On the last he simply sprinted away the life in him. The thin sliver of monorail that had once stretched out to forever now dropped off into a sheer abyss just over the horizon. Once more down the straight, around the far turn, past the pathetic half-pine, into the last turn, flailing now a little, and (all slow motion now), feeling each step of the last fifty yards until it was over.

He staggered about, tightly holding the knees, eyes clenched shut, painfully, for the tears could not get out, while the sweat seemed to seep in easily. Denton stood beside and held him steady, with a gentleness of a medic treating a newly wounded. And, like a casualty, Cassidy seemed not to notice him.

Denton walked him back slowly, talking to him quietly all the way. Cassidy, still deep in his anguish, said nothing. Denton fed him from the blender, let him drink all the liquids he wanted, then gently put him to bed.

"Quenton, you . . ."

"I know," Cassidy said. His eyes were still moist; he turned away. "But it is a very hard thing to have to know."

Denton nodded, smiled at him as he swatted him once on the fanny (the muscles there were quivering, he thought, *just like it was for me*) and left. Cassidy was in a deep sleep by the time Denton was out the door.

Cassidy awoke only once during the night, filled the toilet with bloody urine (something Denton told him might happen) and went back to bed. He slept seventeen hours altogether and when he awoke at last, the runner, paragon of fitness and efficient mobility, *this* runner at least, had trouble getting around. He went back to bed.

33. Orchids

I must have human contact," he told Denton. "And I'm not talking about your standard Newberry barmaid who mixes better metaphors than drinks."

"Chasing it," Denton said, "is more of a pastime than a runner can handle, generally speaking."

"Well, if you don't get me out of here among people who talk with recognized syntax, I'm liable to do something rash, like set fire to your little dream retreat and hop a freight train."

And that is exactly how Cassidy found himself at, of all things, a cocktail party, beginning to admit to himself a certain degree of social ineptitude of the variety that usually culminates with your pants cuff inexplicably in someone's lemon meringue pie. Yet there it was: People clearly made him nervous.

Denton had abandoned him early in the evening—intentionally he now suspected—and he had struggled through several conversations with guests who, though sincere and intelligent enough, gave off a carefully cultivated aura of university town bohemianism. Though they would surely rise in the morning, gargle, and proceed to their offices to fill teeth, draw wills, grade papers and otherwise keep the cogs of the republic whirring away, still they might at any moment (given the appropriate argument) grab up a thirty-aught-six and a slab of jerky and take to the hills to fight the good fight. Most of it struck him as bizarre, and at the same time he was observing all of it, he was worrying about the fact that even after several days of light workouts, he still had not recovered fully from his interval ordeal.

And he tired quickly of this standard party fare that goes: "You run 20 *miles*? Without *stopping*? I couldn't run 20 *feet* har har har har . . ." He would have to bite his tongue to keep from saying that it had been real humorous the first four thousand times he heard it. He had forgotten what it was like, this thing with the stupid jokes. And too there were the

189

questions: What did he eat? Did he believe in isometrics?
Isotonics? Ice and heat? How about aerobics, est, ESP STP?
What did he have to say about yoga, yogurt, Yogi Berra? What
was his pulse rate, his blood pressure, his time for the 100-yard
dash? What was the secret, they wanted to know; in a thousand different ways they wanted to know *The Secret*. And not
one of them was prepared, truly prepared to believe that it
had not so much to do with chemicals and zippy mental tricks
as with that most unprofound and sometimes heart-rending
process of removing, molecule by molecule, the very tough
rubber that comprised the bottoms of his training shoes. The
Trial of Miles; Miles of Trials. How could they be expected to
understand that?

When he finally heard the one about how "I couldn't *drive*
as far as you *run*" he thought: *death on a plate*. Fleeing to the
kitchen he was fishing around in the ice tub for a non-diet
beer when he noticed that the dark-haired girl had followed
him in. She stood with one fist on her hip, watching him with
faint amusement, but in a nice way, her head cocked curi-
ously, and this: a flash of white carnivorous teeth against her
dark face. I'm not up to this, he told himself.

He was fumbling around in the tub a little more than was
called for and since he figured she was waiting for him to get
his ass out of the way, he dived in with both hands and finally
speared a normal beer. His hands were stiff and numb from
the ice.

"Good old fattening kind," he said lamely (oh aren't we
just the conversationalist?). He heh-hehed good naturedly,
wondering when he had become a total moron, and was
about to make his hasty escape when she laughed. It was a
remarkably unaffected laugh, throaty-real. It stopped him
pretty quick.

"You wer ot having much fun out there," she said. It
was a statement, not a question. Then he noticed she already
had a drink in her hand.

"I suppose not. Shows, huh?" He cracked the beer,
dropped the tab into the ice, took a manly slug and stuck his
left hand into his back pocket to get it warm. He rocked back
on his heels, looking about the kitchen as if truly absorbed by
its contents. Maybe she's never seen anyone talk to the
cookware, he thought.

"Would you like to see the orchids in the back yard?" she asked.

"Orchids? There are orchids in the back yard?"

"No," she laughed, "not a one. Come on." She took him by the hand and led him back through the living room and out the sliding glass doors. There were no orchids. They sat on the far side of the pool on a child's swing set and listened to the noise of the party, that now seemed somehow distant, faintly ludicrous. Cassidy wondered at first why it seemed so nostalgic, but then remembered: There were grownup parties long ago, and I sat in swing sets and listened to them.

She was a psychology instructor, working on her PhD and she did not in the least want to talk about it. He judged her to be 24 or 25, not as pretty as Andrea, but with her irony-ridden eyes and the amusement obvious in her forehead and eyebrows she might at any moment—he figured—have him sitting back on his haunches more or less barking like a seal. Maybe I'm too easy, he thought.

She was clearly a woman who could take care of herself and for some reason that rattled him.

"You must not go to parties much. At least I've never seen you around before," she said. Cassidy was drawing designs in the frost on his beer can.

"No, I suppose not. When you get right down to it, I don't really do much of anything."

"Except your running."

"Yes, except that."

"Doesn't sound very interesting."

"Oh hey," he sat up straight, "it's not. Take my word for it." Deftly he watched her reaction and then in almost perfect sync repeated her next question right along with her:

"Then why do you (I) do it?"

She remained unflustered however, laughed, and waited politely for his response.

"I wish there were some very clever, eminently acceptable answer to that. It's like when people ask me what I think about when I'm running. I usually say something like 'quantum mechanics.' Sometimes I say music."

"Music?"

"It's as good as any. Sometimes I *do* think about music. Actually when you're training you can think about anything you want, just about. But in a race, everyone thinks about the same thing."

"Which is?"

"The race, oddly enough."

"And what do you tell people who keep insisting on knowing why you do it?"

"I say it keeps me regular. Or I say I'm going out for the Olympics; they can sort of understand that since it's on the teevee."

"You say it as if it were a joke."

"Oh it's no joke, it's just that it's such a hard thing, such a slim chance; you have got to be so *lucky* even after you are so *good.* The odds are just against you, that's all. It's like a little kid landing the part of the carrot in his school play on nutrition, and having it go so well that his mother goes around telling everyone someday he'll win an Oscar. I mean, he might very well do it, but . . ."

"Bruce Denton did it," she offered.

"Bruce Denton got an Oscar?"

She gave him one of those one-knuckle female jobs to the deltoid that brought real tears to his eyes.

"Bruce Denton doesn't seem abnormal to you," he grunted, rubbing the spot painfully, "because he's walking around this very house munching pretzels and telling off-color jokes. But he's probably the only Olympic distance runner for a thousand miles. It is not a . . . normal thing to have one at your party, you know? It is not normal to . . . ah, never mind. It lacks perspective. And that hurt, by the way."

"Hmmm. So you spend all your time doing something admittedly boring that you have no good explanation for, and then when you go out to have a good time, you sit around looking like someone just shot your dog. Interesting."

"Think I'm a head case?"

"No doubt about it. Welcome to Rubber City." She motioned in the general direction of the party, and as if on cue there was a wild burst of laughter and suddenly a man with his shirt tails out went crawling on all fours by the sliding glass door at a startling clip. He was looking back over his shoulder and kind of slinking along. Cassidy recognized him as an opthamologist named Caldwell something who had earlier told him to "hang right on in there."

"Dr. Hodge," she said. "Coyote imitation. It's not too bad, actually. This is what's known as middle-class stoned."

Cassidy turned back, looked at her for several seconds and really couldn't think of a thing to say. It occurred to him that he was a pretty dull guy. She reached over and touched his beard. The intimacy of the gesture was incredibly soothing to him.

"I like the new look. Very Nordic. Much different from those awful crewcut pictures in the *Sun*. They must have been taken when you were a freshman. When did this come about?"

"Last few weeks. Something to do with Bruce's hair-brained scheme to get me into the Relays in two weeks. That was one of the reasons he didn't want me to come tonight. Supposedly everyone here is sworn to secrecy. Actually I think it's all a crock."

"Someone said something about it but I didn't pay much attention."

"I have been banned from competing on Southeastern University's tartan trail, now and forevermore." He held up his hands, a preacher pronouncing benediction; then he burped politely behind his hand. Four beers was about his limit now. But he was beginning to feel pretty good about the evening after all. "Dangerous rabble-rouser that I am," he added, "rabble, rabble, rabble."

"Let me ask you something," she said softly.

"Sure," he finished the can with a flourish, "anything. Anything at all." She put her hand on his knee and ran a fingernail along the ridges on the outside of his thigh. It felt to her like nothing so much as a bunch of tightly bound bridge support cables.

"Did you think I was being brash in there, about the orchids and all?" softly still.

"Uh."

"Well did you?"

His Adam's apple felt like a soggy tennis ball.

"Does it surprise you?" She leaned over to capture his downcast eyes, led him back up to look at her. "Well?"

He hated his idiotic awkwardness, his painful lack of any kind of grace. He was a cloistered monk turned loose among Manhattanites, flap-flapping around in his scrungy sandals high up in the carpeted sky, nervously sipping some strange heady cocktail, preoccupied with his own alarming armpits and responding to the simplest inquiry like this: buh dee buh dee buh dee.

"You have to try to understand," he said miserably, still watching her dark serpentine hand, "I have no moves left. You have got to try to understand how it is . . ."

"Oh," she smiled that carnivorous smile, "I will."

34. Pause . . .

For me? You shouldn't have!" Cassidy said when Denton handed over the cardboard box. It was getting close and Denton had announced it was time for brass tacks.

"You don't know how unfunny that may be. No telling what kind of fiery crap will fill the air," Denton said. But his smile indicated his real degree of concern. As Cassidy opened the box Denton thought: *He really doesn't know what he's done; his lightest day was eight miles when he sprained his ankle that time.*

"Finnish national team sweats! They're beautiful," Cassidy held up the robin's egg blue top. The blue and white flag of Finland was in miniature over the left breast.

"I'd like them back in good condition please, Seppo, as I had to trade them straight up for a pair of USA's."

"Zeppo? Zeppo?"

"Seppo, ninny. Here is your contestant's entrance pass and your number. You are listed as Seppo Kaitainen, a miler from Finland currently competing for Central Ohio Tech. Nobody knows about it but you and me and the guy I got to send in the application and fee from Ohio. Cornwall snapped you right up, Seppo! It appears you have run yourself some outstanding times this year."

"I might have known it would be good and kinky."

"Kinky hell! It's pure genius is what it is. You have no idea how much different you look from the old close-cropped anarchist of yore. You get yourself some wire rims, garble up your English a little more than usual, ask for some pickled herring, and by god the sunbitches will think you're Paavo Nurmi."

Cassidy was holding the sweat top up to himself and trying to see himself in the window reflection.

"You honest to god think it'll work?"

"Fish tread water? Queen gotta snatch? Frog waterproof? Wild dog bay at the . . ."

195

"All right, all right. I sense a little pride of authorship here. What happens if someone catches on? Won't your man at Central Ohio Whatchermacallit get screwed over?"

"That illustrious center of higher learning doesn't exist, to my knowledge. Even if it did, there would be no one there to whom, as my counselor friend says, liability would attach. My buddy was only passing through when he mailed in the application. He is a proud resident of Illinois."

"All this to get into a godamned track meet."

"Not just any track meet, Seppo old buddy, not by a long shot. It's not every day a Finn attending an Ohio school gets to run the world record holder from New Zealand right here in north Florida. You ought to can the skepticism and thank your lucky stars I was able to bring the whole production off."

Cassidy smiled. "Hey. I appreciate it, I really do. But since I have apparently made the traveling squad, I'm going to expect Central Ohio to spring for my varsity letter."

"Say no more, Seppo, we treat our foreign athletes right," he said as he stood. "Right now I've got to go see if I can salvage what's left of my marriage. I'll be out early and we'll talk strategy."

"Mmmm." Cassidy was off someplace and Denton hoped it was not out on the track, thrashing himself through it yet another time.

"Hey . . . Hey! Leave it alone for awhile. Get some sleep; you might want to take some of that mild nerve stuff in the cabinet. Try to keep your mind off it as much as possible. You know all about this stuff." He started for the door. "Oh, there's a nondescript racing vest in the box in case you don't have one. Seppo wouldn't be racing in his national colors, it's just a plain . . ."

"Bruce, is there any . . .I mean, could there be any conceivable way I might could win this thing? Seriously, I mean?"

Denton stopped. "Hells bells, Quenton. You can put the fear of god into him, I know that. But give yourself some time. You don't have to go out and trounce the best guy in the world just because you've done some great training here. Let him pull you along to a super time." He started for the door again but stopped with his hand on the knob.

"You know those demons of yours you're always talking about? Well, Walton's got armies of them. You can see them in his eyes when he warms up, scrambling around just wailing and carrying on."

"Well," Cassidy said, standing and stretching, "I guess we just let the fiery little bastards loose and *at* each other."

Denton opened the door, looked back before leaving. "Was there ever any other way?" he said.

The next night after dinner they sat on the front porch right at dusk, sipping coffee and staring into the darkening oaks; fireflies winked in the deeper woods and a red tail hawk circled once high overhead and silently floated away to some far off haven, leaving the chilled deep blue of the sky to the earlier stars. There was an unmistakable feeling of something large having passed and something large coming: eye of hurricane.

Cassidy held his mug with both hands and moved closer to the barbecue grill, where coals glowed pale orange, and thought: the adults would sit on the porch like this while we caught fireflies and played tag on the front lawn. The older of his North Carolina cousins would grow irritable and little Quentie would be counseled not to remain so long uncaught.

Only children and dogs, it seemed, were *supposed* to run, and they all shared the sidewalks. Perhaps that accounted for Cassidy's growing sense of unreality out in the cabin. He no longer could claim his activity was an adjunct to scholastic pursuits, a schoolboy's preoccupation. He was now beyond that, but where? A professional in a field where there was no profession? The horrendously physical nature of his days and ways occasionally caused him to stir; intellectual grist of late had been confined to mind candy of the *Lord of the Rings* variety. He had begun to wonder how much of this was really necessary.

You feel like an animal? Denton had asked. Just what Eliot told Cerutty when he wanted to quit. (As if that were some kind of answer.) But there was a day, Denton said, when Cerutty had been caught in a rip-tide at Portsea, and Eliot had grabbed the old man by his white hair and just swam. He swam and swam, not going anywhere at all, just there in place, for what seemed like hours, *until the fucking ocean just gave up.*

Animal's exactly right, Denton had said, but *Jesus what an animal.*

Then Denton had looked over at him and said: let's go run.

And Quenton Cassidy, having not a thing else in the world to do, said okay. So ended the great intellectual revolt of March.

It was shortly after that Cassidy began to notice something very strange in his training: It was nearly impossible to make himself hurt. His ten miles in the morning left him only flushed and hungry; in the afternoon he thrashed himself through his distance run or interval workout and finished feeling somewhat itchy, as if something were up. This night he told Denton about this strange sensation of invulnerability. Cassidy admitted to being very puzzled.

But the Olympian just settled back against the porch step, sipped on his coffee and smiled warmly at the miler.

"How nice," he said, "for you to have arrived right on time."

Now, within 48 hours, he would be lacing very tightly those thin kangaroo skin slippers with pin spikes and he would attempt to overtake the most locomotively efficient *homo sapiens* to yet trod the earth, at the distance of one mile, that is. Among all the swift messengers of the Hellenistic era, among the Masai warriors of the plains of Africa who laughingly run game to ground, among the mustachioed old professional runners of the lunatic marathon dance age who ran for large purses, among all these there was not one who even approached this modern, black-suited New Zealander; the first human to run faster—not than four minutes—but than three minutes and fifty seconds, a barrier without quite the symmetrical poetry for mankind perhaps, but one with such a terrible message for other runners—those who knew best how to interpret such messages—that they wobbled. Some gave up in despair, some sought refuge in other events. Liquori, it was said, went to 5000 meters.

Bruce Denton, sipping his coffee quietly, knew well the carnivorous nature of prerace fears. He sought to relieve what he felt was an ominous silence. The one thing he did not yet know about the miler was his control. Denton feared that during the next few hours the runner, like an aging automobile on a country road, might simply rattle himself to pieces.

"There was the Englishman Oates," he said, "on an expedition to one of the poles, I forget which. Out of supplies and fuel, the men were sitting around in a tent while a deadly blizzard raged and held rescue teams at bay. Several, I believe, had already frozen to death. Oates, tiring of it all, rose and announced: 'I'm going outside. I may be some time.'"

Cassidy smiled over the top of his mug, the coffee now going lukewarm in the chill of the evening, and counted that as the moment he most loved Bruce Denton.

"It's all right, Bruce," he said. "Really. It's all right."

35. The Orb

Saying something about walking off his macaroni and cheese, Cassidy escaped to the evening. There was a bit of marital uneasiness in the air, a strain that he may have had more than a little to do with, but for now all he could think of was closing the glistening, seamless orb, receptacle of his fiercest yearning.

In the afternoon they had gone to a deserted high school track for the last session, a nearly lightheaded tune-up; for the first time in months he was completely rested and strong and when Denton walked over and held up the watch grimly it said: 24.8. That was the fourth and final 220. Denton shook his head disgustedly.

"I couldn't help it," Cassidy said.

"Okay," Denton replied; he would have liked to have been able to show a little genuine anger at such a reckless display, but he knew how it felt and so remained quiet as they jogged a final slow mile around the battered old asphalt track.

During dinner there was none of the usual banter and Jeannie, after trying several times to relieve the tension, finally clammed up, allowing everyone to stew in the awful clink clank, chomp chomp of non-conversing diners who, when the pressure is on, cannot seem to keep their silverware and their own mastication under control. It was nerve-wracking for Denton and his wife, but Cassidy hardly noticed.

Now he was walking quickly, inexorably, towards the place he would complete the orb, set it gently adrift and leave it hard and shining until it was time.

It was one of the early balmy spring evenings when no one wanted to go inside. The campus was bustling; the lighted tennis courts were full and other players sat around waiting patiently, talking and laughing. Groups of three or four made their way to the nearer taverns, loaded cars roared to and fro, cyclists whirred by like mechanical butterflies, with books and Italian sandwiches strapped onto luggage racks.

It was the kind of scene Cassidy would have reveled in before, but the roar was now a tiny faraway buzz, growing by the minute, and as he walked on consumed by it, he was aware only that scenery was moving by as always, steadily and without apparent effort. He walked with the light, brisk, slightly pigeon-toed gait of an athlete, and though he walked very quickly, his breath would not have troubled the smallest candle. He took in even, deep measures of cool air with mechanical regularity, disinterestedly feeling inside his chest the huge heart muscle thumping its slow liquid drumbeat. His legs coiled and uncoiled with rhythm; sacks of anacondas. That part of it was done as well as he could humanly do it. Now he would see to the rest. He had made this pilgrimage many times before and though he would probably do so many times again, he never quite got over the eerie feeling that each time could be the last. Soon he was on the far side of campus where there were few dormitories and hence less activity, fewer lights, and none of the happy spring weekend noise.

Moths fluttered around the single streetlight as he went through the gate, and though the rubbery smell of wintergreen and sweat was as familiar to him as the musky woodiness of his room at Doobey Hall, his heart still jumped. The usual night joggers were out, and if they cast haughty glances at this mere stroller on their turf, the stroller paid no attention. He walked clockwise around the curve to the starting post at the beginning of the first turn, and stood there a few feet behind the parabolic bend of the starting stripe. He looked around and tried to imagine, in Hollywood-style flashes, the skeletal bleachers full, the now dark klieg lights burning down, the pageantry of the multi-hued sweatsuits from a thousand schools flashing by as athletes warmed up. He would be part of that faceless panorama too, until the announcement over the loudspeaker that never failed to twist his heart around with a spurt of adrenalized fear: FIRST CALL FOR THE MILE RUN. The all-consuming roar, the overwhelming psych would begin then and would build up until he stood ready on this line, at once controlled and near lunacy, fearless and terrified, wishing for the relief of the start, the misery of the end. Anything! Just let the waiting be done with! Cassidy toed the starting line there in street clothes and was able to get some of it: A few of the runners would run back and forth in their lanes, some would jiggle their fingers, some would jump up and down (all this more nervous than therapeutic). The orange-sleeved starter would walk among them with his pistol, saying, all right gentlemen, all right. He would talk gently, trying to somehow ease it for them, hoping to prevent a false start by calming them with the soft modulation of his voice. They were not as bad as sprinters, he knew, but they were still pretty skittish. The runners would gather nervously at the starting line, taking care not to look each other in the eye.

The starter would say: "There will be two commands, gentlemen, 'take your marks' and then the gun. All right, gentlemen, stand tall. Stand tall, gentlemen." He would sound a little like an executioner.

And Cassidy stood tall there in the dark, while a cool breeze ruffled the ragged lock of hair on his forehead, knowing that for that one instant there would be a kind of calm in the midst of all that pounding, roaring furor, a moment of serene calm before an unholy storm. There would be a single instant of near disbelief that it would finally be happening in a fraction of a second; finally happening after the months, the miles, the misty mornings; finally happening after the eighth or ninth now forgotten interval along the way somewhere that broke your heart once again. He would be leaning over tensely with the rest of them while the white lights burned down on them and for an awful split-second he would feel as if his legs had no strength at all. But then his heart would nearly explode when the pistol cracked. Cassidy felt a little of that now. He took a deep breath and began walking into the first turn, counterclockwise, the way of all races.

The first lap would be lost in a flash of adrenaline and pounding hooves. They would crash into the first turn in a bunch; the technical rule was that with a one-stride lead, a runner could cut in front. As with many such rules it was honored generally by the breach; the real-life rule of the first turn is exactly this: every man for himself. He would run powerfully into this turn, Cassidy thought, just like always, and he would use his elbows if he needed to make some space. Cassidy walked the turn, trying to imagine the sudden rasping of heavy breathing, the flashing of elbows and spiked feet all around. You had to be calm in the heavy traffic, he knew, hold

back your impatience and control the panic; wait for opportunities. The first lap would be like that the whole way: fast,
scary, with no pain or serious effort. The rampaging adrenaline and pent-up energy did that. The first lap was a process
of burning it off; no one ever won a mile race on the first lap.
Cassidy walked the far, dark straightaway. On the opposite
side from the main bleachers, it was the loneliest part of the
track. This was where the race-acute senses picked up the
single calls of encouragement (usually from teammates),
sometimes the idiotic suggestion called out by those who
knew no better ("pick it up, pick it up"). There would be the
occasional giggling of moronic teeny-boppers who did not
quite know what they were laughing about. But those were
the peripheral toys of a frenzied mind; the real work of the
shining orb was monitoring the steadily droning pocketa
pocketa of a human body hurtling along at a constant fifteen
plus miles an hour. He walked through the far turn and up
the straight to the starting post. Someone would be reading
out times, probably around 57 or 58; assuming that no one
went crazy during the first quarter. You'll hear the crowd
again along here, he thought, particularly after we go through
under 60; they won't be cheering for some godamned Finn,
but you'll hear them just the same.

Whether a psychological thing or not, the second lap was
when it always hit him, either right at the post or as they
rounded the turn. The shocking enormity of the physical
effort descended on him then and he knew from there on in
it would be pretty grim business. At this point the carefully
nurtured mental toughness, tempered by hours of interval
work, would allow him to endure the shock to his system with
relative ease and race on. He would be ready for it and he
would know it was going to get far worse. He could be the
best-conditioned athlete in the world but if his mind was not
ready to accept the numbing wave at the start of the second
lap, he would not even finish, much less hope to win.

Cassidy walked through the turn, and again into the
lonely back straight. By this time he would be concentrating
on pace, not allowing himself to become frightened by the
first hint of numbness and discomfort. It wouldn't be "pain"
exactly, not at this point, but it would not be altogether
pleasant either. It was here the pace might tend to slow,

something he would have to watch, something he would damned well *prevent* if he had to. He would now go into his floating stride, the long ground-eaters, and he would think to himself: cover territory.

No one ever won a race on the second lap either but plenty of people lost them there. This would be the time for covering distance with as little effort as possible. Through the far turn and into the home straight again he tried for the feeling and thought he got it pretty well. Finally around at the starting post again he tried to get the awfulness of the start of the third lap, but could not. He had seen the drawn haunted look on his own face in mid-race photographs and still he could not get that feeling; it was contained there somewhere in the glistening orb, he knew, and would never get out. Denton was right about it, you could think about it all you want but you couldn't feel it until you were there again. He knew only that here, at the halfway point, he would be once again *in extremis*. It would flabbergast him to think (so he would do so only for an instant) that he was only half way through it. He would have run the first half-mile faster than he could run a half mile flat out in high school (1:59.2) and he would have a long way to go.

He walked into the turn of the third lap. Here the real melancholy began, when the runner might ask himself just what in the hell he was doing to himself. It was a time for the most intense concentration, the iciest resolve. It was here the leader might balk at the pain and allow the pace to lag, here that positions shifted; those whose conditioning was not competitive would settle to the back of the pack to hang on, the kickers would move up like vultures to their vantage points at the shoulders of the front runners. It was a long, cruel lap with no distinguishing feature save the fact that it had to be run. Every miler knows, in the way a sailor knows the middle of the ocean, that it is not the first lap but the third that is farthest from the finish line. Races are won or lost here, records broken or forfeited to history, careers made or ended. The third lap was a microcosm not of life, but of the Bad Times, the times to be gotten through, the no-toys-at-Christmas, sittin'-at-the-bus-station-at-midnight blues times to look back on and, however weakly, laugh at if you can. The third lap was to be endured and endured and endured.

Cassidy reached the home straight again, thinking: No matter how bad it is, I can't let it lag here, whatever the cost. If I have to lead the whole mothering thing, I can't let it lag here. Then he was walking back by the post for what would be the gun lap. As soon as the pistol cracked, he would feel a tingling on the back of his neck and the adrenaline would shoot through his system again. A quarter of a mile to go and he would become a competitive athlete again, looking around to size up the situation, leaning a little into his stride and once again, even through the numbing haze then taking hold of his body, feeling pride in his strength.

Cassidy walked through the turn, pumping his arms a little, thinking of the nervous crowd noises as the pace began to pick up. Perhaps there would be only a small group left in it now; three, four maybe. But they would all have ambitions; no one ever ran down the back straight of the gun lap with the leaders without thinking he had a shot at it. On Cassidy walked along the lonely straight imagining the bristling speed as the pace heated up; there would be some last second evaluations, some positioning and re-positioning, and then finally the kicks, one by one or all at once, blasting away for the tightly drawn yarn across the finish line. Into the turn with only a 330 to go, everyone would be into it by then, everyone still in contention. Walton was known to kick from more than a 440 out, so surely his hand would be on the table. Coming out of the final turn just at the place Landy turned to look for the elusive Bannister, Cassidy walked into the final 110 straight and thought: Here, as they say, it will all be over but the shouting; you will fight the inclination to lean backwards, fight to keep the integrity of the stride, not let overeager limbs flail around trying to get more speed, just run your best stride like you have trained ten thousand miles to do and don't for god's sake let up here until the post is behind you. The die would be cast here, and no praying or cheering or cajoling or whimpering would change it. He had lost in this final straight before, but not as much as he had won here; neither held much in the way of fear or surprise once you were there. Such matters, as Denton had often said, were settled much earlier: weeks, months, years before, they were settled on the training fields, on the ten-mile courses, on the morning workout missed here or made up there. Other than maintaining and leaning at the tape, Denton had told him, there is not much you can do about it. Heart has nothing to do with it. In the final straight, *everyone* has heart.

Cassidy walked on past the finish line, across which someone would hold the taut yarn and blink as the runners flashed by. It was still more than 24 hours away, but standing there in the calm anonymous night five yards past the familiar white post, Quenton Cassidy knew at that instant the depth of his frenzied yearning to feel the soft white strand weaken and separate against his heaving chest.

The demons were in control; it no longer made him afraid.

36. The Race

The noise from the stadium carried out here but Cassidy didn't pay much attention. He liked doing most of the warmup ritual out on the cross-country course where he could think. The routine itself was automatic: four miles easy; then long, flowing striders, another mile easy, faster striders, then on with the spikes, some sprints on the track, then jog until time. It was the roar in his head he had to fight.

It had to be contained, suppressed, released only in that slow crescendo of calculated frenzy that would crest when the pistol cracked and he unleashed it all. The orb now floated gently in his mind, glistening, peaceful, hard as spun steel. It would hold all grief, all despair, all the race-woes of a body going to the edge; it would allow him to do what he had to do until there was nothing left.

Yes, he had decided long ago it was better to get ready out here, where things were quieter, more normal, more like his everyday routine. Trying to warm up in the stadium, being close to the crowd, would make him jittery, causing the roar in his head to build in spurts, getting him there too early. It might upset the orb and when the despair descended he would have no place to put it. Or he might be in such a lunatic state as to turn the first 220 in 25 seconds out of sheer screaming hysteria. No, it was better out here, where it was quiet, where he could get ready in the same way he had done all the rest; it gave some comfort, this last bit of quietude.

He jogged slowly by the married student housing area, watching little children play under the trees. It was the eerie, almost magic, post-dinner hour when time stands still for a child, when all existence floats in a cool gray bath of dying day and Order is mercifully drawn from a chaotic infinity by a mother's come-home call.

"Erica! Jeremy!" Two little figures scuttled away in the shadows. He was getting farther and farther from the stadium, but he had plenty of time. Some other runners passed in pairs and threes, but no one spoke. One nodded at Cassidy but looked puzzled. What would they be thinking about this bearded Finn with the ragged blond hair?

Would they think they recognized him from some *Track and Field News* photo?

Cassidy jogged on. It was early May warm and subtropical flowers ruled the air dizzily: the kind of evening so heavy with promise as to make him wonder if his life could ever be quite the same again as it was now, while he was so vital, so quick, so nearly immortal; while his speed and strength was such that he could be called by only a handful of men on earth. Surely there could not be that many of us walking around like this, he thought.

He felt a strange brand of nostalgia now that it was so close; a nostalgia for this moment, for this next hour. The present was so poignant he had begun to reminisce already. He thought of Michelangelo's David pondering the stone: David, too, wondering if life would ever be the same.

Quenton Cassidy could be forgiven the solemnity of his mood. He was a young man about to go to the edge, a young man with every bit of the wherewithal to *get* to the edge. The inevitability of his journey there was never very far from his mind; he knew that before too very long he would be in mortal distress.

The time you won your town the race, we chaired you through the marketplace, he thought. Then a burst for twenty yards just to enjoy the sensation of sudden unleashed speed. He felt flushed and tired. That was common. You never really know how you feel, he thought, until the second lap. Sometimes not even then. Sometimes you don't even know until the last lap, *the stiller town.*

When he reached Lake Alice, he slowed to a walk and then stopped altogether. He stretched out on the grass and did hurdles and butterflies. Stretching was always a pleasant indulgence.

Then he undid the vertical zippers along the legs of his sweat pants and felt up and down both achilles tendons. All the knots and lumps were gone. Soft trails, he thought; godamn Denton and those beautiful soft trails. He had made it through the winter okay, only two colds and no real injuries. He was a man without an alibi.

Two runners in Villanova sweats went by, but he didn't recognize either of them. From far off the crowd yelled as someone cleared a height or broke the tape in a sprint preliminary, and his own body responded by dumping a shot of adrenaline into his system. He caught it quickly. Not yet, he thought, not even close yet.

It was a time for daydreams; the roar in his head was far off now and building, but it would grow on its own. The problem now was control.

There had been a local race a long time ago, a five-miler late in the summer. As the runner tooled along the bicycle path on the Palm Beach side of the lake he was sweating profusely; it flew off in arcs on every stride. True, he was not in very good shape yet, but it was far too early to worry about it. It was still summer and deathly hot.

The child stopped him right in his tracks. It was about a mile after he had made the turn at the Sailfish Club. The kid could have been no more than six or seven, and as he walked towards the runner, it was apparent there was something wrong with him; he moved without flow, all angles and juts. The runner thought: he's so pale. But the child was just beaming. Wispy hair fell back into place as the hot wind blew through it, clear blue eyes stared at Cassidy without fear or self-consciousness. Cassidy stood gasping, dripping puddles of sweat onto the asphalt. He tried his best to beam back. Through his gasping he couldn't help chuckling at how silly this was.

"Hello," Cassidy said.

"Hello," the child said happily, "what are you doing?"

"I'm running a race. What's your name?"

"Allan." The child laughed, put a small hand to his mouth. It was so thin as to seem transparent. The runner looked over his little legs for braces but saw none. The left shoe, however, seemed bulkier on the bottom than the other.

"A race?" The child laughed again, obviously wary of being teased. "But where are your opponents?" He said it oh-po-nuts.

"Oh," the runner gestured back towards the Sailfish Club, "they'll be right along." The child cocked his head in a very curious, nearly feminine manner, but he was still beaming.

"You," he said, "run like a big cat." The runner swallowed.

"You," Cassidy said, "are the finest fellow I have run across all morning, Allan. And I guess I'd better be getting along before my oh-po-nuts come along."

"Goodbye big cat."

"Goodbye Allan."

As he slipped off and gathered speed, he looked behind every few yards to see the child still watching; finally he disappeared behind a curve of high hibiscus a quarter of a mile down towards the bridge. Wonder what he will think when the rest of them come clomping along, he thought. And although he really wasn't in very good shape yet he turned a 4:45 for the last mile, changed from his racing flats and jogged across the bridge towards home before the rest of them got in. If there was a medal or something they would just have to mail it to him.

For a long time after that he wondered what it was about that child.

A shriek from the stadium brought him back. He braked his wildly skittering heart.

Cassidy swooped into a strider, held it until the speed built to racing pace, held it, held it, then eased off, slowed to a stride, then a jog, and finally to a walk a hundred yards away. He was on the flat grass in the field across the street from the stadium; other athletes flashed by in blurs of color. He allowed himself some excitement on one of the striders and instantly felt the goose bumps on the back of his neck. He hadn't ever had it quite this bad before.

The noise from the stadium across the street added to the growing roar in his head but it didn't matter now; it was all right now. He allowed it to come, let it fuel his stride as he started up, slipped into it, and then built up speed until his legs seemed to come detached from him and he flew along without conscious effort. Other athletes were at it too, nervous, casting furtive glances at each other (never looking anyone in the eye). A lot of people talk themselves right out of races now, Cassidy thought. He looked at his watch: 7:38. The mile was scheduled for 8:20 but they were running behind. Still, a few minutes later he heard the call over the loudspeaker: FIRST CALL FOR THE MILE RUN. His heart twisted around in his chest like a wild animal; it was an absolutely wrenching shot of adrenaline. *They were going to run it after all! He was going to have to go through with it!*

Then he got control again and steadied himself. Of course he was going to run this race. Take it easy. It was time to get into the infield and get used to being inside there, do the last touch-ups, put on the spikes: ritual, ritual, ritual. Then the last sprints, the final psyching. Jesus, he thought suddenly, why am I doing this? I ought to be in the three-mile. I've been doing all that bulk work and everything. I can't possibly be ready for a mile . . .

Then he steadied himself again; he thought of the last 220 the evening before and told himself: easy. He took a deep breath and walked over to pick up his bag. He had not spoken one word to anyone during the entire hour he had been out here. Runners flashed by. Everyone looked fast and fit as hell.

Then he caught himself again. Any of these mothers runs 3:58 in a godamn time trial in the dead of night and he'll damned well deserve to eat my lunch. Again he told himself: easy.

Inside the stadium a 178-pound lad who could bench press 300 pounds planted a 16-foot fiberglass pole in a tin box, inverted himself, and was tossed into the air a little more than 17 feet, 8 inches. When the crowd reacted to this feat with a roar, something flipped in Quenton Cassidy: His heart jumped so hard he thought his head was going to pop right off. The tumult in his head was like rush hour traffic in the bottom of a wishing well. He walked to the competitors' entrance and for a split second had a rush of ordinary civilian panic as well. He had forgotten completely about this disguise business.

But the little round face looked up from the clipboard and the cold stump of cigar went round and round.

"Well, let's see here, 242, why I guess that would be you, Seppo! Go right on in there boy and you have yourseff a good race, yuh hear? Say, that ain't true what they say about you Finn boys drinkin' reindeer milk, is it? Didn't think so."

Cassidy heard Brady Grapehouse cackling behind him as he went into the stadium.

How the hell did Denton arrange that, he wondered. But then he was on the inside and the special atmosphere, the

blue-white lights, the wintergreen-la ed multi-colored carni-
val that is a major track meet sent hi senses reeling, just as it
always did. God, he thought, here I an. again; here it all is and
here am I with it all on the line on more time. He looked
back uptrack to make sure it was clea and then jogged across
the lanes to put his bag down. His heart skittered again,
feeling for the first time in weeks the springy Tartan beneath
his feet. Officials were running here and there, hurdle setters
scurrying around, timers checking watches. No one noticed
the tall runner in robin's egg blue as he began the methodical
jogging on the inside grass lane. The infield was a mass of
motion. Javelin throwers were slogging back and forth in their
strange sideways gate, hurling imaginary spears at their long-
extinct enemies, broad jumpers bounded around, high jumpers took their run-ups, and the runners of all sizes circled the
track in various stages of their warmups. It made a three-ring
circus look like a quilting bee.

SECOND CALL FOR THE MILE RUN. *Flash* went another shot of adrenaline through his veins—he took two
gasping breaths that seemed wrenched from his body as if
from one tossed suddenly into an icy sea. He got control
again, this time with difficultly. Two laps, that's what the ritual
called for. The roar inside his head drowned out the crowd
altogether, except when they went wild over some performance. But Quenton Cassidy noticed nothing; he moved
inside his own box. His gaze was starting to take on the trance
quality, so that when he ran by Denton without seeing him,
the older runner was not in the least surprised.

"Seppo!" he called. It took awhile to register. But then, of
course it was all right. Denton would know an international
runner, it would only be natural. Denton held out his hand
when Cassidy circled back. He took it nervously.

"Sorry," Cassidy said. "He here yet?"

"Nope. But he will be. Best get your spikes on. How is it?"

"Banjo string. E flat."

Denton nodded.

"Bruce, I can hardly swallow."

"It's okay. It'll be like all the rest once you get moving.
Beforehand's tougher. I would jog with you but I don't want
to push our luck. Both Prigman and Doobey are here. Guess

Walton's a big enough attraction to get even the football establishment. Anyone say anything to you?"

"No. Guess it's working. I'll be all right. I want to do it alone anyway." Denton noticed he was breathing fast, shallow, nearly gasping. It was not important he knew, so long as he had not torn himself all up inside over it already. It would be all right soon. He gripped Cassidy by the elbow.

"Cass, I . . ."

Cassidy looked Denton in the eye very briefly, then smiled. He gripped Denton's forearm and held it hard for a moment. Then he turned and ran off down the track. So, Denton thought to himself. He had seen the look in Cassidy's eye. *So there it is after all.*

Cassidy finished the rest of the ritual lap. Then it would be off with the flats, on with the spikes, off with the damp t-shirt, on with the nylon racing singlet: ritual ritual ritual. He had done it exactly this way hundreds of times.

A roar came from the crowd that he did not understand. Nothing was going on with the field events, and they were between races on the track. Then he looked over at the competitor's entrance and understood. A knot had formed, a chancre of humanity around the gate that suddenly opened up and expelled in a burst the fastest miler in history. The crowd went crazy as he ambled easily across the track with a wan smile, giving the stands a little wave. But Cassidy could tell, even from where he stood, the kind of look in his eye as he glanced quickly around the stadium and with a shudder dropped his bag to tug up the zipper on his turtleneck warmup. Little fluffs of hair on the back of Cassidy's neck went prickly again as Walton began his striders. He was nearly two inches shorter than Cassidy but looked as if he could run through a wall. He already had his spikes on. Every eye in the place followed him as he began doing his sprints on the back straight. The black suit of New Zealand, Cassidy thought, the silver leaf—*Baillie, Halberg, Snell.* His idols, his Gods! And now Walton.

Then he shook his head violently and swore under his breath at himself: *Godamn you!*

The roar had gone! He had been watching Walton slack-jawed like some high school kid and the roar in his own head

had just gone! He jumped up, spikes on, and sprinted around
the first turn, ignoring (not really seeing) Denton's bemused
expression as he went by. When he slowed to a jog on the far
side, calmer now, his jaw was set, his eyes fixed in a trance,
and the orb rested inside a howling mindstorm. He did not
realize that the figure flashing by on the turn had been
Walton.

Now Cassidy took off his sweat bottoms, jogged around
and left them at his bag; he kept the top on and jogged on.
This was the way he always did it. They were getting ready to
run off the high hurdles, the last race before the mile.

THIRD CALL FOR THE MILE RUN. ALL MILERS
REPORT TO THE STARTER.

The last leap of his heart jounced him as he heard the
announcement but by now he was accustomed to the shock.
He made no move for the starting line, nor did any of the
other milers. The high hurdles hadn't even been run and
there would be several minutes of confusion afterwards while
the timers sorted things out. The milers knew all these ancient
rhythms, so they kept doing their striders and jogging. The
gun cracked for the highs and they looked across the track at
the race in the mildest sort of curiosity. After the hurdlers
had swept past the finish line the announcer was after them
again: ALL MILERS REPORT TO THE STARTER IM-
MEDIATELY. LAST CALL FOR THE ONE-MILE RUN. It
no longer jolted him because it was *all* jolt now. He barely
heard the loudspeaker, such was the roar in his head. When
he took off his sweat top he realized he had not put on his
racing singlet. He was still in the wet t-shirt! Godamn it! How
the hell could I have . . .

Then he got control again, jogged rapidly over to his bag
and changed. There was still plenty of time even though most
of the milers were on the track milling around. The timers
were in disarray from the previous race and the starter was
walking among the runners as Cassidy knew he would. All
right, gentlemen, he was saying, all right, listen to the starting
instructions gentlemen, as the runners paced back and forth,
jiggling and jumping up and down, avoiding eyes, gasping
their little shallow gasps, shaking out legs that didn't need
shaking, and generally living their last few seconds of torment. Cassidy jogged out among them, feeling feathery light

now in just racing nylon and spikes; he felt as though he weighed about 10 pounds. He wore the white and blue Adidas 9.9's that had never been second.

Cassidy, too, took up the jiggling and pacing. The announcer was making introductions, but no one seemed to be paying attention. Walton was in lane one, so naturally they started with the outside lane. All eyes were on just one person, the powerful looking Kiwi in the all black nylon with a little silver fern over the breast. There was polite applause for the Finn in lane three, but when the announcer started on the final introduction, he didn't get to the gold medals, the world records, the endless titles, before the place was a madhouse. Everyone knew it all already. Walton jogged out a few steps and waved. Denton stood by the first turn in his navy blue USA team sweats, watching. You have to learn the little smile and wave, he thought, that's one part of it maybe you don't think about beforehand. I'll bet that's the last thing old John wants to be doing right now. Even before a race like this.

Cassidy thought: easy easy easy. Be careful through the turn and get through the first lap. Then start *thinking*. Easy easy easy. Save your goodies.

"All right gentlemen," the starter was saying in his executioner's tone, gun hanging down at the end of his fluorescent orange sleeve, "a two-command start, gentlemen, 'take your marks' and then the gun. Is that clear? All right gentlemen, stand tall. Stand tall, gentlemen . . ."

The crowd hushed suddenly.

High up in the stands very nearly directly across from the starting post, Andrea sat beside the very excited umbrella man and thought: *It's him.*

The starter was backing out from among them now, still saying. "Stand tall, gentlemen, stand tall . . ."

And Quenton Cassidy stood tall in the night as a very slight breeze brushed his burning face. At last, he thought, at last it is here. It is really here.

The starter began backing off the track in quick little steps, raising his gun arm at the same time. For just an instant, Cassidy looked over to lane one and saw John Walton staring right back at him.

"TAKE YOUR MARKS!"

Cassidy's heart tried to leap out through his thin taut skin and hop into his wet hands. But outwardly it was all very calm, very serene, just as always, and it seemed to last a tiny forever, just like that, a snapshot of them all there on the curved parabola of a starting line, eight giant hearts attached to eight pairs of bellows-like lungs mounted on eight pairs of super-charged stilts. They were poised there on the edge of some howling vortex they had run ten thousand miles to get to. Now they had to run one more.

CRACK!

There was the tiny little flutter during which he thought his legs were going to fail completely, but then they were away, out of their crouches and fairly bolting, bounding out and away, not even smoothly yet, burning off the first rush of excitement and fear. But here Cassidy found himself about two yards in front already and probably right on schedule for his maniac 25-second 220. Standing on the inside of the curve, Denton flashed by and said quietly: tuck in. Cassidy tucked in.

He didn't recognize the green singlet, but it occurred to him that it had to be the runner in lane two. Walton was obviously behind them somewhere, unworried and un-rushed. Then Cassidy glanced again and recognized the Irishman. Of course! He had hardly paid attention to anyone else in the race. The first 220 went by as always, giddily, and as they flashed by the white post someone gave them an unofficial split: 26.2 Yeeow! Too fast! No wonder Walton didn't hop right on up there. But there was no chance to look around, Cassidy could sense runners on his outside shoulder and twice he felt someone clipping his heel. He was running almost abreast of the Irishman, sharing the lead actually, but the real truth was that he was more surrounded than anything else. As they came out of the second turn he dared a quick glance to the inside and saw Walton, striding comfortably, head down, watching the feet flashing by in front of him; all business. Okay, thought Cassidy, stay right there. Right where you are.

It was an untenable attitude, he knew, but at this moment before it all got wild and bad it was easy to entertain such facile delusions of control. The crowd shrieked as they passed the starting post in a knot. But did he hear that? Probably not. He thought he heard one single shout: Go Cassidy.

". . .fifty SIX, fifty SEVEN, fifty EIGHT . . ." They were going by the post. Denton, flashing by again on the inside, said quickly: "Fifty seven five too fast." Remarkable, he said it almost in a conversational tone, but Cassidy heard it distinctly. All right Bruce, it's too godamn fast, what the hell am I supposed to do about it?

The announcer was saying: "O'RORK, THEN KAITAINEN, HARRIS, AND JOHN WALTON OF NEW ZEALAND . . ."

Then it started to come on him, as it always did here. He usually felt it in the gut first; a slow, acid kind of strain, systems beginning to panic down there; intestines, other organs closing down for the duration, preparing for whatever dire project was in progress. And the legs now started to get the first wave of lactic acid numbness, the start of a deep ache that would all too soon become the ambulatory paralysis of the final straightaway. Even this early he was getting all the old feelings, thinking: God here it is again! Back in it again and I had forgotten completely what it was like. Forgotten altogether. Shoulders and arms starting now. Pay attention godamn it!

The orb bobbed gently, taking it all in, retaining it, keeping it quiet inside the steely interior and allowing him to think. He concentrated on his task.

Even from the far straightaway he could hear the crowd grow uneasy and then erupt, but before he could react he sensed a body coming up on his shoulder and then flinging by to take the lead. A roar came from across the field. Cassidy pondered calmly. Who was it? It wasn't Walton. A short runner in all red. Wisconsin? St. Johns? He racked his brain, but came up with nothing. Was he a rabbit or just some guy looking for a few seconds of glory, leading John Walton in a mile? Cassidy hung where he was all through the turn coming into the home straight for the second time, then glanced back to the inside and saw Walton, this time a little more labored, but still running casually, eyes cast slightly downward, watch-

ing the feet in front of him. The roar was deafening as they
went by, but this time he was sure he heard it, there was no
mistake, several voices called out: Go Cassidy!

". . .one fifty SEVEN, one fifty EIGHT, one fifty NINE
. . ."

Then two things happened almost at once. First Bruce
Denton flashed by, said calmly: one fifty seven good. And a
split second after that the crowd erupted again as a black-
suited runner bolted by in a savage burst of speed: *WALTON!*
What the hell is he doing, Cassidy thought.

The announcer, excited, came on: "AND NOW WAL-
TON HAS TAKEN THE LEAD FROM HARRIS AS THEY
WENT BY THE HALF IN . . ." Cassidy couldn't hear the rest.

Jesus, what is he doing, Cassidy thought as he watched the
black-suited figure easily slide by the runner in red, and keep
on, showing no sign of slowing down. Cassidy was really
feeling it now, starting the third lap, the old intestine-sliding-
down-the-leg *extremis* that comes at the precise middle of a
race when it dawns on you that there is a long melancholy
way to go. But there was Walton, *pulling away.*

Quenton Cassidy did not know it, of course, but here was
the decision for all time, the decision that led him up the path
to the higher callings or off on a side road to end up in the
bushes somewhere. There was really no thinking to it; his face
now set firmly in the race mask, showing nothing more than
a detached strained interest, he let out a surge and found
himself fairly flying around the Irishman down the back
straight. Red shirt was already fading badly from his burst and
Cassidy was by him quickly too. He pulled into lane one and
thought: that was too fast! You could have done that better.
But it was too late for recriminations, he set about hauling in
the black suit in front of him, even now blending into the
night, spikes flashing in a blur ahead. And this: from across
the field, the calls, more of them, louder, most positive,
beseeching now: CASSIDY! CASSIDY!

The announcer: ". . .WALTON OF NEW ZEALAND
WITH KAITAINEN SEVEN YARDS BACK . . ."

His shoulders ached now with the heavy strain of lactic
acid, so he pumped harder, concentrated on his form, trying
to cover ground smoothly. Now was the time he wanted to be
floating, covering ground with as little effort as possible, but

he found himself straining just to hold pace. And Walton looked so easy! Was he of this earth? Could it really be this much of a joke to him, running this pace without a care in the world?

Cassidy could not feel his legs but that was all right. He was flying along in the night concentrating so hard on the black-suited demon out there that he was actually surprised to hit the second turn. He cursed mentally when he found himself flung by his own momentum out into the second lane, then got it under control, leaned into the turn and got back on pattern. A stupid mistake, he thought, and it cost me two yards.

But coming out of the turn into the straight he felt it. He had contact. Walton had come back to him some and he had contact from five yards back. And he had the power. He knew that too as they sped down the straight, really feeling it now, the lactic acid aching through his body, but also starting the build-up, getting excited knowing that this time it would not be long, that it wasn't going to go on forever after all.

Down past the stands and this time Cassidy heard, unbelieving, what they were chanting as the two figures went by the white starting post: CASS-A-DAY! CASS-A-DAY! CASS-A-DAY!

Even the announcer no longer played the game: ". . .IT'S WALTON FOLLOWED BY . . . CASSIDY OF SOUTHEASTERN . . ."

Dick Doobey, nearly blind with rage, blood vessels standing out on his soft red face, jumped up from his seat in the officials' section and started out the gate onto the track to do God only knew what when he ran smack into the really quite startlingly muscled arm of Mike Mobley, that was stretched across the opening, his huge hand holding the far post in a death grip. Mobley challenged him for an instant with a gaze full of contempt and pity, then the giant turned back to the race and the chant: CASS-A-DAY! CASS-A-DAY! CASS-A-DAY!

His face ashen, Doobey slumped into the nearest seat he could find. Up in the press box, in icy silence, Steven C. Prigman turned to look at the gentlemen of the press, some of whom waited for his reaction; he smiled ruefully, turned back to the race.

And Denton flashing by now: Two fifty five flat. Wait.

Then the gun: CRACK! And the hair on the back of his neck standing up as it always did. Cassidy thought: four hundred yards to go *jesus god what a cost just to be here and he's slipping away if I could just hold him now he's been flat out for* . . .

But Walton was not flat out at all. He suddenly looked back at Cassidy and Cassidy thought he saw a tiny flicker in those hard eyes: surprise. Not concern. Just a mild kind of surprise.

And that followed by a little burst so powerful and quick it broke Cassidy's heart. *God how can he do that?*

Quenton Cassidy, sadly now, was starting to tie up halfway down the back straight and all he could think was: *son of a bitch what has he been doing running from the front? He never does that.* Now Cassidy's arms and shoulders getting worse and worse as the orb strains and bounces around inside, trying to hold it all, Cassidy feeling now the process of his form starting to degenerate involuntarily, he wanly remarks to himself that this must be how death is, *and look how easy dear god he looks up there. So this is how it is, this is exactly how it is, how he beats you and beats you and beats you.*

She had stood with everyone else the last time by and though she knew umbrella man was unobtrusively observing her reactions now, she studied Cassidy's face when he went by and saw in it the totally dispassionate look of the runner at his toil; alert but not excited, full of strain and some unnamed misery, but so obviously showing no emotion, masking darker secrets. What was it he had said about demons? She had some idea of what Cassidy and Walton were experiencing because the other runners, some twenty yards behind, did not hold it as well as these two. Walton to her looked simply intimidating, as if he had been born at full stride; his torso was powerful for a runner and his every stride suggested merciless strength held in reserve. He was haughty in his power and it was somehow chilling to watch.

But then she had looked at Quenton Cassidy, saw the same objective, emotionless look about him, watched the sleek, machinelike workings of legs that were longer than Walton's. And suddenly she had seen him from a different perspective: he too looked intimidating. And something very deep inside her turned a little as she realized that she was, after all, frightened for him, for this task he had taken upon himself. Her eyes had flooded and she stood there in her confusion and turmoil, not caring that umbrella man was staring at her.

CASS-A-DAY! CASS-A-DAY! CASS-A-DAY!

He was starting to get the white haze even this early; it would be very bad when it all caught up, but of course that was no consideration now. *Come on you son of a bitch,* he thought, but he knew he was just hanging on. It was all going slowly downhill and Walton had about eight yards on him still. Cassidy could feel the muscles in his neck start to tighten, pulling his lower lip downwards into an ugly grimace; he knew this was one of the last signs, this death sneer. *So this is what happens! You just don't get him, that's all! The son of a bitch just keeps on going and it ends and you don't get him ever!*

Cassidy adjusted his lean a little forward; that seemed to help some, but the neck was getting tighter and he felt his arms beginning to stiffen. By the time they got out of the turn and into the last straight, he knew they would be really bad. All down the back straight Cassidy tried to reel him in, but it was no good. Eight yards. Eight yards, *Eight yards!* The strain was apparent to those close to the track, on the exhale breath he made little gasps: *gahh! gahh! gahh!* His eyes were starting to squeeze up shut but he could hardly see through the white haze anyway.

The chant roared across the field, beseeching, hopeful, frenzied.

CASS-A-DAY! CASS-A-DAY! CASS-A-DAY!

Shut up! Shut up! I'm not your godamned hero! All down the back straight he stared at the fleeing black suit through the wrinkled slits he had left for eyes, stared at the black suit and wished they would all leave him alone. Just leave him the hell alone with his misery and defeat.

That's when he saw it.

Almost imperceptible, but there it was just the same: the left shoulder dipped suddenly, then the right leg shot out a little further than usual, and that was it: back to normal stride.

Walton was tying up too.

So that's the way it is. Not so casual after all.

Cassidy bore down, bore down, and finally began reeling him in, all during the final turn, all the way around he pulled him in, inch by inch, as his mouth was drawn more and more into the ugly grimace by the spastic neck muscles. Inch by inch the black suit came back until finally they broke clear of the turn and there it was: John Walton was three feet ahead of him with a hundred and ten yards of Tartan stretching out in front of them to the finish line. There was utter pandemonium in the stands as the chant degenerated into a howling, shrieking din.

Quenton Cassidy moved out to the second lane, the Lane of High Hopes, and ran out the rest of the life in him.

37. A Stiller Town

All through the last 50 yards he had looked through the two fogged slits of windows at the howling slow motion nightmare going on around him as he rigged up in true fashion, getting the jaw-shoulder lock and the sideways final straight fade as he began to lose all semblance of control; he peered out at all this as the orb was about to burst letting all the poison flood out, peered at it and quite calmly wondered: *when will it all end?*

He felt more than saw Walton come back up to his shoulder, entertained an idle curiosity about who would get it, but then went back to wistfully concentrating on those green inches of Tartan passing slowly, slowly beneath his feet.

The last 10 yards his body was a solid block of lactic acid, with those straining neck muscles pulling his lip down and his back arched, trapezia trying to pull him over backwards. And all the way Quenton Cassidy is telling himself:

Not now . . . it hurts but go all the way through do not stop until you are past it you cannot afford to give the son of a bitch anything . . . so holdit holdit holdit jesus christ hold it holditholditHOLDITHOLDIT HOLD IT . . .

Finally with a scream and a violent wrenching motion he shook himself loose from this terrible force that gripped him, forced himself into a semblance of a lean and it was over . . .

. . .or at least he thought it was over if it was not all some bad dream and he is gasping simply wrenching air from around him feeling death surely imminent here beside him crying and going hands-to-knees, stumbling please leave me, please I don't want, please I need to breathe . . .

And then Denton has him around the waist and is lifting him up off the ground, please Bruce put me down I can't breathe but Denton is taking him off, away from them, dragging the tall brown limp doll which apparently cannot stand on its own, holding him up painfully and saying: Remember it Quenton, godamn you better remember it because it doesn't ever quite get any better are you listening to me godamn you? and Cassidy forcing his eyes open finally and seeing Denton through the white haze and seeing that he is crying too. *Oh Bruce I'm listening please let me go jesus it hurts* and Denton lets him go hand to knees to pray to the runner's finish line god but Denton leans over and whispers: *three fifty two five, Cass. He kicked from 500 yards out but it was you, Quenton Cassidy, it was YOU all the way. You know you beat him don't you, Quenton godamn it?*

But Cassidy can't do anything but hold his knees and make his little gagging noises and nod, wishing everyone would just leave him the hell alone so he could see if he was going to live or not.

Walton walks by and they touch hands; Walton regards Cassidy with curiosity but no fear. He nods to Denton.

"Bruce," he says.

"John."

This is no game for upstarts or big surprises and Walton's look is clearly more of curiosity than anything else. There will be time, his eyes say, time for decisions and revisions.

"Later mate," he says to Quenton Cassidy. A respectful nod to Denton and he is gone.

Later, Cassidy says to himself.

When, after the countless flashes of cameras and the rude pushing, the well-wishing and the endless questions (still wanting to know *the Secret*), after all of that he finally got away from them and talked with Bruce Denton quietly for a few moments, he pulled the zipper up all the way on the sweat top against the evening chill and stepped out onto the track as those remaining in the bleachers roared. Quenton Cassidy looked up, gave a little smile and wave and thought: *I have nowhere to go.*

It was then that Bruce Denton turned with a sigh and walked alone towards the gate, thinking that Quenton Cassidy's smile was sad indeed.

38. . . . A Runner

The young man walked steadily through the far turn, the darkest part of the track, and entered the final straightaway. Here, he thought, it is usually all over; just a matter of throwing what is left into it. It would be exciting to the onlookers perhaps, but the runners would be calmly playing it out.

During the second and third laps he had tried to conjure up the old feeling of despair and pain, but as always could not quite get it. It had to be experienced, not remembered.

Now he was walking the last 50 yards, unconsciously swinging his arms a little more vigorously, trying to conjure up some of that helpless frozen broth of the last few yards, when the arms and shoulders, legs, and hips seem to bind themselves up together and the jaw locks into the tight grimace as if in supplication, and all of life is reduced to a simple desperation, a pleading for the last pathetic twitch from simple clay. How well he knew these things.

Then he was by the post, telling himself for the last five yards: go *through it*, go all the way through it. He stopped and looked around. The pain would catch you here, of course, the orb would shatter as soon as you crossed the line and it would overwhelm you for those first few seconds. That, of all the feelings, was the one that your mind protected you from the most; later you wouldn't even be able to get a hint of it.

But he supposed that even as bad as it was then, there must be some kind of pleasure mixed in with it, some desperate relief. Joy, perhaps, in knowing that it was over, one more time, with nothing held back.

He took several deep breaths of the warm September air and then walked to the infield to get his travel bag. He looked around once more at the vaulting pits, the oblong sandbox of the horizontal jumpers, the concrete rings for the weight men, and finally back at the starting post. His eyes then took in the track, slowly following the rubberized surface all the way around the first turn, down the long lonely back straight past the 220 post, around the far turn, and then back up the final straight to the finish post where he had long ago beaten the great John Walton. Uncomplicated dimensions that had for some years now defined his life.

A quarter of a mile that he knew by the inches. There was much to be left behind here, he thought. But I can live with that.

He walked straight across the infield, across the track and out the gate, leaving the joggers to their nightly toil. The moths still worried the streetlight.

The young man stopped momentarily amidst the dancing insect shadows and opened the small travel bag. He reached around under the passport, clothes and toilet articles until he found it. He opened the flat thin oblong box under the streetlight and looked at it once more.

The heavy round disk reposed against pink satin, its thick purple ribbon curling up and behind the soft material. The writing around the edge was in Greek but the general import was clear enough.

In the pale light the silver metal glowed dully. It no longer stabbed at him.

This I can live with too, he thought. Primarily because I no longer have any say in the matter. He smiled faintly, closed the box and replaced it in the bottom of the bag. He turned without looking back and walked away from the track.

There was a very old gnarled tree somewhere he wanted to find and then he would be on his way.

How often do you hear about someone borrowing a friend's book, then later buying his own copy because he liked it so much? Or a book so treasured that it gets passed from friend to friend until it simply falls apart from so many readings? *Once a Runner* is such a book.

It has become a cult classic and remains our all-time best seller. It has been acclaimed over the years by Frank Shorter, Bill Rodgers, Alberto Salazar and many other top runners as the best running novel ever. The story of college runner Quenton Cassidy's battle to the top is widely regarded as the most accurate portrayal yet written of the little known world of world class runners.

Many readers say they learned more about running from this novel than from all the training books they have read.

It won *Running* magazine's award as the best book of the year, and has been highly acclaimed by *Running Times, Racing South, and Track & Field News*, as well as by writers like Joe Henderson, Don Kardong and Kenny Moore.

"I've read *Once a Runner* six times and still enjoy it immensely. It continues to renew my heart to 'go after the fire, not the smoke.'"
—**J.A. Sandoz**, Olympia, WA

"Please send me two more copies of *Once a Runner*. It makes an excellent gift to my running friends. It might interest Mr. Parker to know that one [copy] is presently circulating among the members of the München Ost (East Munich) Track Club in West Germany. I had two of their members stay with me as exchange students last year and gave them a copy upon departure. One of them, a 1500-meter man and miler, wrote that his pulse went to 130 during the description of the last race. 'That's *exactly* how it is,' he said. In return

I received a t-shirt from the Greek marathon from Marathon to Athens—an equitable trade. My thanks to Mr. Parker for a great book."
—**Dave Slaughter**, Florence, KY

"I have just finished reading *Once a Runner* and would like to tell you how much I enjoyed it. I am an assistant cross country coach in Jacksonville at Bishop Kenny High School. Our runners are preparing for the state cross country meet in two weeks. As part of this preparation a lot of them are reading *Once a Runner*."
—**James Bryan**, Jacksonville, FL

"Perhaps the best novel ever written about running. There are parts of *Once a Runner* that are pure poetry. I enjoyed it thoroughly and have never read descriptions of what it is to run and race as accurate and compelling as Parker's. . ."
—**Tom Jordan**, *Track & Field News*

"I hate to use a cliche, but I couldn't put it down." —**Joe Henderson**, *Runner's World*

"I'm jealous. This is very close to the kind of book I've wanted to write for years. . . [Parker] has shown an ability to find that vein in that runners have within them, and write about it better than anyone ever has." —**Don Kardong**, of *Runner's World*

"By far the most accurate fictional portrayal of the world of the serious runner. . . a marvelous description of the way it really is." —**Kenny Moore**, of *Sports Illustrated*

Once a Runner, the novel
By John L. Parker, Jr.
©1978, paper, 194 pgs. $12.95
Code: OAR

A Quick, Easy, and Inexpensive Way to Get into Heart Monitor Training . . .

This great technology has finally become user-friendly and reliable enough for us to recommend these particular products as an invaluable tools for the athlete in serious training.

In my opinion, the Polar Favor and the Polar Edge represent milestones in this technology.

The No-Brainer Solution

The Favor has no buttons to push, nothing to set, no beeps, chimes, or little computer voices. It doesn't even have an on-off switch. When you hold it up close to the chest strap sending unit as you would naturally on a run, it simply pops on and gives you your pulse. Not only that, it is so water resistant, you can wear it during a swim workout or a water running session!

The prices have also fallen out of the stratosphere so that just about anyone can afford to get into the same high-tech training concept now in use by many of the top endurance athletes in the world. The list price is $119, but we are offering it for $99.

The other model we carry is also simple, but The Edge allows you to set a "zone," and then beeps at you when you're above or below it. I have to admit, it's pretty handy to have that reminder when you haven't been training a lot, and you're not yet able to gauge effort very accurately. It also has a memory playback feature that tells you what percentage of your workout was spent in the set zone. The Edge normally sells for $189, but we offer it for $159.

Free How-To Booklet

Buy any Polar heart monitor (we carry all models–just call) at our reduced prices, and we'll throw in a copy this this book, *Heart Monitor Training for the Compleat Idiot*, a $4.95 value.

No matter which monitor you use with our easy-to-understand program, you'll be doing cutting edge training in a matter of minutes!

Polar Favor Heart Monitor & Book
$99 + $4 shipping and handling
Code: POL

Polar Edge Heart Monitor & Book
$159 + $4 shipping and handling
Code: PO2

Heart Monitor Training for the Compleat Idiot (book only)
by John L. Parker
paper, ©1993, 64 pgs. $4.95
Code: HMT

The Polar Edge   The Polar Favor

For the others, it may have been a race, but for Brad Townes it was a quest for salvation. He had run all the way from death's door and he had lost everything along the way. In the final mile, he had nothing left to lose except the race. You'll find your heart racing right along with the protagonist in this compelling story, beautifully told by a veteran runner.

The grand daddy of all marathons is the backdrop for this exciting story, with the chapters taking you right through the Great Race itself: Brookline to Hopkinton, Hayden Rowe Street, Hopkinton to Ashland to Framingham, Framingham to Natick, Natick to Wellesley, Wellesley to Newton Falls, The Newton Hills, Brookline, and finally Boston. When you finish, you'll feel as if you'd just run the race alongside Bradley Townes!

Reading this book is a great way to prepare mentally and spritually to run Boston.

"I admit it. I couldn't put the book down. I needed to know——did Bradley Townes win? Did he beat Rodgers and Seko in the premier non-Olympic 26-miler——Boston?. . .Tuckman draws you quickly into the Townes' story and his quest for victory over 26 miles and death." ——**Chuck Morris,** *Maine Running*

". . . enough true details and a fast enough pace to please even an envious writer who looked hard for ways to be critical. I read the book in one sitting, which has only happened two other times in the past ten years. . ."——**Joe Henderson,** *Running Commentary*

An excerpt

Brad could still make out snatches of the radio coverage over the crowd noise. So they still don't know who I am, he thought. They can just call me Mighty Joe from Hannibal, Mo, he chuckled to himself, despite the fire now spreading through his lungs and back muscles.

Twenty yard ahead he could see Seko and beyond him in the distance, Rodgers. In front of Rodgers was only the motorcycle policeman. Now if I can just tie myself to Seko with an invisible cord, and slowly start to pull the son of a bitch in, he thought, just like Bannister did to Landy. He focused on the rhythmically moving shoulders of the Japanese champion, established contact in his mind, and then grimly set about his task.

Rodgers has just passed the 23 mile point, folks, and still looks as loose and easy as he did when he took the lead back on the hills. Seko is behind him but looks tired. And then there's that mystery man. We still don't have. . . . Oh, excuse me. . . . They're trying. . . . Uh, here it is, I have it. I now have the information! Number 2022 is. . . Bradley Townes. . . whose name is not familiar to me. Nor. . . I'm just checking now. . .No? Nor to anyone else on the press truck.

Repeating: Bradley Townes is in third place. He is from Boston. He is 28 years old, and his best previous time is 2:22:35. He is not affiliated with any club and he lists no sponsoring company or product. I hardly need emphasize that he was not included in any of the pre-race publicity information handed out by the Boston Athletic Association. Again, I apologize, but that is all the information that has been released. We are trying to find out more and we'll let you know as soon as we do.

Brad reached the bottom of the hill and now was just three miles out. Twenty-three down and three to go, he thought. Good God! Just give me the strength. He gave Seko a little tug on the cord. . .

Long Road to Boston
by Bruce W. Tuckman
©1988, paper, 169 pgs. $12.95
Code: LRB

RUNNERS
& Other Dreamers

by John L. Parker, Jr.

What really made Jim Ryun tick? Why did Jim Fixx really die? What is the Cinnamon Bun Theory and what does it have to do with Pat Porter, high altitude sickness, and four national cross country championships?

Parker's writing is as powerful as ever and his many readers will find the answers to such questions and a great deal more in his latest work.

This one is destined to become a cult classic like *Once a Runner* and *Runners and Other Ghosts on the Trail*. In fact, this latest collection of Parker's non-fiction pieces contains everything that originally appeared in *Ghosts on the Trail* (now sold out) plus much, much more. Profiles on Jim Ryun, Pat Porter, Barry Brown, Frank Shorter and others. Incisive essays on Courage, Coming Back, The Aging Athlete, and Missing the Poetry, all from his highly regarded *Ultrasport* columns. Lighter moments like "The Great Dragon Run," "The TeeVee Olympics," "Training in Greece," and "Getting Beat by a Woman."

". . .Parker excites and tantalizes the reader. . . Every runner should read this jewel." ----**Ruben Flores**, *San Antonio Light*

". . .a collection of true stories about runners, for runners, by a runner. John Parker knows running from the inside out and knows how to tell a story." —*California Track and Running News*

An Excerpt

A high desert, like a war, is a very good place to find out some things about yourself that you may not have wanted to know.

How you handle it is your business.

It has always been a favorite of Saints and Madmen and Lost Tribes. A lot of people just leave. The Light gets to them. Or the Space. Or something quite a bit less ethereal, such as the way rattlesnakes like to crawl into your sleeping bag to stay warm. The letters back, though, are always wistful:

. . .I was born and raised in Alamosa. I love every inch of the valley and all the happy memories it holds, and yes, even the sad ones. . .

And:

. . .My grandfather settled in the valley not awfully long after the Indians left! Talk about "soul" —

Mine lies deep in that river land surrounded by the Rockies. . .

Those from a literary magazine called *Alma*, Spanish for "soul," published out of Alamosa, Colorado, a small town on the floor of the San Luis Valley. "Floor" here is deceptive usage. Alamosa is one and one-half miles above sea level. And anywhere you go from here is up. To live in such a place is to break yourself of your oxygen habit.

And there is something else about the high desert, something you think you already know, but which if you haven't been there you can't really *feel*. It is this: the desert doesn't care what kind of hurry you're in or how fast you're going, it's not going to let you get anywhere. You can sit in your rent-a-car going just under a hundred in a perfectly straight line toward the airport at Denver and after a couple of hours you will still be, relatively speaking, in the same place.

You cannot breathe here and you cannot make any progress against the backdrop. It is the long distance runner's most perfectly articulated nightmare.

Pat Porter, a 26-year-old Olympian, a four-time national cross-country champion, voluntarily lives in Alamosa. He *likes* it. Are you beginning to get the idea?

—From "Rare Atmosphere, Astringent Light"

Runners & Other Dreamers
By John L. Parker
©1989, paper, 178 pgs. **$9.95**
Code: RDR

The best writers in the sport of running take up a fascinating subject, the last frontier of long-distance events: races longer than a marathon. Who runs these 50-milers, 100-milers, multi-day events, multi-event events? And *why* do they do it? And (okay, admit you're a little curious) what's it like to do one?

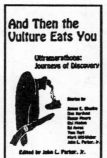

And Then the Vulture Eats You

Ultramarathons: Journeys of Discovery

Stories by
James E. Shapiro
Don Kardong
Kenny Moore
Ed Ayres
Tom Hart
Mark Will-Weber
John L. Parker, Jr.

Edited by John L. Parker, Jr.

James Shapiro, a long time ultra-runner, whose *Meditations from the Breakdown Lane* is a classic piece of running literature, begins by relating with heart-rending detail his experiences in a 6-Day Race in "Swifts on the Wing."

In "To the Limit and Beyond," Kenny Moore takes you through a gut-wrenching experience in his first-person account of the Great Hawaiian Footrace, a horrendous 6-day ordeal that seemingly changes his life.

Don Kardong, one of the wittiest and most personable writers in the sport, in "Le Grizz" goes the 50-mile distance at the infamous race that gives this piece its name. Along the way this former Olympic marathoner, like so many participants in these events, makes startling discoveries about himself.

Ed Ayres, editor of *Running Times*, takes on the Western States 100 in "Wings of Icarus," and the event turns out to be a kind of catharsis in his life.

In "Road Warriors," Hal Higdon's report on his group's informal attempt to run across the state of Indiana is another kind of ultra tale: a light-hearted, self-imposed challenge that turns, like most ultra events, into a revealing spiritual odyssey.

Tom Hart's self-imposed challenge, to run a solo 37-miler on his 37th birthday, is the basis for his ultra story. He finds out, as do the others, that an effort on the magnitude of an ultra is more than a feat of endurance, it is a journey into self.

John Parker ends with "And Then the Vulture Eats You," an uproarious analysis of today's ultra runners ("Mystic Ultras"). Your sides will ache from reading his account of the war between the "Track Men" and the "Mystic Ultras" in the Jackson, Michigan Ultimate Runner contest, in which the entrants race a 10K, a 440, a mile, a 100-yd dash, a mile, and a marathon, all in the same day.

If you are an ultra runner, have ever been even *mildly* curious about such events, or if you are just a lover of great writing, you will greatly enjoy this book.

An Excerpt

From Shapiro's "Swifts on the Wing"

Most of us would be on the track 16 to 18 hours a day. Some would sleep in a trackside tent that swarmed with activity; others like myself would dash off to nearby hotels for a few hours of troubled sleep, tormented by burning feet, sore joints and overtired bodies. Some runners would say much later, when we emerged on the other side of this trial, that they didn't dream about the race while it was actually on but that they did during the first free night.

Certainly there was no way to escape the feverish intoxication of the race. Only once during those six days and nights did the number of competitors sink to just one. At every moment somebody or some bodies moved round the track, ceaselessly at work, so that no matter when you slept, the relentless advance of your competitors seeped through the chill night air, made you awaken with that sobering sense that not another instant could be wasted. It was like war.

Awonderful novel about a mysterious, reclusive runner haunting London's Hampstead Heath. And would you believe, A long-running hit. This enchanting novel was written by Boulderite Paul Christman, editor of the *Running Stats* newsletter. This is one of those hard-to-find books that you will treasure for years.

"Anyone who considers himself (or herself) a hopeless running nut is going to get a serious kick out of it."— *Running Times*

"Great fun to read and the climactic conclusion boldly rewrites running history, and predicts the future as well." —*Women's Sports & Fitness*

"There are parts of the narrative that are so familiar you'll feel as if you've been caught thinking aloud." —*Rocky Mountain Running News*

"This book is like a good race: it starts out easy, picks up in the middle, and finishes with a dazzling sprint. Runners everywhere will enjoy it."—**Lorraine Moller**, Olympian

"An exciting yarn that holds the reader to the tape. . ."—**Dick Quax**, Olympian

An excerpt

God dammit! she thought to herself as Christa and a pack of men began to ease by her like a formation of drenched egrets. *You're not slipping by that easily!* Solian tried picking up her knees, but her mind was making a promise her legs couldn't keep. Christa and company evenly receded from her grasp.

Oh, no, not you too! Solian mentally lashed herself as Mary struggled by her 90 seconds later. *I'm going to drop out. . .no,*

got to keep going. . .third woman. . . you can still break 2:50. . .

Minutes later she stumbled to a stop at a feed station just beyond the 38-kilometer mark, gulped a cup of water, then grabbed a sponge and squeezed it over her head. Her first few steps made her feel nauseous. She probably needed some salt, but in the last few miles of a marathon replacement drinks upset her stomach worse than water. Solian could feel the water sloshing around in her stomach and she was getting very dizzy. The sun seemed to be penetrating right through her AUCKLAND UNIVERSITY singlet and navy-blue nylon shorts. *Don't do it! Don't!* Her mind and body were engaged in a contest: the former urging her to keep running, the latter telling her to walk. *Just make it to the 39-kilometer mark. . . you might start feeling better. . . .* But 100 meters later she found herself walking. God, she hated those pitying looks from the spectators when she wasn't doing well.

"C'mon, Solian, only three kilometers to go!" a man supporting himself on two metal arm-braced crutches shouted from the side of the road. Solian felt tears well up in her eyes. Here was a man who would give anything to walk properly, and she was walking when she could still be running. *But, there's no disgrace in saving yourself for another day. Why kill yourself? Walk off the course and admit you just didn't have the miles.* But it was no go: she knew she would have to finish; the man on crutches merely a reminder of what a gift it was to be able to use her legs. Painfully she began to run again. . .

This critically acclaimed novel, first published in 1969, has for years been regarded as one of the true classics not only in the literature of footracing, but in general interest literature as well.

THE OLYMPIAN
By Brian Glanville

Glanville's beautifully portrayed relationship between runner Ike Low and the eccentric and charismatic coach Sam Dee has become a set piece in the tales of athletes: *Rocky, Chariots of Fire,* even *Long Road to Boston* owe a debt to this work.

There are echoes of *Loneliness of the Long Distance Runner* as well. You will be captivated by the story of the working-class stiff, Ike Low, as Sam Dee "discovers" him thrashing through inconsequential races, a mediocre sprinter at a local running club.

"The first time I met him, I thought he was a nut case," said Ike of his coach.

"You are built to run the *mile,*" Dee told him. "You are the perfect combination of ectomorph-mesomorph; long calves, lean, muscular thighs and arms, chest between thirty-seven and thirty-eight, and broad, slim shoulders. A miler is the aristocrat of running. A miler is the nearest to a thoroughbred racehorse that exists on two legs."

And thus begins the relationship that will transform Ike into one of the great distance runners in the world.

"Until *Once A Runner,* this was my favorite running novel." —Bill Rodgers

"When I was a miler in college, this book was my *Once a Runner.*" —John L. Parker

An Excerpt

This thing, this pain thing, in a way I saw what he meant, but in another way, I didn't understand it. Why run at all if it was going to hurt you? Sport, to me, was something you enjoyed, and if you didn't enjoy it, you packed it in. On the other hand, I could see he was right, that this sort of attitude wasn't going to get you nowhere, not with everybody else so dead serious and more or less dedicating their lives to it. Either you did it properly, or you might as well let it alone.

And mind you, it wasn't like there was no enjoyment in it at all, that it was all slog. The training was hard, of course, and all the things you had to give up, but the races, they could really be great, if things were going well; so exciting that everything else in the world seemed dead; that moment when it was time to go and you felt this power thrumming away in you like a great, big engine and you knew you were going to do it, beat the lot of them. In a way it was better than actually doing it, like a meal or making love to a bird; I mean, it usually looks better beforehand. Though winning was great, too, breaking that old tape, the little, light touch against your chest, and the first feeling you always had, didn't matter how tired you were, was always this flutter in the guts, like to say, I've done it.

The other way I could see Sam was right was obviously if you want something, you ain't going to get it for nothing, not unless you inherit it, and you can't inherit running, and there was a hell of a lot to want in athletics——breaking records, running for Britain, traveling abroad, and maybe one day, please God, an Olympic medal. Because records, they were here today and gone tomorrow, but an Olympic gold medal they could never take away from you.

This is the wonderful autobiography of Clarence DeMar, seven-time winner of the Boston Marathon. In an age that had not yet conceived of masters running, his last Boston victory came in 1930 when he was nearly 42!

Originally published in 1937, this little gem was nearly forgotten for many years. It was discovered and reprinted in 1981, then forgotten again. Charmingly written in DeMar's own heartfelt words, it provides a fascinating glimpse into an America of a simpler time.

Perhaps the best-known distance runner of his era, DeMar never profited monetarily from his prowess. He prided himself on his simple New England values: his work as a typesetter, his leadership of a Boy Scout troop, his church work. Much of his training was accomplished during his runs to and from work each day.

He discusses a great many of the unsolicited suggestions about diet, training, and lifestyle he received over the years, a few of which he dutifully tried on himself by way of experimentation. He was a shrewd analyst, open to new ideas, yet with enough skepticism to give weight to his findings. Amazingly enough, *nearly all* the conclusions he reached over 50 years ago about these complex issues have been validated by subsequent research.

In so many ways, DeMar was way ahead of his time. You'll be fascinated by his story.

"Clarence DeMar may have run through—and to the top of—another era, but his story will ring true to all modern marathoners. Today's runners will not only enjoy reading about the way it was; they may even learn a little about the way it should be."

—Amby Burfoot, *Runner's World*

"Long after many of the current running books are forgotten—and deservedly so for some of them—*Marathon* will continue to be in the front of the pack. That's where Clarence DeMar always was himself."

—Colman McCarthy, *Washington Post*

> MARATHON by Clarence DeMar
> ©1937, paper, 156 p. **$9.95**
> Code: **CDM**

There has never been another Pre.

Steve Prefontaine, a true American original, captured the imagination of running fans in the 70's like no one before or since. An American record-holder many times over, the charismatic, fearless, outspoken Pre attracted hordes of fans to the University of Oregon's Hayward Field to watch him take on the best in the world. They were called Pre's People. Thousands of others around the world were avid followers of this magnetic personality. They still grieve his tragic death in a 1975 car wreck, just hours after winning his latest 5000-meter race at Hayward.

Jordan covers Pre's meteoric career from his early high school races in Coos

Bay, Oregon (where he set a national two-mile record of 8:41.5 in 1969), through his college days racing the likes of Frank Shorter, Kenny Moore, Greg Fredericks, Harold Norpoth, Don Kardong, Lasse Viren, and Rod Dixon. He covers Pre's agonizing fourth in the '72 Olympic final (13:28.3 to Viren's winning 13:26.4), his great '73 and '74 seasons (six American records), and the start of what should have been the greatest racing year of his career.

> *PRE!* by Tom Jordan
> ©1977, paper, 129 pgs., $12.95
> Code: **PRE**

Long-time *Runner's World* editor and one of the true veteran commentators of our sport, Joe Henderson, reminisces about how the running boom all came about. This book was unavailable for years and has now been brought back by Cedarwinds. Many insights and helpful suggestions about training, racing, and living the life of a runner.

An excerpt:

I got lucky. First, I was lucky to find running. We were suited for each other, and I have no doubt that it has made me a better person. I don't mean better than anyone else. I don't make those kind of comparisons. I mean better by far than I would have been if I never had started again after dropping out of my first race in April 1958.

Next, I got lucky when I started to write. I learned the craft without really trying. It grew out of record-keeping for running. I learned to write the way I learned to run—by doing it, by building from each day's little defeats and victories until I had a foundation much bigger and stronger than I ever tried or expected to make.

I won state championships in high school, ran miles in the 4-teens, went to college free, traveled the country for races. I wrote for newspapers, magazines, booklets and books. I edited the most important journal in running publishing history. But all the while I knew: It was luck and then persistence that took me there, not talent.

I don't say any of these things to demean myself. I like myself and I'm proud of nearly everything I've done. I'd be a fool to say I didn't enjoy winning seven state high school championships, running four sub-4:20 miles, running in two national cross country meets and competing in almost half the states when I still took racing seriously.

I'd be denying what I am if I said my ego didn't like seeing my byline on top of articles, my name on the front of books, myself being applauded as I stood up to speak, or being asked my advice and opinions—first by letter and phone, and later on radio and TV.

But when I review the things that have given and continue to give me real pleasure, the few big moments aren't anywhere near the top of the list. When I think back on the best day of my running life—May 20, 1961, when I won the Iowa mile and half-mile in record times—it seems it happened to someone else. When I see one of my books on a store shelf, I feel little parental attachment to it. The book was mine only as I wrote it, then I gave it up for adoption.

I get my real pleasure from the words flowing from pen to paper in just the right sequence. I get it from the flow of steps down from my head, through my guts and legs, out through my feet to the good earth.

The Running Revolution
by Joe Henderson
paper, 205 pgs. ©1980 **$6.95**
Code: RRE

A no-nonsense approach to the basics of racing on the road, including training. A good first reference work for soeone thinking about racing or inthe early stages of competition. Contains photos and an appendix with pacing charts and metric to yard conversons. Chapters include: The History of Road Racing, Selecting Races, Training for Road Races, Racing, Injuries, and Auxiliary Aids for Runners. The

writers are the well-known University of Oregon women's coach and his athlete/journalist wife.

**All About
Road Racing**
By Tom and
Janet Heinonen
©1979, paper, 126 pgs.
$7.95
Code: AAB

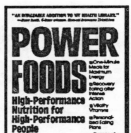

This is Parker's newly revised humor collection, originally published as Aerobic Chic & Other Delusions. This book containns everything in the original, plus eight new hilarious chapters, including "Flo Jo's Folly", "Life Among Skinflints", and classic Parker commentary on runners' gadgets, his trip to Greece, and the sport of cross country.

There is also his classic "Aerobic Chic" quiz the status-seeking runner can take to determine just how "with it" he or she is. (Hint: If you think a Rosa Mota is a new four-cylinder Japanese roadster, you lose 50 points.) Here's a rundown of the other chapters: "Harry Winkler and the Awesome Attack of the Toothless Shark" is about a phony shark attack pulled by some of Parker's skin-diving buddies. "Won't you come home, Irv Taylor?" is the story of an old-timey runner who retires in disgust because of all the newcomers in their

fancy running togs. "Big Stakes at Twin Lakes" is about Parker and a friend running a mile relay against four other guys. "My Latest Marathon" is a survivor's account of his first 26-miler. "Mountain Climbing in Florida" tells of Parker's quest to reach the highest point in his not-so-mountainous home state of Florida. "The Blister Derby" recounts his first and last attempt at race-walking. "Stalking the Wild Pelota" is Parker's side-splitting account of playing Jai Lai for the first and last time.

Needless to say, this is a great gift or back-of-the-john book.

"I laughed till I thought I would have to send out for a truss. . ." —**Ron Wiggins,** *Palm Beach Post*

Run Down Fired Up & Teed Off
By John L. Parker, Jr.
©1993, paper, 80 pgs. $6.95
Code: RDF

For ultrarunners as well as us mere 10kers and marathon-ers. This is the fascinating, true story of the legendary Ted Corbitt, a pioneer ultra-distance runner of the 1950's. More than a compelling personal story of a black athlete in a little known sport, this book is also filled with Corbitt's hard-earned wisdom from thousands of miles of training and racing in the "pre-boom" days. Corbitt's courage and determination will enthrall and inspire you. This hard-to-find book makes a great gift.

An Excerpt

The gun barked and they were off. They had to circle the track 3 1/2 times before heading out of the stadium and onto the road.

After two laps Ted noticed a familiar figure cruising alongside him.

The famous facial contortions were missing, but his powerful stride was unmistakable. The "Prague Express" [Emil Zatopek] glided by without effort, gradually moving up on the leaders.

At the head of the long procession, England's Jim Peters cut himself loose from the pack with a devastating burst. Ted's dream of glory ended almost before it began. Leaving the stadium at the fastest pace of his life, he felt an agonizing pain in his right side. It was the worst stitch he had ever known.

Maybe it was the exceptional pace or the terrible tension he had suffered all these weeks. Immediately the pain slowed him and he started losing ground. Yet, despite the stitch he remained with men who would eventually finish in the top ten. Then Jones and Dyrgall swept past. Dyrgall called out, "Watch the pace, it's awful fast." At that moment the pain was at its worst, but even when it eased there was a binding sensation which persisted throughout the remaining distance. . .

Corbitt By John Chodes
paper, ©1974 154 pgs. $8.95
Code: COR

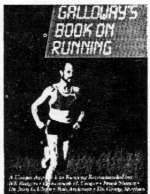

Kenny Moore, aside from being an Olympic marathoner, is perhaps the best crafter of non-fiction prose ever to write on the subject of running. His book is a continuing source of joy. His style is informative, as befitting a *Sports Illustrated* staffer, yet has the grace of carefully crafted poetry. He zeroes in on such venerable subjects as renowned Oregon coach Bill Bowerman, legendary Aussie record-holder Ron Clarke, first four-minute miler Roger Bannister, and friend and fellow Olympian Frank Shorter.

Best Efforts
World Class Runners and Races
by Kenny Moore

The classic late 70's mile confrontation between Filbert Bayi and John Walker, multiple gold medalist Lasse Viren, Boston Bill Rodgers, Mary Decker Slaney, Henry Rono, Grete Waitz, Eamonn Coughlan, and Sebastian Coe are all marvelously brought to life by his pen. He writes poignantly of the death of his friend and teammate, Steve Prefontaine in "A Final Drive to the Finish," and recalls the first defini-

tive physiological mass-testing of elite runners (he was one of them) in the early 70's in "Muscle and Blood." There is one piece called "Concentrate on the Chrysanthemums," about one of Shorter's early marathon triumphs, that is worth the price of the whole book.

Moore brilliantly captures some of the most fascinating runners from a particularly interesting era in distance running. This book contains some of the best non-fiction writing ever done on the subject of running.

"This book is delicious. It is ambrosia for the mind."
----John L. Parker, Jr.

> *Best Efforts* by Kenny Moore
> ©1982, 1992, paperback, 199 pgs.
> **$12.95**
> **Code: BES**

This is the first book to address in depth the *underpinning* of a successful training regimen. Long-time fitness writer Sleamaker has analyzed the world's best systems of endurance sport training and combined their most effective elements. He deals with principles that apply across all endurance sport boundaries, but also includes sport-specific advice for runners, as well as sections directed at cyclists, swimmers, bi- and triathletes, and others.

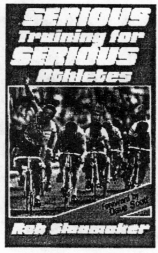

SERIOUS Training for SERIOUS Athletes
Rob Sleamaker

"Whether your aspirations are to pursue endurance sports at the local level or to become a world champion, this book is a marvelous resource for analyzing, evaluating, and critiquing your training program."
----Dave Scott, 6-time Ironman Winner

> *Serious Training for Serious Athletes*
> by Rob Sleamaker
> paper, 247pgs.
> ©1989 **$15.95**
> **Code: STS**

If anyone should know how to approach training as a masters runner, it's Hal Higdon. The author of *On the Run from Dogs and People* (and 23 other books) covers it all, from the question of health dangers to base training, minimizing injuries, masters secrets, motivation, diet, and maintaining your youth. Higdon, a Senior Writer for *Runner's World* and a contributor to many other magazines, is perhaps the first athlete ever to hold national records in the junior, open and the masters divisions. He has participated in six Olympic Trials.

This book has already been widely praised.

Mike Davis of the *Indianapolis News* wrote: ". . .it's tough to read the first chapter and not get an urge to slip on a pair of shoes and go for a run."

Maurice Hobbs of the *Minneapolis Tribune* wrote: "It would have been nice to have had Higdon's newest book 12 years ago when I started running."

Two of the great masters runners of our times (with the help of *Runner's World's* Joe Henderson) have put together a truly comprehensive, informative, and interesting book on after-40 running. They not only tell you some of their personal backgrounds, but also give you some feel for masters running historically. Did you know, for instance, that Clarence DeMar won the 1930 Boston Marathon at age 41 and is still its oldest winner? Or that 47-year-old Finn Vaino Muinonen won a silver in the European Championship Marathon in 1946? Or that Evy Palm of Sweden PR'd with a 2:31:05 at age 47?

John Campbell, Joyce Smith, Jack Foster, and Miki Gorman are all accorded their proper place in the constellation of masters stars.

The book also gets into the nitty-gritty of training for the mature runner: "What the Years Give to Performance, and What They Take Away"; "The New Way to Train without Injury"; "Nutrition Advice to Keep You Running Smoothly"; "Racing: How to Start, How to Finish"; "Breaking Personal Records"; "What it Takes to Make It Through a Marathon"; "Mastering the

Mile"; and "The Joy of Training and Racing Cross Country" are among the many topics covered. The book also provides handy pacing charts, record listings, and training charts.

The authors hardly need introduction. Rodgers is a four-time winner of both the New York and Boston marathons. At 43 he is now one of America's top masters runners. Welch, now 46, began running at age 35. Within four years she made the British Olympic team and in 1987 won the New York City Marathon. Henderson is the author of 13 books on running and fitness and has been running himself for more than 30 years.

Whether you're training for your first 5K, or planning your umpteenth marathon, you'll not only enjoy your first read of this jam-packed book, you'll keep it handy for future reference.

Still the old champ

The highly compact design made the old *Runner's Log* a favorite since 1981. Now an updated, even more feature-filled version has been released with Bill Rodgers' imprimatur. At 8½ X 5¼, it's almost small enough to slip into a back pocket, yet features nice thick, card-stock type pages. If you're not into verbose entries and are looking for a really efficient design, this log's for you. Features: 1) Undated; 2) One week per page; 3) Daily slots for course, distance, workout type, time, temperature and humidity; 4) weekly slots for total mileage, week's average, cumulative. 5)3 comment lines per day; 2 for week; 6) handy mood symbols, weight section; 6) Short sections on training tips;

7) Yearly records include: races, mileage graph by the week, cumulative mileage graph; 8) pace charts for two miles through marathon

> **Bill Rodgers' Classic Running Log** by Jogalite
> ©1993, spiral paper, 86 pgs. $9.95
> **Code: LG7**

The contender

Sports Log Publishers puts out some of the most popular logs in sports. Their Runlog is compact at 6" X 9", and nicely laid out, with inspiring color and black & white photographs. Features: 1) Undated pages; 2) Two pages per week, total of 56 weeks; 3) Open format with plenty of room for daily notes 4)

Weekly summary section, with body weight, cumulative mileage and weekly mileage; 5) Short sections on stretching, nutrition, training, etc.; 6) Pace charts, Race result summary log, Map to Race Day Worksheet, and Cumulative Mileage Chart.

This is the one for the verbose runner who's tired of writing in the margins of all his/her past logs.

> **RunLog**
> by Tim Houts & John Cronin
> ©1994, spiral paper, 166 pgs. $9.95
> **Code: LG1**

Kick Ass Log Software

There are a *lot* of programs out there that will promise to keep track of your training for you. We think *The Athlete's Diary* is the best.

Why? It's easy to use, yet powerful; it does what you want it to, but doesn't overwhelm you with useless bells and whistles. It's smart enough to digest weeks and months of training data and then paint the big picture for you. Plus, it's been around for years, it comes in Mac, DOS, and Windows versions, and it's reasonably priced at $49.95. It's so efficient, you don't even have to have a hard drive. It will run from a floppy. And hey, the manual is written in English!

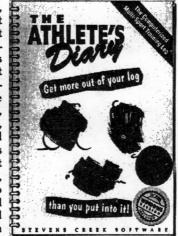

This program keeps track of times, distances, paces, routes/workout types, and comments. It is also versatile as all get out. You can use it as a straight runner's log, but it'll also handle your occasional cross-training entries. Then when you get injured enough to become a full-time triathlete, you can keep right on using this program–it was actually designed for it. It's billed as "The Computerized Multi-Sport Training Log," and the description fits.

The program allows you to plan your training in advance, print out your workouts, then modify the entries to reflect what actually happened.

Pop-up menus allow you to change your report format from weekly to monthly, from all sports to one sport, and from summary form to graph form. If you really want to *see* how your training has been going, this program will show it to you.

Software designer Steve Jamison is an athlete as well as a computer guy, and his knowledge of training and attention to detail really shows in *The Athlete's Diary*.

Continuing support for the program is provided directly by Stevens Creek Software.

"The Athlete's Diary has provided me with an efficient and user-friendly means of measuring my training progress in order to maximize by athletic potential."
—Andrew Kelsey, *Age Group Tri World Champ*

"I would like to say this is one of the most user-friendly programs I have ever used. I am sure there are many more runners that cross-train and are looking for software such as yours. . ."—**Ralph D. Ramos, *Cincinnati***

". . .works as well with one sport as it does with eight." —**California Computer News**

". . .does everything but run for you." —**Running Times**

". . .lots of features, very few weaknesses." —**Triathlon Today**

The Athlete's Diary
by Stevens Creek Software
©1993, **$49.95**
Codes: DID (DOS),
DIW (Windows), DIM (Mac)

The Stim-o-Stam Secret

Back in the early days o Track Club in Gainesvi the runners used to notice th what kind of shape you were really hot weather came, you get sore and your training wc suffer. If you were lucky soi might take you aside and let you in on a genuine training secret: Stim-O-Stam. Sounds like some kind of kid's toy or something, but it's really your best defense against hot-weather electrolyte deple-tion and general weariness in all conditions. Marty Liquori and other Gainesville runners have been swearing by it for years. Oh, sure, you could sit around and drink two gallons of Exceed every night, but the truth is that you still prob-ably wouldn't get replenished as well as with Stim-O-Stam. These amazing little tablets are made from a well-guarded for-mula of dibasic and monobasic sodium phosphates, potassium and vitamin C. The company recommends it as a year-around supplement, and says double-blind experiments have shown Stim-O-Stam improves stamina by "main-taining a neutral acid-base balance (pH) in the muscle and blood; making more oxy-gen available; reducing lactic acid build-up, while accelerating ATP production."

The recommended dosage is three tab-lets before, three tablets after workouts, but as many as 12 per day may be taken in extreme heat or workout conditions.

The Xtrnr sports bar is a new product that combines the basic Stim-O-Stam phosphate formula with the fructose, glucose polymers, and branched chain amino acids needed for no-nonsense ath-letic refueling. Frankly, this honey-nut flavored bar is not as palatable as the PowerBar, its nearest competitor (prob-ably because the phosphate ingredients themselves don't taste all that great), but it offers the same nutritional value of PowerBar with the added electrolyte re-placement benefit of the Stim-O-Stam phosphate formula built in. This is an incredibly powerful product for hard-core performance support and enhancement, not a trendy snack item.

Please specify flavors: Honey Nut, Ba-nana Nut, or Chocolate Toffee.

Stim-O-Stam tablets (500 tab bottle, 4-6 month supply) $27.95 + $4 shipping
Code: ST1

Xtrnr Sports Bar (24-pack) $39.95 + $4.00 shipping
Code: ST2

This is simply the most comprehensive book on endurance training ever compiled. Somewhere in its 832 pages is a discussion of nearly every conceivable topic of interest to the serious athlete. Noakes is a medical doctor and exercise physiologist as well as a long-time runner, with more than 70 marathon and ultramarathon events in his log.

He explores the physiology of running with entire chapters on muscle structure and function, oxygen transport, energy metabolism, and control of body temperature.

You'll discover important new ideas in research, such as recent doubt about the VO2 max concept and its implications for predicting running performance, and the newly realized importance of drinking patterns during exercise in determining fluid and energy replacement.

Noakes considers all aspects of training, offering practical guidelines on shoes and apparel, tips for beginners, and advice on finding the right races for your skill level. He includes fascinating insights from pioneer training theorist Arthur Newton, chapters on training the mind, the problems of overtraining, and the approaches taken by 34 of the world's greatest runners.

Noakes also deals with the down side: injuries and other health considerations. He demonstrates convincingly that injuries don't "just happen," and tells you how to recognize, diagnose, avoid, and treat them. He includes chapters on nutrition and weight control, as well separate chapters dealing with issues relating to both women and children.

Finally, he examines both the benefits and hazards of endurance training as it relates to the body's major systems, including the respiratory, gastrointestinal, genitourinary, endocrine, immune, and central nervous system. He devotes considerable space to environmental hazards, coronary heart disease, longevity issues, and instances of sudden death in athletes.

Dr. Noakes is the Liberty Life Professor of Exercise and Sports Science, and director of the Bioenergetics of Exercise Research Unit of the Medical Research Council of the University of Cape Town. He is an editorial board member for many international sport science journals and the 1991 president of the South African Sports Medicine Association as well as a Fellow of the American College of Sports Medicine.

"Noakes has a training, an intelligence, a sensitivity, and experience that few writers on the athletic life can equal. On every page we see the work of the scientist. . . "
—**George Sheehan, MD**

The world's leading distance experts set out to write a book aimed primarily at coaches, but to their surprise, runners as well began to discover this remarkably complete and up-to-date text.

Sebastian Coe's rise to the top of world-class middle-distance running was no accident. It was the direct result of an approach to training that combines practical principles with scientific knowledge---- the approach described in this book by Coe's coach/father Peter and by Dr. David Martin, one of the sports leading physiologists.

The book's 82 photos, 72 figures, and 40 tables make the extensive technical information easy to understand. You'll find practical examples of how this training approach transformed Coe, Keith Brantly, Wendy Sly, Pat Porter, Tom Byers, Janis Klecker, and others from fast runners into world-class winners.

This book bridges the gaps between scientific information and the day-to-day realities of training.

You'll learn about the biomechanics and biochemistry of running; goal-setting for competitive runners; developing a plan for total body fitness; the importance of multitier and multi-pace training; strategies for successful racing from the 800-meter through the marathon; integrating psychological and physiological aspects of athlete

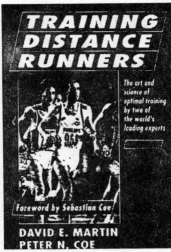

TRAINING DISTANCE RUNNERS

The art and science of optimal training by two of the world's leading experts

Foreword by Sebastian Coe

DAVID E. MARTIN
PETER N. COE

development; techniques for scientific assessment of fitness; stress management to avoid burnout; and the dangers of over-training.

The chapters include:
1. The Coupling of Movement and Metabolism
2. Heart, Lung, and Blood Dynamics During Exercise
3. A Unified Strategy for Training Distance Runners
4. Comprehensive Conditioning for Runners
5. Successful Racing: Preparation and Achievement
6. Stress Management in Training

"A Rolls Royce of running manuals. . .This is certainly the most complete work I have encountered that tackles the multi-disciplinary demands of training runners." ---*Athletics Today*

"I can honestly say that this book is, without a doubt, the best presentation on the subject of distance preparation and training I have ever read." ---Joe Newton *Head Track and Cross Country Coach, York High School, Elmhurst, IL*

Training Distance Runners
By David E. Martin and Peter N. Coe
hardcover, 312 pgs. ©1991 $32.95
Code: TDR

A no-nonsense approach to the basics of racing on the road, including training. A good first reference work for soeone thinking about racing or inthe early stages of competition. Contains photos and an appendix with pacing charts and metric to yard conversons. Chapters include: The History of Road Racing, Selecting Races, Training for Road Races, Racing, Injuries, and Auxiliary Aids for Runners. The writers are the well-known University of Oregon women's coach and his athlete/journalist wife.

All About Road Racing
By Tom and Janet Heinonen
©1979, paper, 126 pgs. $7.95
Code: AAB

A Literary Gem Collection

What a wonderful idea! Runner/editor Garth Battista has gathered together all the memorable (and widely scattered) jewels of running literature he could find into one volume.

Frankly, we were surprised to find stories and poems we never knew existed.

In addition to the expected excerpts from *Loneliness of a Long Distance Runner, Long Road to Boston, The Olympian,* and *Once a Runner,* Battista has reclaimed prose and poesy from such eminences as Walt Whitman, Evelyn Waugh, W.H. Auden and Joyce Carol Oates, from one-time Olympic sprinter Jackson Scholz (a short story called "The Winning Bug"), and lesser knowns like Richard Wilbur (a wonderfully nostalgic poem called "Running") and Harry Sylvester (a short-story about a gallant war-time race through enemy lines).

Battista, the gem collector, has done his gathering admirably. Nor does he falter when it comes to presentation. Rather than structuring the book mundanely according to literary discipline, he has wisely—for a book meant to be read in joyous spurts—mixed short fiction, novel excerpts and poetry together, and sorted instead by topic. Some categories are predictable—The Milers; The Marathoners; The Sprinters—others are intriguingly off-beat—Murder, Malice & Madness; Form and Motivation; Time, Memory and Age.

There is a slice of Homer's *Iliad,* there is Rina Ferrarelli on Joan Benoit Samuelson's gold medal. There is Max Apple waxing hilarious on his conversion: "...I had been a beer man for a decade. When I finally started to run I felt like a washing machine." There is A.E. Housman's poignant and unfor-gettable ode to a dead runner that we are forever having to dig out of our college anthology to reread.

Now it will abide at close hand, as this book will never be far from our bedside table.

> **The Runner's Literary Companion** ed. by Garth Battista ©1994, hardcover, 332 pgs. $22.95 Code: RLC

Ten Million Footsteps

Arnold Schwarzenegger read it. He couldn't believe his eyes and read it again: the story of a 73-year-old man named Paul Reese running across the United States, a marathon a day for 124 days straight and covering 3,192 miles.

Now the story of the retired Marine Corps officer from California is one of Schwarzenegger's favorite sources of inspiration. "Truly, the running shoe has replaced the rocking chair as a national symbol for healthy aging," said the former chairman of the President's Council on Physical Fitness and Sports.

Reese's personal journal, meant only as a record book of his adventure, found its way into print with the help of *Runner's World* writer Joe Henderson. Slimmed down, it retains all of the immediacy and intimacy of Reese's heat-of-battle report.

The History of Boston!

This is the first complete history of the world's oldest and most celebrated marathon. Veteran writer and marathoner Tom Derderian takes readers on a 640-page tour of the race from 1897 through 1993. Readers will find out little known facts about the athletes who shaped each race—how they trained, the problems they encountered, how the competition unfolded. Derderian's engaging writing style recreates the moments that have made history. Readers will experience the triumphs and highlights: Clarence DeMar's seventh seventh win in the 1930 race, 19 years after his first Boston victory. Katherine Switzer's 1967 run as the first officially entered woman. The addition of prize money in 1986. Readers will learn how the race fared during the Great Depression and the two world wars. And they'll feel the disappointments and defeats, from the death of 1914 winner Jimmy Duffy on the battlefields of France to the Rosie Ruiz scandal in 1980. More than 100 photos, dating back to 1896, help to bring this panoramic story to life.

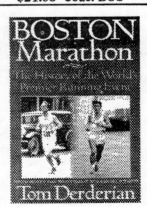

Running & Being, & Much More Sheehan

Over the years we've received many requests for copies of Dr. Georgie Sheehan's earlier books, particularly *Running and Being*, but the books have long been out of

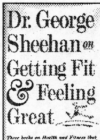

print. But now because of a recent printing by Random House, Sheehan's classic *Running and Being* is available again as part of a triple book combination that also includes *This Running Life*, and *How to Feel Great 24 Hours a Day*. These are not condensations, but the complete text originals, attractively bound in hardcover, and at an amazing price.

This is Dr. Sheehan at doing some of his best and earliest work. If you appreciate the literature of running, this book belongs in your library.

Dr. George Sheehan
on Getting Fit
by George Sheehan ©1992,
hardcover, 661 pgs. **$16.95**
Code: GFF

He's been called "Mark Twain in sneakers." He's perhaps our greatest philosopher/ athlete, and certainly one of the best-known figures in the sport. Running guru and general all-around fitness expert George Sheehan draws on 70 years of living for pungent and personal

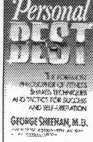

commentary on ways to live better, happier, and more productively. His credo for fitness (and in large part, life), "Whatever you do, it should be fun—because if it's not, you're not going to do it well" comes through in his main message: Energy breeds energy, and if you want to achieve excellence, you have to first manufacture a fit body. But this is a book about life, not just athletics—a *why* book, not a how-to, written for thinking men and women who *use* their bodies.

Personal Best by George Sheehan
©1989, paper, 256 pgs.,
$12.95 Code: PBP

The Philosopher Laureate of the sport of running weighs in with another of his delightful works, this time expounding mostly on how to achieve superior performances.

Sheehan takes the long view, and he starts with the core question, What makes runners run? Then takes you right through the program,

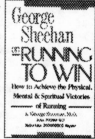

physical and spiritual training, cross-training, injury avoidance, psyching up and psyching down, dealing with illness, rest and recovery, approaching competition, how to coach yourself, and just about every other topic a serious and thoughtful runner might be concerned with.

Running to Win by Dr. Sheehan
hardcover, 230 pgs., © 1992,
$19.95 Code GSH

University of California's track and cross-country coach Vern Gambetta lays out personal background, best marks, annual progression, and both competitive and non-competitive season weekly schedules along with a narrative description of each woman's approach to training.

Women included are: Kathy Adams, Tena Anex, Evelyn Ashford, Diane Barrett, Joan Benoit, Karen Bridges, Ruth Caldwell, Fran Castro, Carol Cook, Kris Costello, Doreen Ennis, Eryn Forbes, Linda Goen, Ellison Goodall, Jennie Gorham, Judy Graham, Doris Brown-Heritage, Lynne Hjelte, Tara Hobbs.

Also: Pam Jiles, Maggie Keyes, Deby LaPlante, Sue Latter, Sandra Levinski, Wendy Koenig-Knudson, Susi Meek, Molly Miller, Deborah Mitchell-Pearson, Molly Morton, Sue North, Jan Oehm, Phyllis Olrich, Debbie Quatier, Cindy Schmandt, Jarvis Scott, Grete Waitz, Leann Warren, Kathy Weston, Cheri Williams.

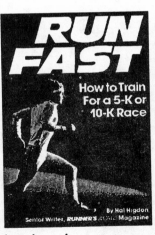

> **How Women Runners Train**
> By Vern Gambetta
> paper   ©1980   128 pgs. $7.95
> Code: HWR

One of the most experienced and accomplished writers in the sport takes on the subject of getting better results in the shorter races.

Higdon explains: "While numerous books told people how to start jogging and how to finish their first marathon, less attention is paid to running short races faster. Many of the millions of participants in the current fitness boom skipped high school track and cross-country, where they might have learned the necessary skills. They didn't run in college, either. As a result they missed the training you get at that level. They never learned to warm up properly. They don't have a coach. They don't know about interval training, fartlek, and bounding drills."

This book fills that gap, and does it in Higdon's familiar highly readable, highly personal style. This book covers just about everything the intermediate runner needs to know to start running faster in races shorter than the marathon.

"Vintage Higdon. He brings perspective to his discussion and demonstrates every point with a story from his own experience or that of other runners, coaches and scientists. A wealth of information." —**David L. Costill, PhD**, author of *Inside Running*

> ***Run Fast*** by Hal Higdon
> paper, ©1992, 212 pgs., $14.95
> Code: RFA

Shipping Rates
(please add to your order form)

Type of Service	FIRST BOOK	EACH ADDITIONAL
Standard Book Rate U.S. Mail	$3	$.50
Priority Mail in U.S. (delivery in 3-4 days)	$4	$1
UPS Ground	$4	$.50
UPS 2nd Day	$7	$1
UPS Overnight	$12	$4
Canada & Mexico Surface	$4	$1
Air Mail	$5	$2
Other Western Hemisphere Countries Surface	$4	$2
Air Mail	$6	$3
Europe Surface	$4	$2
Air Mail	$8	$6
Asia, Africa, Pacific Rim, etc. Surface	$4	$2
Air Mail	$10	$8

Cedarwinds Publishing Company
P.O. Box 351, Medway, OH 45341
Credit Card Orders only:
800-548-2388
Hours: 9 am to 6 pm EST
(or use recording after hours)
Information: 513-849-1689
FAX Orders: 513-849-1624
(Prices subject to change without notice.)

Editorial Offices:
Box 13618, Tallahassee, FL 32317
904-224-9261 fax: 904-561-0747

Quantity	Title	Amount

(Note: Shipping is already added in price of non-book products) Sub-total	
Florida and Ohio residents please add 7% sales tax	
Standard Shipping: Add $3 for first book, $.50 for each additional	
Special Shipping, please specify from box at left:	

TOTAL ENCLOSED $

NAME_____

ADDRESS_____

CITY_____STATE_____ZIP_____

Important: please furnish telephone numbers below in case we need to contact you.

Day phone: _____

❑ Check or money order enclosed (do not send cash)
❑ Visa/MC

Card No._____

Expiration _____
Signature _____

To order by mail, send check, money order, or
credit card authorization above----payable in U.S.
funds----to:
Cedarwinds Publishing Company
P.O. Box 351--- 1305 Park Dr.
Medway, OH 45341

FAX: 513-849-1624
Phone Orders: 800-548-2388

Quantity	Title	Amount

(Note: Shipping is already added in price of non-book products) Sub-total	
Florida and Ohio residents please add 7% sales tax	
Standard Shipping: Add $3 for first book, $.50 for each additional	
Special Shipping, please specify from box at left:	
TOTAL ENCLOSED $	

NAME_____

ADDRESS_____

CITY_____STATE_____ZIP_____

Important: please furnish telephone numbers below in case we need to contact you.

Day phone: _____

❑ Check or money order enclosed (do not send cash)
❑ Visa/MC

Card No._____

Expiration _____
Signature _____

To order by mail, send check, money order, or
credit card authorization above----payable in U.S.
funds----to:
Cedarwinds Publishing Company
P.O. Box 351— 1305 Park Dr.
Medway, OH 45341

FAX: 513-849-1624
Phone Orders: 800-548-2388

Quantity	Title	Amount

(Note: Shipping is already added in price of non-book products) Sub-total	
Florida and Ohio residents please add 7% sales tax	
Standard Shipping: Add $3 for first book, $.50 for each additional	
Special Shipping, please specify from box at left:	
TOTAL ENCLOSED $	

NAME_____

ADDRESS_____

CITY_____STATE_____ZIP_____

Important: please furnish telephone numbers below in case we need to contact you.

Day phone: _____

❑ Check or money order enclosed (do not send cash)
❑ Visa/MC

Card No._____

Expiration _____
Signature _____

To order by mail, send check, money order, or
credit card authorization above----payable in U.S.
funds----to:
**Cedarwinds Publishing Company
P.O. Box 351--- 1305 Park Dr.
Medway, OH 45341**

**FAX: 513-849-1624
Phone Orders: 800-548-2388**